GLOSSARY

Kees	Short for Cornelis pronounced as case
Moeke	Little mother used like Mama or Mummy
Mevrouw	Madam
Dankjewel	Thank you
Reichsschule	Hitlers Elite School for Boys
Oma / Opa	Granny / Grandad

Food

Erwtensoep	Pea soup
Gevulde koeken	Almond paste cake
Kletsmajoors	Biscuits with caramelised sugar
Haché	Meat stewed with cloves
Hete Bliksem	Potato mash mixed with apples
Pepernoten	Spice/gingerbread nut
Puddingbroodje	White soft breadroll with a custard filling

Abbreviations

DEMAG	Deutsche Maschinenfabrik AG
NSB	National Socialist Movement (Nationaal Socialist Beweging)
SD	Sicherheitsdienst (security service) the intelligence agency of the SS
SGA	A grammar school in Arnhem

THE BONE SCULPTOR

THE BONE SCULPTOR

A.S. Mink

Books AS Literature

ISBN:

Paperback | 978-9-0833-4881-0

Hardback | 978-9-0833-4882-7

Cover and interior design by Rob Wickerhoff

Cover illustrations by Tabuki

Published by Books AS Literature Publishing

First edition 2024

For Rob

CHAPTER ONE

Kees

The bones knocked against the belly of the pot as he poked them, pushing them into a solution of hot water, bleach, and Lux soap. When he decided the water was about to boil, he tapped the wheel of the petroleum burner with his index finger until the flames sputtered and objected. He slid the metal cap over them, depriving the wick of oxygen. Smoke spiralled towards the cobwebs dangling from the ceiling. The smell reached its long arm down his throat. He turned to the broken window, breathing deeply, sucking clean air into his lungs.

His anatomy book was open and ready, with the pages turned to the illustrations of human skulls from all sides and angles. He had prepared his worktop as an operating table, arranging his instruments on a grimy old sheet. At least now, his tools would come in useful – three scalpels, four pairs of scissors, and even his tissue forceps and clamps of all shapes and sizes, instruments he needed no more now medical school was out of the question. So much had changed since Hitler had invaded Holland. But Hitler wasn't the cause of his academic failure.

He took the wooden tongs from the nail in the beam above the window and picked out the bones from the pot to dry them on the windowsill. Then, he dug his favourite tool from his pocket – his sculpting knife – folding his fingers around its handle. The smooth wood on his skin fitted so comfortably in the palm of his hand. He raised the steel blade upwards towards his puckered lips as if to kiss it and felt its coolness press on his mouth; the metal smelled of blood.

He turned to what he had been working on – three tiny skulls, perfect miniature replicas of human skulls the size of the distal phalanx of his thumb, and admired his work. The intricate detail of the jaw, the hollows he had carved for eye sockets, and the fine zigzagging cranial sutures running across the tiny scalps. He smiled, picked up a fresh piece of bone, a femur segment, and started to carve a ribcage.

The door behind him creaked, and fresh air whipped around his neck.

'Corrie said you'd be here,' Ab said.

Kees turned on the wooden stool to face his friend and smiled.

'Hello stranger,' he said.

'If the mountain won't come to Mohammed, Mohammed must come to the mountain...' His voice trailed off as his eyes caught the bones in Kees's hand. 'What are you working on?'

Kees glanced at his finished project as if through Ab's eyes. He picked up a box from his worktop. 'I think this is the best one yet,' Kees said, holding up the walnut box and showing it to Ab. He had arranged several skeletons at various stages of development – an infant, a child, and a teenager with wings between the arms and the ribcages. The bones of the arms were adjusted with tiny pins on the backing.

'Don't you ever tire of making these things?' Ab said. 'I thought you wanted to be a doctor above everything else.' He turned and glanced around the garden shed – 'So this is the new surgery?'

Kees scratched his neck. 'Moeke banned me from working in the house... because of the smell.' Kees stood up, 'Anyway, what are you doing here? Shouldn't you be back in Amsterdam studying the real thing?'

'Don't you read the newspapers anymore?'

Kees squeezed his lips together in a false smile. Ab was right. Kees had stopped reading newspapers since the Nazis ruled the country. The news made him sad.

Kees and Ab had always been friends, ever since junior infants. They both studied medicine in Amsterdam and would have been going on to the second year in the new semester if Kees hadn't returned home in the spring because of finances and Ab a few months later because of the Nazis.

'Banning Jews can't go on forever,' Kees said. 'You'll resume your studies soon enough.'

'We'll see,' Ab said. 'At least you have a hobby.'

Kees returned the box to his workbench. 'They're not ordinary puppets. They're special. The souls of the deceased animals transfer into them.'

'Do animals have souls?' Ab picked up the box and peered at Kees's sculptures. 'Wouldn't it be something if it were true?'

'Corrie says they come to life when no one is watching.'

'As do her dolls and teddy bears, I'm sure.'

'Children have a sixth sense, you know.'

Ab stared into the box as if trying to see what was happening in those hollow skulls.

'Consider using human bones,' he said. 'See what happens?'

'Human bones?' Kees asked. 'Where would I find human bones?' Kees sank into thought. He saw the bins after autopsies at the university in his mind's eye. Hands and fingers. All he needed was one digit. It would be small, but he could carve a skull from that.

Ab cleared his throat and punched Kees's shoulder. 'Have I started those wheels of your mind turning?' Ab asked, smiling. 'Anyway,' he said, shrugging his shoulders. 'I wouldn't mind a chance at immortality. When I'm dead, you may cut off, say, my little finger.' Ab raised his pinkie. 'Sculpt something from this, a skull, or I don't know... you decide. You're the bone sculptor. As long as I turn out pretty and I can fly.'

Kees shuddered. He glanced into the sky through the opened door behind Ab. The sun was shining in a faultless blue sky.

'It could be the last day of summer,' Kees said. 'Want to go for a swim?'

He walked around Ab, out of the shed, and loped across the

3

lawn. The trees rustled, and leaves were falling. A faint smell of decay lingered on the warm breeze that swept in from the Nether-Rhine. Kees entered the French windows of the breakfast room and returned a couple of minutes later with a red and yellow checkered blanket and two swimsuits. He tossed them to Ab and spread the blanket on the lawn by the pool.

Ab chose the dark blue swim suit and changed while holding a towel around his waist. He walked to the pool and dived in. Kees followed. He took off his shirt and tie, flipped off his shoes, and, not bothering to change into swimming trunks, he plunged into the pool expecting the water to be warm. But it was freezing. He clenched his jaw as he swam, slicing through the glistering surface towards the steps. Ab was the first to climb out of the water.

'When did that pool turn so cold?' Ab said. He noticed Kees was still wearing his trousers. He looked away, glancing up at one of the bedroom windows on the first floor.

Kees followed his friend's eyes to his sister, Punica, who was looking down at them, her face veiled in the lace curtains. Ab waved for her to join them. She pulled back.

'Don't encourage her,' Kees said, finally changing into his dry swimming trunks.

Ab sat on the blanket and smiled, taking a cigarette from his trouser pocket. Kees watched him as he tried to hide his delight at hearing Punica liked him.

Not five minutes later, Punica came prancing through the open French windows of the breakfast room and scudded down the few stone terrace steps, taking the last one with a hop, landing on the lawn with both feet.

'Why does she always do that?' Ab whispered, obviously enchanted by Punica's entrance.

'Do what?' Kees said. 'Follow us?'

'No, I meant never taking the last step of anything, whether it's the rung of a ladder or the last step of the stairs. She always hops down with both feet.'

Punica took off her bathrobe and dropped it onto the blanket by the boys' feet. She wore a white bathing suit with a bow under her breasts and looked like a fashion model; she trampled over the blanket, hurrying towards the pool. She paused on the tiles, and as she curled her toes over the edge, she pulled a white bathing cap with rubber floppy flowers over her blonde curls.

'Should we warn her?' Ab whispered, smiling.

'Why are you whispering?' Punica asked.

She spoke confidently and sounded older than her age.

'Yes, why are you whispering, Ab?' Kees asked, mimicking her low, hoarse voice. She had a cyst nestling on her vocal cords since she was twelve.

'What did you want to tell me?' she asked.

Kees threw a towel into Ab's face to shut him up.

She bent forward and dived into the pool. Her flowery bathing cap popped above the glistening surface a few seconds later. She let out a loud, hoarse screech.

'We tried to warn you,' Kees said, laughing.

'Oh,' she shrieked, tiptoeing towards the steps, keeping her arms above the water. She pulled herself up quickly, almost falling on the silvery, slippery steps. Then, hugging herself, she ran towards them. She tried to wipe the cold water from her skin and pulled at her bathrobe, but Kees was sitting on it. He heaved himself up a bit, leaning on one hand, but she could not pull it free from under him.

'It's freezing,' she gasped, shuddering.

Ab yanked the bathrobe from under Kees and wrapped it around her. He rubbed her back to warm her up. Kees looked away – she was only fourteen, for God's sake. He bit his tongue to keep himself from commenting.

Ab sat down beside Kees and nudged him. 'Tell her what I said about using human bones for your sculptures,' he said.

'Human bones?' Punica asked, eyebrows arched. She peered at Kees, anxious for him to tell her.

The hair on Kees's neck rose, and his cheeks started to glow. Punica glanced at Ab, who looked away.

'Okay,' she said, turning towards the house, 'I'll leave you two to

5

it.'

'No... no, come, sit down,' Ab shoved over, making room for her on the blanket.

'So, Kees, how have you been sleeping recently?' Ab asked him.

Ab was trying to get a conversation going; Kees knew that. Usually, he would have loved to talk about his dreams. At university, they kept discussing what they could mean. But after having returned home, everything about them felt off. And he felt weird for dreaming such nonsense. His stepmother had told him all the Russian fairy tales as bedtime stories when he was still a child. However, owning up to still dreaming about children's fairy tales in front of his younger sister embarrassed him. He turned crimson.

'Are you still hoping to travel to Russia someday?' Ab asked.

Kees helped himself to one of Ab's cigarettes, thinking hard about how he could change the subject. Ab automatically handed him a lighter.

'Kees has told me all about the snow maiden at university,' Ab said to Punica.

'His nocturnal adventures.' Punica sighed. 'Do you have one for me too?' she asked Ab, pretending to hold a cigarette between her index and middle finger. He reached her one, and she slipped it between her lips. She leaned in as he flicked the spark wheel of his lighter.

'Last night, I dreamed I was a stag,' Kees said, pretending coolness.

'I'm going back in.' Punica bent down, picked up her bathrobe from the grass, and started towards the house.

Ab stopped her, taking her arm.

'They're just dreams. It doesn't mean anything. It's just his head. His mind is always so full of thoughts—'

'I know. But—,' she whispered and glanced at Kees, who pretended to be busy, wringing out his trousers as he listened closely. 'He is so sensitive,' she said, sighing. 'He hasn't been the same since my father had him come home from university. Carving those weird skeletons at all hours, unable to sleep, and when he finally falls

6

asleep, he has crazy dreams. I think he's losing his mind.'

The gate screeched open, and Ab and Punica jumped in fright. Kees and Punica's father entered the garden. He was wearing a black uniform they hadn't seen him wear before, a collaborator's uniform of the National Socialists – the Dutch Nazi movement known as the NSB.

Ab's face turned white; he avoided Mr Mandemaker's eyes as he gathered his clothes. Punica stared at her father, her mouth hanging open.

'I have to go,' Ab said, putting on his trousers.

'Hello, Ab,' Mr Mandemaker said. 'It's been a while since we saw you here.'

Punica laid her hand on Ab's sleeve, holding his arm. 'Please... don't be offended,' she said softly. 'The uniform can't be serious—'

'I better get back,' Ab said to her. He pulled the jacket over his shirt, rolled up his tie, and put it in his pocket.

'Stay for dinner,' Kees said. 'My mother would love that. You know how fond she is of you, and you haven't even been in to say hello to her.'

'I can't,' Ab muttered, crouching while sliding his bare feet into his leather shoes. Straightening his back, he rolled his socks into a ball and slid them into his other pocket. Ab shook his head, pinching his lips together. He touched Punica's arm lightly before he hurried away, leaving the gate open behind him. He disappeared behind the garden wall. A steel screech of a whistle; a German voice shouting, 'Halt!'

Punica gasped and sprinted towards the gates.

Two men in an SS uniform were holding an old gentleman at gunpoint. The man, dressed in a black overcoat and a high black hat, sank to his knees. Ab passed the Jewish man and disappeared around the corner into Arke Noach Street. The SS men pushed the old gentleman to the ground, and one of them raised his army boot above the old man's head. He lowered it onto the man's neck, where it froze, pinning the man onto the cobbled street like an animal.

'Oh my god,' Punica said.

Kees had followed her to the gate and would not let her go out onto the street.

'Punica, come inside!' their father shouted.

'Pap wants you inside,' Kees said.

'Kees, please? We can't ignore what is happening around us.'

'Come with me, Pun.' Kees held out his hand to her.

He hadn't called her Pun for a long time, not since returning home from university.

'I never thought I'd see Father wearing... a Nazi uniform,' Punica whispered, biting back tears.

'He's been out of work for ages. People do what they need to do.'

'So, you're making excuses for him now?'

Kees squeezed his lips together, lost for words.

Her hand slipped into his. 'Are you his puppet?' she asked.

'What do you mean?'

'His puppet? Always doing what he wants you to do, pulling your strings whichever way he wants? You should be in college. You always wanted to be a doctor. Wasn't that what those bones were about? But all you do these days is make puppets and now maybe you are becoming a puppet yourself, doing exactly what Pap wants you to do. I know about you...'

The chill of the approaching winter swept over the garden. Kees placed his arm around her shoulder and steered her towards their father. Kees stopped by the red chequered blanket on the lawn and picked it up. He wrapped it around Punica's shoulders. 'Your lips have turned blue,' he said.

'Kees, you need to stand up for what you believe. Even to him,' she said, gesturing to her father. 'Even him. Do you understand? Or you'll lose everything.'

Kees nodded. 'Go inside. Ab should be safely home by now.'

Their father waited for them by the French windows. Punica stared at Kees.

A lorry came to a rumbling stop, the brakes puffing and gasping, and men roaring in that awful language of theirs. Machine-gun fire rattled for never-ending seconds. Punica pressed her hands on her ears and screamed from the pit of her stomach. Kees raised his hands to her face, but she pushed them away. She ran past him over the lawn, onto the gravel path, and past her father, who still awaited her on the stone steps to the breakfast room and disappeared into the house.

CHAPTER TWO

Petronella

Petronella Mandemaker kept a special box in her dressing room; it stood on a mahogany table by the windows. Her grandfather had crossed three frontiers to find it. He, too, had the gift, she would explain, of finding magical objects just like she had. Her Opa – her grandfather – would lose his way when searching for new treasures, sometimes roving as far as Germany or Belgium. Once, he strayed into France and seemed to have lost his mind, let alone his way. Petronella thought she would never see her favourite Opa again.

The box was made of cherry wood and carved with a botanical theme. On the front, leaves wrestled to free themselves from the wooden surface. On the lid, a magpie crouched, spreading its wings as if to hop up and fly away. An imaginary wind ruffled its feathers, and its claws trampled the leaves and cherries underneath them. The box had three drawers. The bottom drawer had a brass lock and key. As a child, Petronella loved to close her eyes and let her fingers trace the carvings like a blind person reading Braille, and while examining the box with her thin fingertips, she found its magical portal.

Underneath the magpie's protective claws, hidden in the lid, was a secret compartment. Only Petronella mastered the intricate series of pulling and sliding ornaments to open it – if done in a precise order – the magpie clicked upwards, and the lid snapped open. There, carefully wrapped in a rich blue velvet cloth, she discovered two silver birds with beating hearts.

On Petronella's wedding day, years later, Cornelis told her, while travelling back from the ceremony in a horse-drawn carriage, that his very young son was coming to live with them. He hadn't even told her he had a son, or that he had been married before. They detoured and collected a scared little boy with feathery raven hair at the railway station. He was waiting for them on the platform, wearing clothes too big for him, shoes too big for him, and a sign with black sooty letters saying, child Mandemaker and underneath in brackets Cornelis. When she set eyes on the tiny, frightened little bird of a boy, she fell in love with him instantly.

Once home, and after having fed the boy, she remembered her silver birds and took him to her dressing room to help him settle in. She introduced her prized little companions to him, balancing both in her outstretched hands. Petronella told him how the wings had been moulded from a solid plate of silver; their wings were engraved to resemble real wings, the feathers catching the light. She gently held his hand, spreading one finger, and guided his touch over the sinuous detail.

He picked one up – the mother bird – and listened, his ear pressed to its chest.

'Boom... boom... boom,' he whispered as if he could hear its heartbeat.

Only then, crouching by him, did she lift the cardboard sign hanging from a string around his neck and slid it over his head. How could a mother send her infant son away on a train packed with strangers with no identification except a piece of cardboard bearing his name?

'This little mother bird will always protect you,' she whispered in his ear.

Kees pressed his ear on his shoulder, puckering his face. He touched the mother bird's feathers, cocking his head as he studied it. A puzzled smile played on his lips, enchanted by the bird as he stroked its beak. Its silver eyes followed his moves, and the light shifted in them.

'Take her to your room and keep her safe, and she will, in return for your love, always keep you safe.' Petronella raised a finger to her lips. 'But this will be our little secret,' she whispered. He nodded, his eyes glowing with an inner light. She returned the baby bird to the box. 'In the meantime, I will look after her chick for her,' said Petronella.

Kees smiled and watched Petronella return the box to her dressing table. She took the mother bird from Kees's hand and slid it into his pocket.

'Even though,' she whispered, 'it will miss its Moeke dreadfully, she knows I will keep it safe while she protects you with all her heart and all her might.'

She took his hand and led him to the spare room, removed his trousers, socks, and shoes, and put him into bed. A bath could wait until tomorrow. She kissed her new stepson on the forehead. Tomorrow, she thought, tomorrow, she would re-decorate the guestroom for her son. Kees was a splendid gift given to her by her husband on her wedding day.

She closed the heavy damask curtains and told Kees a bedtime story about a Russian snow maiden who could not let herself fall in love because love would warm her heart and melt her from the inside out. When the child was fast asleep, Petronella tiptoed onto the landing, and there she saw Cornelis waiting for her. He glanced at her from under his heavy eyebrows and cleared his throat, diverting his gaze to his cigarette. He still wore his wedding suit, his tie slung around his neck. She had fallen in love with his self-confidence, but now, standing there, avoiding her gaze as he tapped his legs, she loved him even more. She searched his strange eyes and tried to decipher what they told her.

'Why didn't you tell me you had a son?' she whispered.

'I thought you knew.'

'No. How am I supposed to know if you don't tell me?'

'You knew about the house?'

'Gossip, I thought.'

'They said I stole it, didn't they?'

'I don't listen to gossip, but now I wonder if I shouldn't start when you're keeping things from me.'

'I bought this house fair and square. The jewel of the city, as they call it now, is owned by such a lowly fellow.' He raised his hand to her cheek and cupped her face. 'I bought it for you. I've always recognised the beauty of this place, even when it was derelict and vagrants and prostitutes used it. The mayor wanted to demolish the estate and build slums for the poor. The city council thought they'd outsmarted me. They hoped the cost of demolition would bankrupt me, and they'd save themselves a packet. It never occurred to them that the house could be restored and would be beautiful. The ink wasn't dry on the deeds when their first letters arrived to order me to clear the land. They tried to force me to pull down the house.'

'So, you've entered a battle with the mayor?' she said. 'You are aware of the fact that he is my father?'

'It was mentioned once or twice,' Cornelis said, smiling.

'Now,' he waved his arm as if including everyone, 'they say I stole it from the city.'

'Darling, I'm not talking about the house. The house is like something from a fairy tale. It is magnificent. But why didn't you tell me you are divorced? That you fathered a son with another woman?'

Cornelis stared at the floor. 'I should have told you,' he whispered.

The evening sun shone through the hallway's stained-glass windows, and Cornelis's face lit up orange and blue. Only the stroke of light over his eyes had a natural colour. Petronella glanced at the restored stained-glass windows – a landscape in evening colours.

'The window,' she said. 'How on earth did you restore it? You've created a masterpiece.'

'You inspired me,' he said.

'The day I met you at that New Year's party...' Petronella thought for a moment. 'I was so ashamed of what my father did to you. I wanted to apologise for my family's behaviour but couldn't catch you up. I called out to you. But it was midnight, and the fireworks exploded above our heads.' She sighed. 'The colours of the fireworks on your back, the way you walked, so proud. I followed you then, and I'll keep on following you. I remember standing on the street right outside this house, and I noticed a light coming out of the front room, and I... I saw you working on the ceiling, the plaster falling around you. You didn't see me. You looked so handsome in your anger. Your determi-

13

nation. A ring of burning candles around you. I... I loved you... My love for you is strong enough to defy anyone, even my father. I would give up everything for you.'

Cornelis took her into his arms.

'I am your wife, and I'm not going anywhere.'

He embraced her, kissing her neck under her left ear. She snuggled into his arms.

'Six bedrooms and all but two in need of a child,' she said.

CHAPTER THREE

Kees

Kees was sitting on a wooden stool, waiting for his precious bones to boil. Thick cobwebs covered the windows. Nails in the ceiling looked like the devil's eyes as they glared at him. It was December, and the wind pounded on the door. Kees raised the collar of his coat and huddled by the warmth of his petroleum burner. The Nazis had sent many young men home from university, but his failure was different: nothing to do with religion or even the Nazis. His situation was a personal defeat, for which he blamed his father's incompetence in finding work.

Acorns exploded onto the iron roof of the shed, sending the chickens into a frenzy at Kees's feet. The wind burst through the door. A chicken escaped onto the frosted grass on pale legs, flapping its wings wildly, trying to find refuge in the frozen winter garden. Kees got up and closed the door behind it. He sat back onto the stool, trying to shake off the memory of that horrible evening with his father. Kees had done something so out of character it seemed as if someone had taken possession of him. If he had been alone, he would never have signed his name, but his father was with him, urging him, telling him to take the pen between his fingers.

He wiped his clammy hands on his trouser legs and took a deep breath. He heard the bell of a schillenboer – a peeler's cart – screech above the wind, shaking him from his thoughts. It sounded like a train conductor's whistle. His legs trembled. To calm himself, he whispered aloud: It is just the peeler collecting potato peels for animal feed, and he imagined the cook, Mrs de Vries, with her tub filled to the brim with discarded vegetable peels and scrapings, rushing out to meet it.

The boiling water bubbled and spat over the rim of the pot onto the blood-stained surface of a butcher's chopping block. The metallic smell sickened him. He stood up, patting his pockets on his hips, and pretended he had received his orders to report for training to see how it would fit his mind. He wondered if he could turn his fear into something else. Anticipation? Could he make his departure seem like an adventure? He had always wanted to go to Russia. And only cowards stayed home with their mothers, he told himself. He was not a coward. His eyes traced the details of his surroundings. The bones ticked and thumped monotonously. He sat back on the stool again, listened to the sounds surrounding him, and let them mesmerise him and take him into a dreamlike state. The warm, moist air wrapped around him like a veil. He felt himself drifting into sleep.

His mind searched for that of the deer. And changing into a deer once more, he entered his dreams. He pushed his snout into the snow and searched for grass. There was none. He stretched his neck upward, sniffing the scent of spruce. He heard a branch snap, and as he contemplated bolting away, he saw a shadow move. He rushed into the dense foliage to hide.

A girl appeared. She visited him often in his dreams, wearing a long coat of wolf skin with fur on the inside and suede on the outside. The suede was elaborately embroidered with crimson and saffron thread. Her skin resembled sparkling snow: her eyes were turquoise with yellow rings around the iris. Kees listened to her breathing as he tried to suppress his own. He wanted to talk to her and ask her why she visited him so often, but his voice grumbled in a low baritone sound like a stag, and he wondered if he could speak at all. The girl jumped from fright and bolted away.

Corrie stood on the threshold of the shed, watching him. She wore thick woollen stockings and a beige dress with a bow and frills. A crocheted string dangled across her shoulders from mitten to mitten. Kees smiled. Corrie never came to the shed. She stared at the axe,

16

leaning against the ladder behind him. The hay used for cleaning the blade lay in bloody clumps around it. The pot jittered on the petroleum burner, and he became aware of the odour and how unpleasant the shed must seem to his little sister. Corrie raised her mittened hands toward her face and covered her mouth and nose.

'What brings you here?' Kees said, standing up.

'It's the third of December,' she said. 'Saint Nicolas is coming.'

'The third,' he repeated, frowning his eyebrows, pretending to think hard. 'Sinterklaas. Today?' he asked. 'Isn't the old man a bit late? Shouldn't he have arrived in the middle of November?'

'No!' she screamed. 'There is a war on, remember?' She scrunched her eyebrows. 'You said it yourself. As long as Sinterklaas was here before the fifth of December, he would still be on time, remember? Because of the war?'

Kees sank onto his haunches, and Corrie placed her soft, purple-mittened hands on his cheeks.

'Will you take me?' she asked.

'I... I don't go out onto the street, not since I've enlisted—'

'What's enlisted?'

'It's when you put your name down on a list promising to—'

'What have you promised?' Her eyes were big and curious.

'That I'd go to Russia to free little girls like yourself from communism.'

'What's connumism?'

'Communism is—'

'Do you like going away to free girls like me?'

'I'd prefer to stay here with you,' Kees said, forcing his lips into a smile. 'I suppose I could take you to see Sinterklaas arrive at the docks.'

Corrie clapped her hands, grinning. Kees lifted her into the air and remembered Moeke had once taken him to see Sinterklaas arrive. Kees remembered the steamship, Amerigo, Sinterklaas's white horse, the band playing all the songs, the pepernoten, the gingerbread cubes, and the sweets. He loved seeing the Petes running, jumping, doing cartwheels, climbing the chimney, and running up and down the deck – but then Russia crammed back into his mind, and he felt his heart contract with fear and dread.

'Why did you squish your face?' Corrie asked.

'Have you been good? Sinterklaas writes everything in that great book of his. We don't want one of the Petes putting you in his sack and taking you back to Spain with him, do we?'

'I'm always good,' Corrie said.

'Don't tell lies now,' Kees said, pushing his face against her neck, tickling her sides.

She screamed with laughter, flopping backwards and nearly falling from his arms into the boiling pot. Kees jolted his arms around her and pulled her into a tight embrace. Corrie giggled; not seeming to notice that he had nearly dropped her.

'I know you sneak around my room when I'm working here on my creations,' he said, lowering her gently back to the floor and raising his eyebrows.

'I don't sneak around your room,' she said. 'I would never go in there alone. Your room smells of dead stuff.'

'Dead stuff? And how does dead stuff smell?'

Corrie sighed deeply, rolling her eyes. 'Like the kitchen rubbish in summer.'

'My room doesn't smell like that at all.' He picked up the tongs and took the bones out of the boiling water to dry on the windowsill.

'How do your fairy creatures come to life?'

'Come to life?' His voice quivered. 'They don't come to life. They're just puppets I carve from old bones.'

'Why are they always moving around your bedroom, then?'

'They don't move around my bedroom.'

'I saw them – sometimes they fly, and sometimes they dance.'

Kees shook his head. 'Why don't you fetch your coat and let me finish here?'

She ran out across the hoar-frosted grass towards the French windows. 'Hurry,' she called over her shoulder, 'or we'll be late, and Sinterklaas will be gone.'

Kees remembered the last time he asked Corrie about her sneaking around. He had found one of his skeletons broken on his bedroom floor. She said she had seen it dance on the ceiling while she stood on the threshold. She swore she hadn't entered his room. He remembered how terrified she was, screaming for Moeke. 'Corrie, that's just the draft from the window,' he'd said. 'It catches their silk wings. Like little sails do, on sailing boats on a lake? I know you play with them.'

She'd shaken her head violently, her plaits swinging about her shoulders.

'Not even sometimes?' he'd asked.

'I never touch them,' she said, her arms stretched beside her thighs, her palms facing him. 'They're horrible, scary monsters. One day, you will be sorry you even made them,' she'd said.

'I'm ready!' Corrie called out now, running back toward the shed wearing her coat and her pink knitted hat with the orange pompon. Someone must have helped her pull the string of her mittens through her coat sleeves. She hopped while she buttoned her coat, the mittens flapping by her hands.

Kees turned off the burner. He followed Corrie to the house, buttoning his coat, and entered the breakfast room. Moeke was busy embroidering yet another project, one of her latest commissions. His stepmother glanced up. Her face changed when she saw Kees coming towards her.

'Moeke!' yelled Corrie. 'Kees is taking me to see Sinterklaas. In case you're wondering.'

Moeke got up to hush her. But Kees waved his hand, gesturing that it was fine.

'I need to get out,' he said. 'I'll be leaving soon enough.'

He leaned over to kiss his stepmother's cheek, and she stroked his head, scrunching his hair as if he were still a little boy.

'Don't worry about me,' he whispered. 'I'm fine.'

She pressed her lips together and smiled, but her eyes weren't in it. 'I just don't understand how your father could—'

'We've been through this so many times,' he said.

He followed Corrie into the 'useless room' – a hallway connecting three other rooms with sliding doors. A round couch Petronella had found during the refurbishment of the first-class waiting lounge at the railway station stood at the exact centre of the room. The way she had embroidered the worn material with her luscious floral patterns looked magnificent. A Belgium vase adorned the centrepiece. It had been a wedding present; Petronella's only wedding present. Her wandering grandfather had found it in Belgium on one of his treasure hunts.

The stained-glass windows projected a colourful pattern onto the parquet floor in the hallway. Mrs de Vries returned from the street with her emptied tub. Kees held the vestibule door open for her as she entered the house. He forced a smile.

'Going out?' she asked, with a puzzled look. She watched him take his hat from the hat stand.

'We're going to see Sinterklaas!' Corrie yelled, her eyes alight.

'Really,' Mrs de Vries said, glancing up at Kees.

He nodded as he wrapped the grey scarf Punica knitted for him as a Christmas gift around his neck. He tipped his hat to Mrs de Vries. Finally, for the first time since his father had taken him to those Nazi collaborators where his father had tricked Kees into enlisting in a foreign army, the German SS – an army to which he had no obligations – Kees mustered the courage to leave the house.

CHAPTER FOUR

Kees

Kees loved playing with his little silver mother bird. Balancing it on his outstretched hand, he'd run through all the rooms, imagining it flying above his fingers. At four years old, he was oblivious to the rumours around town about his divorced father and his stepmother.

Kees ran into the master bedroom. He loved the room and the magic box in his stepmother's dressing room; Moeke had hung curtains at the large windows with Chinese hand-painted images of volcanoes and rice fields. Kees saw Papa lying on the four-poster bed, holding a wet cloth on his forehead.

'Papa, look at how the silver bird flies,' Kees called out. 'Look, papa, look.'

Cornelis waved his hand to quieten the boy. 'I have a headache. I'll be down soon,' he said. 'Who's at the door?'

Kees stopped, hunching his shoulders. Realising Papa wasn't looking at him, he said, 'I don't know.'

'It might be guests with birthday presents?' Cornelis said.

'Presents, presents,' Kees called out. He ran out onto the landing.

'Close the door behind you,' Papa mumbled.

Kees reached up to pull the door towards him. 'Someone at the door,' he called out, running down the stairs, through the corridor, and into the dining room where Nienke was hanging party garlands from the ceiling. On the walls, oil paintings of someone else's ancestors, Koopmannen – wealthy merchants – who had made their fortunes centuries ago, looked down on him. They wore collars of starched lace, like excessive bibs; and black coats and high black hats. They had pink rosy faces with stern eyes that always followed him around the room. In the hallway, he smelled Mrs de Vries's pancakes from the kitchen. She was preparing his favourite birthday meal – pancakes with bacon rashers, white castor sugar, and syrup.

'Moeke, the bell, the bell!' he shouted.

'So early... who could it be?' Moeke exclaimed. She rushed down from the spiral library steps. She followed Kees to the door. 'Slow down, Kees. You'll fall over and hurt yourself. The party is not for a couple of hours yet. I'm sure it won't be a guest.'

'Presents all for me!' he shouted.

'No, no, no... no presents, not now. It's too early. Later, you'll get your presents.'

He stopped abruptly in front of her. 'No presents?'

She winked at him. 'Not until the party starts,' she whispered, bending down to him. 'But you never know,' she said, raising her eyebrows, smiling.

He stood by the door and trampled the floor for her to open it, the bird sitting on his left hand.

Moeke brushed imaginary dust from her immaculate skirt and turned to the mirror in the vestibule for a quick check. She pushed a lank curl with the flat of her hand, coaxing it to curl about her ears.

'Now you may open the door,' she said.

Petronella raised her eyebrows in surprise as she glanced at the woman on her doorstep. She wore a brown, wide-pleated skirt and a short coat with an old balding fur collar; her left shoe had a hole in the toe.

Much later, Petronella explained her shock at seeing her husband's ex-wife on that frosty January morning and the rush to get the woman and her freezing baby into the house. She often mentioned the recklessness of sending Kees on a train to them with a cardboard sign with his name around his neck. Kees might have been lost forever, she exclaimed. Now, she had the chance to give the woman the long-awaited piece of her mind; she was wholly occupied in getting her and the baby into the drawing room where the fire was lit.

'Please have a seat,' Petronella said, gesturing to the sofa by the window. The woman sat down, still wearing her coat, holding the toddler close to her bosom. Once seated, she turned the little girl around so she could see into the room. Moeke rang the servant's bell and sat down. Kees stood by his stepmother's side, his left hand leaning on her shoulder. Moeke and the strange women studied each other's faces, and neither seemed to want to talk first.

'Where is that girl?' Moeke said, half standing up and sitting down again. 'Cornelis will be home soon for Kees's birthday party. I don't want a scene in front of the boy.'

'I came here to speak to you,' the woman said matter-of-factly.

Kees raised his hand to his face. 'Moeke,' he exclaimed, 'You're not allowed to tell a fib—'

'Kees, will you ring the bell again?' She glanced at the woman and back at Kees. 'Or go to the dining room and ask Nienke to make some tea for us. We have a visitor.' Looking at the baby, she added, 'And let her bring the child a cup of warm, aniseed-flavoured milk. The poor little thing looks frozen.'

Moeke got up and poked up the fire, sparks spitting into the air.

The woman said, 'Yes, that would be so kind. But...' Pausing for a few moments. 'Could he,' gesturing to Kees, 'Could he,' her voice sounded unsure, 'Could he fetch Willem? He's waiting outside. I tried to get him to come in with me, but he was too frightened.'

'Frightened?' Moeke asked. 'Too frightened of what? You didn't leave him alone on the road? As if he wouldn't be frightened to be outside on his own?' She jumped up and ran to the door, leaving it open behind her and through the hallway to the front door, leaving it wide open as well. She hurried into the street with Kees running to the door after her. He watched his stepmother acting like a stranger and felt like he wanted to cry.

A few houses down the road, Moeke stopped and crouched on the sidewalk, facing a doorway which was concealed by a wall. She stuck out her hand to someone invisible to Kees, in the same way she always did when she wanted the child to accompany her. A little boy appeared. He had grown since Kees had seen him last, but the face covered in freckles and the short stubby nose was still unmistakably that of his little brother.

Moeke said, 'Kees, come see who's here on your birthday.'

The little boy held a shiny brass flute on his chest with both hands, his knuckles turning white. His clothes were clean but muddled; the brown coat was too big for him, and his shorts were much too short, revealing inflamed, blood-crusted knees. His hair meshed at the back of his head. Kees felt embarrassed in his ironed and starched white shirt and the little dickey bow that Moeke adored him in.

'Come on, take his hand,' she said to Kees. 'Oh, where is your mother? Did she not come out with you?' Moeke's eyes searched for the woman. She coaxed the little boy along with her hand on his back. The boy waddled before her as he held hands with Kees. 'Your Mama is inside by the warm fire,' she whispered, bending towards the boy and smiling at Kees. She let little Willem enter the house before her, nudged Kees in after him, and followed them, closing the door behind her. She removed Willem's coat and called out. 'Nienke, Nienke, please, will you take the boys into the kitchen and feed them? And make some tea, will you? We have a visitor.'

Mrs de Vries appeared holding up her hands, which were dusted in flour. She ushered the boys into the kitchen with her elbows while holding her hands up.

'What's happened?' she asked over her shoulder. 'Who is this little boy?'

Moeke waved her hands as if to say, not now. Mrs de Vries closed the kitchen door behind them when they heard Moeke call out again, sounding annoyed. 'Now, hurry with the tea; I've rung the bell a thousand times. How long do we have to wait for tea in this house?'

Mrs de Vries washed her hands and smiled at each boy.

'What happened to your knees, little man.'

'He's my brother,' Kees said.

Mrs de Vries wet a hand towel with warm water from the kettle and walked over to Willem to clean his nose. The boy turned his head away each time she tried to touch his skin. She smiled and handed the cloth to Kees. 'Maybe you can try? If he doesn't want you touching him, leave him alone,' she added. 'I suppose there's no way he'll let me touch those knees. Have you fallen over, little man?' she asked gently. Pointing at the flute, she said, 'Do you play?'

The boy pulled the flute to his side and held it away from her.

'His name is Wimpie,' Kees said.

'No, Willem,' the boy said and blew into the brass tube. Loud musical notes filled the kitchen. He played 'Happy Birthday', knowing each note and getting it right every time.

Mrs de Vries smiled and sliced a loaf of bread. 'He must have been practising,' she said to Kees. 'For your birthday party.'

She pumped water into the kettle, placed it on the stove, and smeared butter on the still-warm slice. The butter turned into yellow cream and sank into the soft bread. She returned with a jug of milk from the pantry covered with muslin and poured some into a saucepan. Kees got a star of aniseed from the spices cabinet and dropped it into the milk. 'It's my birthday,' he said. Mrs de Vries smiled. 'Indeed it is,' she said and walked into the pantry for the tea leaves. 'And isn't Willem playing you a lovely birthday tune? He's talented for a boy his age, isn't he, Kees?'

Willem watched Mrs de Vries with a faint smile as she prepared the tray for the drawing room. She spooned a drop of milk onto the inside of her wrist and poured it into three cups, each with a pattern of the three little laughing bears. The kettle whistled, and Mrs de Vries filled the teapot.

Nienke walked in the backdoor, holding a copper pot filled with coal. 'So, who is this?' she asked, looking at the little boy with wide, curious eyes.

'It's my brother Wimpie,' Kees said.

'Willem,' the boy said, interrupting his playing. 'I told you. I am Willem.'

Nienke smiled and walked into the pantry. She returned with a plate of biscuits. 'Well, I'm sure you would love a biscuit, wouldn't you, Willem? And you, my little Party Pig?' she said to Kees. 'Would you like a biscuit too?'

'I want cake,' Kees demanded, his eyes shiny. 'It's my birthday.'

'Well, your party hasn't started yet,' Nienke said, scrunching his hair. She turned to Mrs de Vries. 'Where did the boy come from?' she asked. Mrs de Vries raised her shoulders, gesturing she did not know. Willem watched the two women, apparently intrigued by their friendly faces. No one was paying Kees any attention, so he picked up the tray from the kitchen table and shuffled into the corridor, careful not to spill anything. He took tiny mouse steps and dawdled through the useless room and into the drawing room. When he appeared at the sliding doors, Moeke jumped up and ran over to him.

'Has everybody gone mad in this house?' she called out. 'Kees, you may not carry boiling tea, you know that. Where is Mrs de Vries?'

'She is busy,' Kees said.

'Well, sit there now,' she said to him, gesturing to the floor by the woman 'and play with your baby sister.'

Kees frowned. Sister? He didn't know he had a sister. But he remained silent. He didn't want Moeke to send him back to the kitchen for being a nuisance.

'I understand,' Moeke said to the woman, 'Of course I do.' What she understood, Kees didn't know. 'I'd appreciate it if you would leave before Cornelis gets home. I'm sorry. I don't want a scene in the house. Not today, of all days.'

'Home?' Kees said, looking at Moeke as if she were talking in riddles.

Moeke ignored him and accepted the mug from the little one as she reached it out to her. The baby had a big milky moustache, which Moeke wiped away with her lace handkerchief.

'She's lovely,' Moeke said. 'An adorable little girl.'

The toddler stirred from all the attention. Kees took his handkerchief from his pocket, unfolded the ironed creases, shook it, and let it land on his fist like he had seen magicians do at the circus. The little girl smiled and flapped her hands. He pulled the handkerchief away, showing her one finger, and let it fall over his hand again. She cooed. He pulled it off, now revealing three fingers, and she giggled.

The woman and Moeke talked in low voices, so Kees concentrated on what Moeke said to the strange woman while he performed his magical tricks. He pulled faces and mimed oohs and ahs like a real magician. And when his little sister grew tired of him, he pretended a corner of the handkerchief was a tiny animal crawling along his sleeve toward his hand. The little girl searched his sleeve, pulling at the cotton hanky.

'You have a magnificent home,' the woman said, glancing around the room.

'Yes, Cornelis was very lucky to buy it.'

'You have a talent for finding things, discarded things nobody wants and making them flourish.' She glanced at Kees. 'My son looks very well.'

'Yes,' Moeke nodded, biting her lower lip. 'It's a miracle we found him at the station.'

'I had written his name on the cardboard sign,' the woman said.

'Little boys blossom when loved and looked after,' Moeke said. She glanced around the room and acknowledged her possessions must seem extravagant to her visitor. Moeke had an exceptional talent for finding the best antique furniture discarded on the street. Few knew she waited on Monday evenings until dark to wander the streets searching for abandoned masterpieces. On Tuesday mornings, the Kraak arrived to collect rubbish too big for the city bins. Petronella made sure she found the best furniture before they came. She washed, polished, and mended what needed washing, polishing, and mending; she embroidered worn-out patches in the once elaborate patterns, brushed stains from dirty materials, tending to them, and making them more beautiful than ever. Word got around, and the town's higher classes came to her when something needed restoration, and paid her well for her services.

'I always see the beauty in everything others take for granted?' she said. 'I restored and embroidered every piece of furniture you see before you. They were all considered worthless and thrown out for the Kraak to collect. So, we aren't as rich as you might think.' Moeke sounded annoyed, but she raised her eyebrows and smiled. 'But I promise we will try to help you if we can. Have you contacted my husband?'

'No, I haven't. You could say' – she gestured to the little girl – 'she was the last time we contacted each other.'

Moeke turned crimson.

'As soon as I found out I was pregnant,' the woman continued, 'I left Cornelis and went to my mother's house in Utrecht.'

'With all due respect,' Moeke said, 'did it ever occur to you that a much younger man never stays with his older wife? You were thirty-seven when he married you?'

'Well, at least he told you the truth about our age difference. Did he describe me as the old hag he married, but I suppose he didn't tell you why he married me?'

'We have no secrets,' Moeke said.

'This is his child,' the woman said. 'His child... he abandoned his four children and, in return, took my lovely home in Bakker Street and my livelihood. You must know I had a shop in this town – a shop my first husband had provided for me. If I hadn't remarried after Evert's death, I would still have had the means to provide for my children. Me and Evert had five children of our own. The youngest was Kees's age when Evert died. But we had a roof over our heads, and I could provide for them. Cornelis is charming, all right. He could charm the devil out of hell,' she said. 'After Kees's twin died—'

'Why have you come here?' Moeke asked.

'Evert and I already had five children before he died, and now, with Willem and Mina here,' she said, stroking her daughter's head, 'I have seven. My mother lives in a one-bedroom house in Utrecht. I have mourned my husband and my little Bartje. I could not bear to lose another.'

'I'm sorry,' Moeke said. 'Losing a child must be devastating.'

'You know Cornelis sold both my home and the shop before divorcing me, and I never saw a cent of the money. And this exaggerated place of yours is big enough for—'

This time, Moeke interrupted her. 'I told you we would help you.'

'You are good at taking from others—'

Moeke stood up. 'I think you should leave.'

'No, please give me a chance to explain. I came here today to ask you as a mother, not as my ex-husband's second wife, but as a mother. A good mother.' She glanced at Kees. 'Would you consider taking Willem into your care as well? So, the brothers can be together.'

'Take him... I thought... I thought you wanted money—'

'I want them to have what they deserve; I'm not a bad mother. But I can't find the money to feed them all. I wish I could say I want them to stay with their father, but no love is lost between us. But I think it is important for the boys to be together. I'm sorry I haven't come sooner, but I couldn't face leaving Cornelis again. I'm sorry.'

Moeke got up.

'I think you are the best mother I could wish for my boys,' the woman pleaded.

'And the little girl?' Petronella asked, gesturing to the baby playing with Kees.

The woman stood up, bent over, and picked the girl up off the floor. 'I could never give her up,' she said, taking Kees's handkerchief from the girl's chubby hands. 'Just the boys,' she said, dropping it into her pocket.

She reached for her teacup, drank her tea while leaning on the table, set the cup back on its saucer, and turned to leave. 'I must go,' she said.

Kees wanted his handkerchief back and was about to ask for it—

'Wait, I'll get Willem for you.' Moeke ran away through the useless room to the kitchen and reappeared with little Willem in her arms, his legs wrapped around her waist. His face was still snotty, his hair still tangled, but the warmth of the kitchen was now glowing on his cheeks.

'Please,' Moeke said. 'Don't go without saying goodbye to your son,' then, gesturing to Kees, 'to them both.'

'Thank you,' the woman said, touching the corners of her eyes. She slipped a letter into Moeke's hands. 'This is Willem's birth certificate. You have received Kees's?' she asked. 'Such a stupid mistake sending you Bart's.'

She kissed both boys' foreheads and touched Kees's cheek a little longer. She stared into his eyes, as if wanting to tell him something.

29

Her hand smelled of camomile tea and fresh newspapers. She opened her mouth, but hesitated and remained silent. She turned away from him and wrapped both arms around her daughter, hugging her close to her bosom, keeping her face turned away from Kees as she walked away.

At the front door, Kees heard footsteps coming down the stairs. The woman looked up. Her face tightened; she screwed her eyebrows in anger. Moeke glanced behind her and saw Cornelis stopping halfway. The baby twisted in the woman's arms. She held out her chubby hands to Kees, wanting to return to the game she had played with him. Her eyes brimmed with tears, and she screeched, pulling at her mother's clothes. The woman held out Kees's handkerchief with the embroidered initials C.v.N. The baby smiled, thick tears tumbling down her cheeks. She took the cloth, flapping it in her fist.

'His birthday is the fifth of February,' the woman said. 'I sent you the birth certificates.'

Moeke didn't understand. 'Pardon?' she said.

'Bart and Kees are twins, so they have the same birthday...'

'I don't understand,' Moeke said.

'Today is the twenty-fifth of January...' Moeke's face went redder than Kees had ever seen it. 'Today is Willem's birthday?' the woman said, her shoulders bowed over her daughter. 'Willem is three today.'

Kees stared at the woman. This strange lady made him feel like crying, too. He closed his eyes and remembered how she cuddled him and tucked his vest into his underpants, smoothing the creases. He remembered her face when she lifted him onto the seat on the train and kissed him on his forehead. She hung the sign around his neck and told him not to touch it or move until the gentleman with the moustache and the shiny whistle fetched him and took him to Papa. 'Never forget my name,' she whispered, 'and that you are my son...' She drew an imaginary cross on her heart and pointed at him. And he did the same, pointing at her. His mother got up from her haunches and turned her face away as she walked out of the train like she had done a few minutes ago in the hallway, trying not to show him her tears. He remembered how she had stayed on the platform at the station by his window until the train pulled away and how she ran along, keeping up by his window until the train went faster, and she couldn't keep up with it any longer. He remembered how her face glistened with tears.

Kees remembered now. He remembered everything now.

He stared at the closed front door and turned to the stairs. Moeke had gone up to Papa. He heard Moeke shout the words birthday and the fifth of February over and over. 'How could you have made such a stupid mistake?' Moeke shouted.

Kees ran into the vestibule and opened the front door.

'Mama!' he screamed, 'Mama?!' But the lady had disappeared. He remembered her name now and yelled as loud as he could, 'Your. Name. Is. Elizabeth! Elizabeth is my real mother's name. I haven't forgotten.' But she was gone, and the tears felt cold on his cheeks.

CHAPTER FIVE

Kees

'What's for lunch?' Kees called out when entering the kitchen. He pulled up a chair and sat down between Punica and Willem, who were in a heated argument. Whatever it was, he didn't much care what they were talking about. Knowing them, it could be about German composers being better than the American ones – Willem was all into American music while Punica loved Strauss – or something idiotically unimportant, like whether the dining room table was made of pine or oak. They were both eating kletsmajoors and they competed to get the most words out. Did they even listen to one another? They cupped their hands around their mugs with steaming milk as if warming them. Kees wondered if there was milk left for him in the saucepan.

Willem took another biscuit from the tin.

'I'll have one of those,' Kees said, pulling the tin towards himself, taking one out, and getting up to check the saucepan on the stove for the milk.

Mrs de Vries gave him a look as if to say, Yes, they are at each other's throats again.

The saucepan was empty.

Mrs de Vries was cutting tomatoes and onions into little squares. Beside her on the stove, butter melted in a frying pan. Kees liked the lunch she was preparing. Fried tomatoes and onions in butter served on toast, which she sprinkled with grated cheese and a sprinkling of nutmeg. It was his favourite lunch.

'Maybe you can tell them to stop?' she said.

'What are they arguing about this time?'

'Tell her,' Willem said to Kees. 'You believe the Nazis are doing good things for this country as well, or you wouldn't have joined the SS.'

'Good things?' Kees repeated. 'I joined because I wanted to get away from you two... and to see Russia,' he said, trying to look content but failing miserably.

Mrs de Vries let out a sarcastic laugh.

'It's just crazy that rich people get to say more about governing a country than its majority who happen to be poor,' Willem continued.

'Tell him, Punica said, waiving towards Willem, 'about what Ab thinks.'

'What does he think?' said Kees.

'Come on,' she said.

'Well, you seem to know him better than I do all of a sudden.'

'Come on, Kees. You know how awful life is becoming for him,' Punica said. 'Stop being childish. Tell him about how Jews aren't allowed into cafés anymore. For Jews prohibited!' she said, faking a German accent.

'Ab doesn't like cafés. He doesn't even like drinking alcohol.'

'Is that the point?' she asked. 'Isn't it about going where you want to go? About freedom? About not being told what you can and cannot do by a bunch of foreigners?'

'He should just man up,' Willem interrupted. 'Every change has its downsides.'

'Bullshit.'

'Punica!' Mrs de Vries interjected. 'Watch your language.'

'There isn't a way forward,' Willem said, 'without someone suffering the consequences. And with so many people supporting this new idea – they must be right. Let's just enjoy the dynamic of this new movement. To me, it seems that they want to improve life for the working classes.'

'My God, are you walking around with your eyes shut? How can you not see? How can you be so blind and spout those stupid opinions?'

'Just read your history book. Every change worthwhile has its downsides. It can't be the best fit for everyone. Ab will have to take it on the chin; it won't be forever; he'll be back at university before you know it. When the Germans win, we all will be the better for it. Even Ab will soon forget any hardship he suffered.'

Punica stood up, holding her hands, the palms facing upwards, looking at the ceiling as if she could see fairies flying around. 'Have you completely lost your mind?' she asked, faking a smile. 'Have you had a knock to the head?' – she knocked her own head – 'What have you got in there, sawdust?' Turning to Kees, 'When have you last seen Ab? Certainly, not this week, nor last week, nor the week before that, or you wouldn't be saying those stupid things. Did you not hear what they do to Jewish families?'

'What has the big bad wolf done now?' said Willem.

Petronella walked in. 'Another discussion?' she asked Mrs de Vries, throwing a newspaper onto the kitchen table. 'Children, maybe you two should read the news first?'

'They own the newspapers. Do you believe they still report what's happening? Isn't there a new word for it now? propaganda?' Punica said.

'There's a word for how you are talking, young lady, and it's not the word "polite" nor "ladylike",' Petronella said.

'Moeke, you're the one that said that Nazis aren't to be trusted,' Punica said, raising her voice. 'You wanted Kees and Willem to stay inside as much as possible where it is safe. Those were your words.'

'I'm just a mother hen; I worry about the boys,' Petronella said. 'Wait until you have children of your own.' She turned to the stove. 'Any milk left?'

'Punica?' Mrs de Vries said. 'What have you heard about Ab?'

'Thank you very much for asking. At least someone in this house cares,' Punica said, throwing up her arms and sitting down again. 'Ab's relations in Amsterdam have been put to work in Germany ages ago, and his family is still waiting for word from them. They promised to let them know as soon as they arrived at their new destination, but they haven't yet sent back one word.'

'So, what are you saying,' – Willem looked at Punica – 'is that the Nazis kill whoever they send to Germany? That's absurd. They need the workforce to keep the war going.'

'I'm not saying they're killing them, but come on, you must acknowledge they're not treating Jews with kindness? I saw a boy, maybe eighteen but certainly not older than Kees, being picked up last week. They stopped him on the street for no reason, asking to see his identity card, and when he gave it to them, they weren't showing him any respect. They threw him into the lorry. I'm frightened, Willem. What do you think he could have done to deserve such treatment?'

'Maybe he's just a common criminal? Who knows, maybe he robbed someone? Some Jews do commit criminal acts. They're not all saints like your Ab.'

'What's going on between you and Ab?' Petronella interjected.

'I've heard those stories as well,' Mrs de Vries said, 'I have Jewish relations, and they tell me that a lot of medical people, doctors, and dentists, are committing suicide. There seems to be a surge in suicides.'

'Why only dentists and doctors?' Moeke asked.

'The anaesthetic?'

'They sedate their children?' Punica asked.

'Before they—?' Moeke said. 'Where did you hear this?'

'My cousin,' Mrs de Vries said and nodded, looking worried as she glanced at the teenagers sitting around the kitchen table.

'What could make parents do something so horrific as to kill their own children?' Punica said.

'Punica, please,' Moeke said. 'We don't know that for a fact. I have read nothing about it in any newspaper. Could be just gossip.'

'Moeke, Ab told me his aunt and uncle have been ordered to move in with their family who live in Amsterdam. The Germans forced them, Moeke. They forced them to leave their home and their possessions. He said they had paintings by Old Masters and antique furniture and had to leave everything behind. His aunt even had to leave her engagement ring behind.'

'I thought you just said they left for Germany?' Willem said.

'He has more family, you know,' Punica said.

'That's so far away, darling. Nothing like that will happen here. Remember, my father – your grandfather is an important man in this town. He wouldn't let it get that far.'

'Moeke? You haven't spoken to him in what, sixteen years?'

'Well, at least we're safe in this house,' Petronella said. 'Just remember that this house your father has provided for us has stood the test of time. The last war this house witnessed was when Napoleon invaded this country, and it's still standing. That's more than a hundred and thirty years ago. We are quite safe inside these walls.'

'I will leave soon,' Willem said.

'What?' Moeke looked at Kees. 'Does your father know?'

Kees gave Willem a look.

Willem shrugged his shoulders. 'She has to know sometime,' he said to Kees.

'I'm sorry, Moeke,' Kees said. 'Pa swore us to secrecy. He knew you'd be upset. At least it's only ten kilometres outside the city. He won't be leaving for Russia any time soon.'

'Where to? Not that damn Nazi school I thought I had set you straight on?' Petronella faced Willem, waiting for an answer. 'Willem?' she said.

'It's called a Reichsschule. Do you know how many boys get in and how many want to get in?' Willem said, smiling. 'Pap was so proud.'

'I do not know, and I have no wish to know. Where is your father?' Petronella said, obviously trying to control her voice so that it would sound normal.

Petronella

Petronella left the kitchen; her appetite was suddenly gone. Cornelis was nowhere to be found, so she entered the breakfast room and worked on a new commission. How could she prevent her boys from leaving home? There wasn't a way she could think of to keep them out of Hitler's claws. Both were now signed up. She could not keep them from going without Cornelis's help. Or was there a way? She rushed to the coat stand, pulled her coat from the hanger, and pushed her arms through the sleeves. She looked at herself in the mirror and wiped away tears from her cheeks. She took her compact from her handbag and patted the powderpuff underneath her eyes. Her skin looked cakey and fake. Should she go upstairs and redo her make-up and try to conceal that she had been crying? She decided there was no need for a brave face and stepped out into the chilly afternoon to visit the house she had vowed so long ago never to enter again.

That evening, she returned just before dinner and strolled into the dining room, where her family waited for her. She sat down on the chair with the mouse carvings. She remembered how she had wished a child for every bedroom in the house. Sitting around this beautiful oak table eating dinner with all her children present, she did not regret leaving her father and marrying Cornelis. Even though her father had threatened it would be his death if she went on with this buffoonery, she went through with the marriage anyway. Her father had cut all ties and distanced himself and his family from those common basket weavers to which his daughter now belonged.

She looked at her eldest son, the son she had raised from age three, his younger brother sitting beside him, her son for the last thirteen years. Her eldest boys were not born from her womb but were as much loved as the ones who were. Kees, Willem, Punica, and little Corrie. She could not tell whom she loved the more. Taking each face in, each lovely face, their beautiful innocence, their happiness, she felt a lump form in her throat. She could never turn her back on any of them because they were a happy family, even though money was tight. She had no regrets.

'I saw my father,' she uttered. She wiped breadcrumbs from the tablecloth into an opened matchbox, a tiny dustpan.

Cornelis stopped eating and let his knife drop from his hand onto the plate.

Petronella nodded, biting back tears. She didn't want to cry in front of her children. She didn't want them to leave her feeling scared. What chance would they have in Hitler's army if they were frightened? How much longer was this war going to last? How much damage to her precious family could she endure? She tried to swallow, but nearly choked.

Cornelis reached for his wife's hand. 'Darling, what's the matter?'

'How could you?'

'What are you talking about?'

'Willem told me.'

Petronella got up from the table. 'I'm working on a commission. You promised me on my wedding day that you would not keep secrets from me, and yet today I found out that for the second time in a month, you have kept the most terrible secrets from me.' She turned and walked out of the dining room.

'Don't overreact!' Cornelis called after her. 'They are boys. Boys leave their stepmothers.'

'I have work to do!' called Petronella. 'You know, work? So, I can continue putting food on this table to feed this family.'

Cornelis got up.

'Please don't follow me!'

'Children, finish your meals,' he said, following his wife into the breakfast room, closing the door gently behind them. She sat at her hobby table by the French windows in the corner of the room. He lumbered towards her, his hands in his pockets, watching her sob into her hands. He took her left hand and lowered it from her face.

Petronella gestured to the two sofas in the centre of the room, standing on the Persian rug.

'Do you remember how we sat there with our dinner plates on our laps? The doors to the garden open and Kees running in and out onto the lawn and coming back to play at our feet, pushing his little train set on the Sarouk, tracing the design. We had everything we wanted. How little he was and how wonderful. Aren't you afraid of losing him? How could you encourage him to enlist? The enemy's army? How could you push him towards his death—?'

'He... I—'

'Don't bother denying your part in this. You knew Kees was vulnerable.'

'Don't make more out of this than it needs to be. My boys want... they hunger for adventure. They're at that age when they want to go out into the world and find their own way.'

'Your boys? Did I hear you call them YOUR boys? How dare you?!' Petronella screeched and slapped his face. 'You have no idea what you've done, have you? You have absolutely no idea.' She stood up, wiped her burning hand on her skirt, and pushed past him. She stopped and turned, standing in the centre of the Persian rug, her back erect, her palms facing him at her sides like the Holy Mother, and said, 'I went to my father this afternoon to ask him to help me. I begged him,' she said, lowering herself to her knees. 'I begged him to get Kees out of this stupid, stupid decision, and Willem, my dear Willem, still so young. And you know what? My father, the man I had turned my back on, whom I hadn't spoken to in sixteen years, started calling all his friends and associates to save YOUR son. But all in vain. There was nothing he could do. Nothing,' she said, tears brimming her eyes. 'My father and what you call his snobby associates have refused to join the Nazi party. Therefore, the Nazis have sacked all our good men from the council. And yes, my father called all this an invasion because that is what it is.'

Cornelis walked over to her and seemed hesitant, as if he wanted to kneel by her side.

'It seems,' she continued, looking up at him, her mascara darkening her cheeks, a string of slime running from her nose onto her fingers, 'that the Nazis determine the law in our city now – madmen

39

are governing us. And there is nothing we can do to reverse Kees's decision. And now Willem is leaving us and going into their clutches, and we won't have any say about him either. All that is left of our government is a gang of collaborators, of which you are one, wishing our fine young men into war. A hell that will terrify them for life if they should be so lucky to return, and all we mothers can do is pray to the Almighty God to please, please keep them safe, for their fathers have offered them to the devil to further their own careers. Cornelis, we talked about this, months ago. I thought you agreed that it wasn't a good idea?'

'Darling, he'll be fine. He'll be just fine. Don't worry about the boys so much. And Willem won't be going to the Eastern Front – he's only fifteen. They don't send children to the Front to fight for them.' He tried to hug her.

'He's sixteen. Why can't you remember their birthdays? Do they mean so little to you?'

'They need their adventures. They're young men; they need to discover the world.'

She pulled away from him. 'Please... please... just don't play the fool with me. Please,' she said, wiping her face with both hands, 'don't pretend to be more stupid than you really are. I don't find your stupidity endearing anymore, not now it threatens our family.' She looked at the husband, who was dressed in the NSB uniform. 'Is it any wonder?' she said. 'Is it any wonder?'

She got up off her knees and walked out of the room.

CHAPTER SIX

Petronella

Petronella walked into the kitchen and saw Mrs de Vries getting their breakfast ready. The house was quieter than usual.

'Moeke, do you know where Punica is?' Corrie asked, sticking her head around the door.

'Isn't she in the breakfast room?'

Punica usually started her day in the breakfast room, sitting on the little custard-coloured sofa by the French windows, reading a book, or watching busy blackbirds eat old breadcrumbs, which Mrs de Vries sprinkled on the lawn for them every day.

'She isn't, and she's not in bed either. Or in her bathroom,' Corrie said. 'In case you're wondering.'

'Where's Kees?' Petronella asked Mrs de Vries.

'They have both gone out,' Mrs de Vries said while stirring porridge. She added a lump of butter and a pinch of salt. She turned her face away and cleared her throat.

'Before breakfast?' Petronella asked, scrunching her face in disbelief. 'Did they mention why they had to leave the house so early?'

Mrs de Vries stopped stirring and turned to Petronella. 'They're both worried sick. When I went to the bakery, they were gossiping about lorries collecting people on Eusebius Buiten Singel. I happen to mention it to them. I'm sorry, I should have spoken with you first—'

'Eusebius Buiten Singel, where Ab lives?'

'Everyone talked about it at the bakery.'

'What lorries? What were they saying?'

'They said that lorries had pulled up at the Singel. I should have kept my mouth shut in their presence, but it was out before I knew it. Ab is such a lovely young man—'

'Where's Punica?' Petronella asked.

'Punica said she had to run some errands this morning. And Kees rushed out after her.'

'They didn't say they were going to Ab's house?'

'I said not to go there, but they said they weren't. They truly had errands to run.'

'And you thought this was normal behaviour for her when usually she can't pull herself away from her book? Is there something you're not telling me?' Petronella thought for a few moments. 'Ab's family is okay, though? The Nazis didn't deport them to work camps, did they? Mrs de Vries, will you stop stirring for a moment and look at me? Were they deported?'

'Well, I don't know for certain, but—'

Petronella rushed out of the kitchen. She pulled her coat and shawl from the hook in the vestibule and ran out into the street. They might walk straight into the Nazis clearing out Ab's house. Punica can never hold her tongue and would challenge anyone, even a Nazi. Petronella can't lose a moment and must hurry; she must get there before something terrible happens.

Not until she had passed the church and turned into Beek Street did she notice Corrie following her. She stopped. 'Corrie, what are you doing?' she said.

Corrie hunched her shoulders.

'Come on,' Petronella said, reaching out her hand. 'You might as well come with me before you get lost.'

Punica

Punica stared up at the tall building hovering above her. She looked at the black glass of Ab's bedroom window. Something had changed in the house, like someone had stolen its soul. Punica climbed the steps and pulled the doorbell. It echoed through the hollow building and made a dog bark. She lifted the lid of the letterbox to peer into the hallway. A cold draught wafted over her face. Nothing seemed different; the elaborate flower arrangement still welcomed her with vibrant colours, and the smell of jasmine tea and beeswax lingered as always. The marble entrance shone from all the polishing, but something was different, and she couldn't quite determine what it was. She listened through the letterbox. There was an eerie stillness. She'd expected the sound of clacking heels from somewhere deep within the house. She ran down the steps and crouched by the basement windows to see if Mr van de Berg was at work in his practice. The lights were off, and although the window had a broad stroke of milky glass, she could see that the dental chair was empty.

Punica ran back up the stone steps and climbed onto the railing to peer into the drawing room. The room looked like it had always done: too much furniture and too many plants. The curtains seemed rushed open; they hung over a little desk beneath the window and folded over a fern, bending the branches downwards. Ab's father's pipe lay on an ashtray, his small leather tobacco pouch beside it. She saw something move out of the corner of her eye; she jumped, and her right foot slipped. She jerked forward and clenched the wall to stop herself from falling off. But it was her own reflection in the mirror above the mantelpiece, and she looked ridiculous the way she was standing there, all nosy and curious, peering in. She got down to ring the bell once more. The bell echoed through the building, bellowing into every room, downstairs, upstairs, and even the attic. But there was still no sound of clacking heels or the soft padding of Ab's slippers.

She sat on the steps, pulled her skirt over her knees, and crossed her legs. She leaned her chin on her hands, thinking about what she could do. They must be home. They must be. On a Monday morning, before school? Even Ab, who was back from university, must still be upstairs in his bed. He is as bad at getting up early as Kees is. She glanced over her shoulder, up at his window. She got up again and rang the bell once more. Mrs de Vries must be mistaken. They couldn't have been deported; Ab's father was a dentist. Do they even need dentists in bomb factories in Germany? She glanced up once more. Crows scurried on the gutter, their feet clicking on the zinc. Their heads appeared over the edge, and black eyes peered down at her. A dog yelped in the distance, short sharp snaps, as if desperate and calling someone to help him.

'Darling.' Her mother was standing in the street behind her with Corrie gasping for air by her side. Moeke had tried to hide her curlers under a pink silk scarf, but it had got caught up at the back. Her curlers were visible. Usually, her mother wouldn't even answer the front door with them in... and now she was standing in the middle of the street in broad daylight holding Corrie's hand.

'I have a stitch,' Corrie complained, pressing her hand on her side.

'Moeke, nobody is answering. I've rung the bell three times,' Punica said.

'In case you're wondering,' Corrie moaned.

Punica looked at Corrie. Why was she with Moeke and not getting ready for school?

'Mrs de Vries told me you'd be here. I thought I'd meet you, darling.'

'Do you think the Nazis deported them?'

'Come away from there.'

'Moeke, I have to know where Ab is. I have to find out what has happened. Aren't you worried?'

The curtain moved at the window of the neighbouring house. The door scraped over the marble tiles, and a woman came out.

'Have they...?' Moeke hesitated, looking at Punica's face, 'have they... was there a truck in the street here, early yesterday morning?

44

They say the Germans come on Sunday mornings?'

'I wouldn't know,' the woman said. She looked lemony.

'You heard nothing, no trucks, no commotion?' Petronella said.

'Their dog is in the back garden,' the woman said. She walked toward them, keeping her voice low. 'It's barking like mad. But I'm too afraid to get it.' She looked over her shoulder into the street. 'The Nazis arrest you if they catch you in a house they cleared.'

There was a loud clang of a metal bin lid slamming shut. The woman jumped.

'I have to get back,' she whispered. She ran to her house and closed the door behind her.

'I'm scared,' Corrie said. 'Everyone is acting so weird.'

'We'll get that dog; it must be Blackie,' Moeke said. 'At least we can do that for them. Come along, girls. I'm sure they're all okay. Let's get the dog and go home. They so doted on Blackie.'

'Moeke, where have they taken them? Not to... not to Germany?'

'I don't know, Punica. Let's just get the dog and get out of here.'

Punica ran towards the alleyway, with Moeke and Corrie rushing after her.

'Are we even allowed around the back?' Corrie asked.

'Hush now.'

Moeke pulled Corrie along behind her. It was too narrow to walk side by side. They heard their footsteps echo against the walls of the tall buildings, even though they tried to tread as lightly as possible. Blackie yelped from the walled garden. Petronella walked to the gate and called the dog, sitting on her haunches blocking his route for escape with her body. But Blackie had no intention of escaping, and as soon as he saw Petronella at the gate, he ran back towards the kitchen. The door was open, and the curtain flopped and bellowed out in the wind.

'Blackie, come here, boy,' Moeke called out to him.

But the dog ran into the kitchen and came out again, barking like mad. Punica offered to catch him, but when she moved toward him, he ran back and disappeared into the house.

'Punica, come back. Go to the alleyway and wait by the wall for me.

Take Corrie with you and stay out of sight, both of you.'

'But I want to visit,' Corrie protested.

Moeke stole into the kitchen and disappeared. The dog stopped barking.

'Come on,' Punica whispered, taking her little sister's hand.

A lorry rumbled on the road – the brakes screeched, and it came to a puffing halt. Doors rammed open and slammed shut. Punica froze, her heart thumping in her throat.

'Stay here,' she whispered to Corrie.

She crept through the alley to the end and peered around the corner onto the road. Two men in uniforms got out of a car parked in front of the lorry. They were Dutch police officers. The two men getting out of the truck were SD men, the German Sicherheitsdienst, known for their cruelty and violence. The driver stayed in the lorry and lit a cigarette. Punica turned and tiptoed to Corrie. She took her hand and raised a finger to her lips. She took her in the other direction, away from Ab's house. 'Come on,' she whispered. 'Go there,' she said. 'That blue bicycle shed. The one furthest away. Hide inside and stay there until I give the signal, then you can come out'.

'All the way there?' Corrie complained.

'Not so loud,' Punica whispered. 'Go!'

'What signal?' Corrie asked, lowering her voice.

'The signal. Now go!' Punica whispered.

Punica watched Corrie run to the shed. When she arrived, she turned to her, smiling proudly. Punica pulled a grave face and waved with both hands for her to hide inside it. Corrie disappeared, and Punica ran on tiptoes back towards the garden gate. It creaked as she pushed it open. She saw one of the SD men in the kitchen; he heard the gate and looked out at her. Punica swallowed. Moeke was inside that house, and there was no way she would let anything happen to her mother, so she ran towards the kitchen, calling out another name, Fluffy. They might know Ab's dog was named Blackie.

The man stuck his head out between the curtains, peering at her.

'Excuse me, sir,' she said. 'But my dog ran into your house. I'm sorry to disturb you, but can I get him back?' She tried to sound as young as possible, speaking with a higher voice than usual and letting her knees lean into each other.

'Your dog,' he said.

'Yes, a black cocker spaniel.'

'Fluffy?'

'Yes,' she whispered. 'Fluffy.'

'You better come in,' he said. He had a round face with thin, greying hair. Beads of sweat sparkled on his forehead. He took out a red and white gingham handkerchief to wipe it away. He had a scar on his eyebrow, a line of bulging white skin where no hair grew. On his cheeks, small purple veins gave him a blueish glow.

She approached the threshold and hesitated, but he waved her on to come to him.

'Couldn't I call him from here? I... I don't want to disturb your morning.'

Her knees started to shake, and her gut made weird noises inside her tummy.

Moeke appeared behind the man holding the cocker spaniel in her arms. Punica's heart throbbed in her throat; what should she do now? The man was sure to see her mother. Her mother's face looked so white and scared, unlike her usual relaxed demeanour. The man sensed her behind him and swung around.

'Pardon me, sir,' Moeke said, her voice cracking, easing herself between the man and the black and white tiled sink, pulling the curtain under the sink with her. 'I'll get out of your way. Darling, I've found him for you,' she handed the dog to Punica. 'Luckily, he didn't get very far – the pantry. Well, goodbye,' she forced a watery smile.

'You were in the house?'

'Yes, I ran after my daughter's dog. He ran away. He's naughty.'

'Identification?' the man ordered, his face stern. He held his hand out to her for the document.

'As you can see, I hadn't quite finished dressing when my daughter came to me crying. Her dog had run away, and when we ran after him, we saw him slip into this house. The backdoor was open,' Moeke

47

said, waving her hand slightly towards the door.

'You were crying for your dog?' he asked Punica. 'How old are you? Papers.'

Moeke pulled her identity card from her pocket and laid it quietly in his outstretched hand. 'Do you not have children? I have four. My youngest son is starting the Reichsschule in Schaarsbergen, and the oldest has joined the SS.' She swallowed. 'He's going to Russia as soon as his orders come in...' Moeke's face was a yellowish-white. 'My daughter is the girl's—' she whispered.

'The girl?' he said. He peered at her. 'Take off your coat,' he ordered.

Tears fell from Moeke's eyes as she removed her coat to give it to him. He scrunched it from collar to hem and looked at Moeke's clothes. She wore a tight pencil skirt and a soft jumper, accentuating her figure. He handed her coat back to her and stared at Punica.

The girl? To what girl were they referring? Ab's little sister, was she upstairs? Punica shut her mouth, offered her mother the dog, removed her coat, and held it to him. He grabbed the coat from her.

'I have an adolescent daughter, too,' he said. 'She was a handful when I left. I haven't seen her for a long time. This godforsaken war.' He looked shocked by his own words. He handed Punica's coat back to her. 'Put your coats back on and get out of here,' he ordered, the softness in his voice gone and now sounding harsh again.

Moeke's eyes brimmed with tears. 'The girl,' she whispered. 'The girl upstairs,' she repeated, her mouth contorting. 'What will you do with her?' She hesitated, the corners of her mouth pulling down. 'My husband is a member of the NSB.'

Ab's little sister was the same age as Corrie, Punica thought. Had they deported the family to the work camps, leaving her all alone upstairs?

'Get out of here!' The officer waved them away, turning his back on them.

Moeke handed the dog to Punica. 'Come along, Maria Cornelia,' she said, her voice shaky. 'Mrs de Vries is waiting for us.'

They walked to the back gate and closed it behind them, fastening the clip. Once they turned the corner and were out of sight, Moeke wobbled to the wall, leaned her back against it, and spread out her hands to hold herself upright.

'Moeke, what's happened?'

'Where's Corrie?' Moeke mumbled.

'She's hiding in a shed. Is Eva upstairs? Has something happened to her?'

'Not now, Punica. Fetch your sister!'

Punica crouched and put Blackie on the ground. She pulled the belt from her coat with one hand as she held Blackie's collar with the other. He kept jumping up at her, licking her face, as she tried to make her belt into a leash. Moeke bent her head forward and started to faint. Punica pushed her back, 'Breathe, Moeke. Breathe deeply,' she said. 'Breathe.'

'Where is Corrie?' Moeke whispered as her gaze flickered about her.

'There,' Punica said, 'She's there. Come on, let's get her.' She pointed to the sheds at the end of the lane. Moeke regained her strength and scurried ahead along the earth path, calling Corrie with a breathy voice. Her knees jiggled as if she could no longer walk straight on her stiletto heels.

Punica ran after her, and by the blue shed, she called out Corrie's name. When Moeke saw Corrie, she fell to her knees and hugged her, crying quietly.

Punica didn't know what to do. Should she pull her mother back to her feet? Could she even walk now?

After a few moments, Punica hooked her arm in Moeke's and tried to pull her up. 'We have to get home now, Moeke. Let's... let's just go.'

Corrie stood motionless like a statue, shocked by Moeke's sudden outburst of love.

'Moeke, you're scaring me,' Corrie said.

Punica pulled her mother up from her knees, but she fell back to the ground.

'Come on, Moeke. Please stand up, let's go home. Come on, stand up.'

Her mother rubbed her face hard.

'Come along,' Punica said. 'Corrie, you take Blackie. Hold Blackie tight now, don't let him get away.'

Moeke finally got back to her feet. Punica put her arm around her mother's waist, urging her to walk with her. The dog hopped along, wagging its tail as they followed the path through the park toward Eusebius Cathedral.

They passed the ducks, quacking loudly. Blackie barked back even louder and tried to get at them. Punica helped Corrie hold the dog with one hand, and with the other, she kept her mother close to her. When they emerged from the park, a tram passed, and they had to wait to cross the road. The passengers inside looked out at them with empty gazes. Were their lives still the same? For Punica, everything had changed. She had never seen her mother like this. Moeke was a child who obeyed Punica instead of the other way around. She felt she had lost a part of her mother as she held her arm and steered her back to the house on Kerk Street.

CHAPTER SEVEN

Kees

Kees had been searching for Ab all morning. He thought of the lane not far from town going into the woods and hills behind the city. On one of the slopes was a place with a view they called Little Switzerland. Ab loved the view of the farmhouses in the valley below, with the cows and goats and the farmers attending them as if nothing had changed. Before the war, they often came there and watched the farmers at work.

Kees bought half a boiled, smoked sausage at Hema and started the long walk through the city, eating his lunch from a paper bag. The sausage warmed him. He entered Sonsbeek Park, leaving the main paths; he walked the muddy lanes into the hills. Taking a right turn, he scrunched the bag into a ball and flicked it away. He climbed the steep, overgrown path over collapsed trees and new hedges, his breath fast and heaving, to where he hoped Ab would be.

Finally, after searching everywhere, Kees found Ab sitting on a bench. Approaching him from behind, he walked around it and sat down beside him.

'So, there you are,' Kees gasped, 'I've been searching for you all morning.'

'Here I am,' Ab answered, not looking up but squinting into the distance, concentrating on the horizon.

There was a sense of unease in the air Kees had not experienced with his friend.

'Before the invasion, we had so many plans for our future,' Kees said.

Ab remained silent.

'So many hopes and dreams,' Kees continued. 'Do you remember how we had pledged to learn Russian from old books? You had the translated edition of Anna Karenina, and I had the Russian version. We'd alternate reading a sentence out loud. Do you remember how, after one chapter, we were convinced we could speak Russian?'

'Yes,' Ab said and looked away.

Kees took out a packet of cigarettes from his inside pocket and handed one to Ab; he placed another between his lips and struck a match. He lighted both of their cigarettes.

'Do you remember Sint Nicholas Day last year?' Ab asked. 'When I had come with Eva without our parents. I think I told you that my mother was ill. She wasn't. They had spotted your father wearing the NSB uniform. I had kept it from them, but the truth always comes out no matter how hard you try to hide it. That evening, I felt unsafe in your house.'

'I can't blame you after what my aunt said about informing the police about your family. She even told us how much they'd pay her for the information.' Seven guilders fifty cents per Jew. Consider the amount of money you'd make. Thirty guilders for the complete family. Kees remembered her words distinctly.

'Your mother was silent.'

'My mother was speechless from shock, as we all were, but my father made enough noise to make up for all of us. Do you remember how he yanked my aunt and uncle by the arms from their seats at the dinner table, threw them out onto the street in the rain, rushed back for their hats and coats, and threw them onto the road after them? Do you remember that very expensive hand-painted silk shawl landing in the middle of a muddy puddle? The pink and orange flowers slowly sinking into the filthy water?'

'I remember,' Ab said solemnly.

Kees had hoped the story would make him laugh, but no reaction came, not even a smile.

'My father shouted he would not tolerate this behaviour from anyone, and least of all from his sister!' Kees shouted, doing a stern voice; but losing his wish to be funny halfway through, he whispered the last words.

'I remember how everyone returned to the dining room. It was freezing after they had left. And the half-eaten dinner on the plates and nobody having any appetite left—'

'The food Moeke and Mrs de Vries so joyfully had prepared all day for what should have been a celebration,' Kees interrupted.

'How were they before the war?' Ab said, turning his face to Kees.

'Who?'

'Your aunt and uncle.'

'Kind... generous. Affectionate, I suppose. We enjoyed their visits. We looked forward to them and were always sorry to see them go.'

'How do you explain those kind and generous people becoming monsters willing to turn us in for just a few guilders?' Ab started to cry. He scratched the filter with his thumbnail and threw the half-smoked cigarette into the bushes, sobbing.

Kees watched his friend, his stomach tightening. Kees was the sensitive one, the one who cried, not Ab. Ab was tough, and no one dared hurt him. He hadn't even been bullied at school because he was always so self-confident.

Kees squeezed Ab's shoulder to comfort him. 'This won't be for-ever,' he said.

'You have no idea,' Ab said. 'You have absolutely no idea, with your lovely gentile family who can go wherever they like. Ride trams. God damn me!'

'Listen, let's make a plan,' Kees said. 'Couldn't you go to your fam-ily in Amsterdam, stay there till all this blows over?'

Ab grimaced.

'Tell me what I don't know.'

'The Nazis imprisoned them in Westerbork. They're waiting to be deported to Germany.'

'They'll survive the work camps. Nobody ever died from working hard,' Kees said.

'You can't be that naïve, can you?'

'Do you think they kill Jews?'

'All I know is that we haven't seen anybody returning, even for a short holiday. The Nazis rob the houses after clearing out the occupants. Do you think they put the paintings, antiques, furs, and anything else of value in storage for them?'

'What will your parents do?'

Ab cried again. 'They're gone,' he mumbled, wiping his nose with the back of his hand.

'Where?' a word Kees regretted because Ab raised his hands to his face and groaned as if trying to ban a recurring nightmare.

'Listen,' Kees said. 'The best place to hide is in full view.'

Ab looked at Kees, his face blank.

'Have you never hidden anything before?' Kees tried. 'The further away you bury it, the faster it is discovered. But no one finds it if you put it between your other bits and bobs on your bookshelf. How often have you searched for something that was right there under your nose?'

'So where am I to hide, on your bookshelf by your bed?'

'Join me and come to Russia.'

'Come on, that's just plain stupid.'

'Not stupid. It's your ticket out of a bad situation.'

'They'll know I am Jewish the moment I have to identify myself.'

'But how will they know?'

'The big red J in my passport is bound to give me away.'

'But I know a way. And it will succeed. Trust me.'

'Yeah, yeah... succeed, unless you have a spare passport lying around with my picture in it—'

'I do.'

Ab raised his eyebrows. 'You have a spare passport in my name?'

'I have the next best thing. Your birth certificate. My twin brother died when he was a few months old.'

'And you have it?'

'My mother packed it in the suitcase when she sent me to live with my father. It must have been a mistake. Moeke only found out when my mother sent the correct one to her. All you have to do is use it to get a new passport, and you can be my twin brother. Do it this week and come with me. Sign up.'

'I don't know, Kees. The SS? It'll never work.'

'No, not the German SS. It's a Dutch division to help them win the war. You never know, we might even win some medals. The two of us, together, who knows what we can achieve?'

Ab looked from under his eyebrows, his head bent down. 'Any chance of another cigarette?' he asked.

Kees lit one and handed it to Ab. 'In the meantime, you'd better stay at my house. Your street isn't safe anymore.'

CHAPTER EIGHT

Willem

Willem was the first to leave home. Obsessed with his music and studying with the conservatoire's greats, he was delighted to learn about a new school through a news bulletin on the radio. A Germanic version of the English Public School, and this school would open its doors to everyone. The school wouldn't be far from Arnhem, only a half-hour's bike ride away.

After the broadcast, Willem scoured the newspapers and cut out every item he could find on Nazi boarding schools. He liked the idea of a Dutch version of the English public school. Better still, the article said regardless of class, finances, or intelligence, all applicants would be accepted if they passed the physical exams. Strong boys originating from the countryside, it said, would have the same privileges, although their standard of education was below that of city boys. Willem had seen what not going to university had meant for Kees (a life filled with boredom and weird hobbies), and if going to a Nazi school meant he could study music at the conservatoire, he was willing to enrol in one.

But Moeke wanted nothing to do with this new infatuation of his. 'Be patient and be content with what you have achieved so far. You still have your entire life ahead of you,' she said. 'The war will be over sooner or later, trust me—'

'The school classes are called unities as in united students,' he said, not listening to her. 'And the teachers are called up-raisers, like parents, Zugführers in German. They think a strong and healthy body and good character are the most important things they can teach at school, more important than academic subjects. They cut the academic subjects to a minimum, and there's more time for music. Music. Music. Moeke, did you hear me? And sports like swimming, athletics, fencing, horseback riding, boxing, and sailing. Pap, listen to this' – Pap was sitting in his saffron armchair, reading the newspaper – 'shooting, driving cars, rowing, the list goes on and on. There's so much I can learn there.'

'You don't even like doing sports,' Moeke said, getting up and straightening her skirt. 'I have to finish embroidering that chair for Mrs Janssen, or there'll be no money coming into this house anytime soon. We'll talk about this later.'

Willem looked at his father. 'Pap, this would be such a great opportunity. It says that they only accept the crème de la crème. And once I've finished my final exams, I am eligible to study with skilled musicians, and I can go to any conservatoire I like as long as it's in the Third Reich.'

'What about tuition fees?' his mother called back from her hobby table in the breakfast room.

'It states the institute pays for everything: tuition, food, travelling, uniforms, books, everything,' Willem called back to her. 'And it says I can study anywhere after graduation.'

Pap winked to his son, reaching out to take the newspaper clipping Willem was citing. 'Sounds like any teenage boy's dream,' Cornelis said, looking at the clipping.

'But he's intelligent,' Moeke called out. 'It would be such a waste of his intellect. Be patient, Willem.'

'This sounds wonderful...' Cornelis said to his son. 'And indeed, it says passing the final exams makes you eligible to study anywhere you like within the Third Reich. Anywhere,' he called out to his wife. 'Ah, if I were young...'

His wife called back. 'It might be true you'd be eligible, but how can you study if all you've been doing at secondary school is playing the boy-scout? Willem, you are a grammar school student, so don't forget that accomplishment. Not everybody gets into Het S.G.A. Any boy would be happy to trade with you.'

'Moeke, please read the newspaper clippings—'

'Don't underestimate yourself and what you can achieve. Study hard, and the opportunities coming your way will be limitless. And Cornelis, stop encouraging him.'

'But Moeke, you said the school was too expensive now Pap is out of work. And this school has no tuition fees?'

'I said so expensive, not too expensive. And your father will soon find a new job.'

'We'll let you work in peace, darling.' Cornelis got up to close the door to the breakfast room.

'Pap,' Willem said. 'It says you can get more information through the Department of Education. They have a new division called the Institute for People's Education in The Hague. Look, it says no fees. Here's the address. Will you write to them and ask them if I may sit the entrance exam?'

Willem passed all what they called bravery tests, wrestling older and bigger boys, diving from the highest diving board, ten metres above the swimming pool without hesitation, and he won at boxing. He had never boxed before in his life. The examiners said Willem was a natural athlete. Of course, all this remained a secret between the Mandemaker men, and no one was to tell the female half.

A man in a white coat called out Willem's name. He had to report for a medical examination. With a weird instrument, a fork type of thing, they measured his skull, compared his irises to colour swatches on a chart, and compared the shape of his nose to examples in a notebook. The doctor said his hair was fine, a middle blond colour, although Willem had always referred to himself as a redhead.

The doctor wrote 100% on the report in the column Herrenmensch. He asked Willem if he spoke any languages. German? He said half the school would be German, and they liked to do exchanges with students from other European countries to encounter diverse cultures.

'Do you do exchanges with America?' Willem asked.

'Of course,' he said, 'as soon as they swallow their pride and become a Third Reich country. Next!'

When Willem finally told Moeke that he would start after Christmas in fifth class or fifth unity, he said, correcting himself, Pap had signed all the papers, and everything had been finalised. Willem wanted Moeke to accompany him on his first day, but she refused to go with him. But Pap would bring him all right, and Kees walked them out, holding Blackie by the collar while he closed the gate behind them. Blackie barked like mad at the gate, and Willem stuck his hand through the bars to stroke his nose, holding his bike with the other hand to say goodbye to him.

Punica asked him before breakfast if he really was joining the enemy, and when he said he was, she shook her head and wondered aloud how the men of their family could all be so stupid. She sat upstairs in her window and looked down at him straight-faced, without waving back when he had waved to her. Ab tried to talk Willem out of it the night before, but to no avail. Willem said he was a fine one to talk now that he had enlisted in the German army along with Kees. Moeke gave up trying to talk sense into her boys. She gave up talking to them altogether and even refused to say goodbye to Willem. He saw her working on one of her commissions while her back stayed turned to the window when he got his bike from the shed. He slammed the shed door to get her attention. Nothing. Even after he tapped on the window to let her know he was there, she did not turn around.

Willem wrapped his scarf over his mouth and pulled his knitted hat farther over his ears so only his eyes were visible. He and Pap got onto their bikes, pushed off, and lumbered out of town along the long, straight road, leaving Arnhem behind. White breath puffs left their mouths in slow rhythms. His father shone with pride as they started their journey through the bitter cold to Schaarsbergen. It was minus ten degrees Celsius during the day and at least minus eighteen at night.

They sliced through the cold forest and progressed towards Schaarsbergen. The odd farmhouse along the way looked empty, but the smell of burning wood lingered in the air, and black smoke billowed from the chimney. It had started to snow again. Their bikes creaked. The road became difficult to manoeuvre, with snow and ice gathering around their wheels and slowing them to almost a standstill. Willem stopped talking, putting all his strength into pushing the pedals and moving the bike forward. His heart grew heavier with each push as he felt more and more disappointed about Moeke and Punica not hugging him before he left. He missed the final intimacy of saying goodbye to them. The image of Moeke's back, without turning to see him go, and that of Punica sitting in her window upstairs, her face serious and disapproving, had hurt him more than he'd thought it would. Why couldn't they understand he was doing it for his music, his talent? A small sacrifice now meant he could go anywhere after the war. And he wanted to go to America so much; he was prepared to make any sacrifice possible. But he hadn't told either of them about what had happened at Hotel des Pays-Bas and his excitement about meeting the American swing band.

His mind wandered back to the evening he had sat at the bar, drinking a beer, his eyes fixed on the band performing on stage. Moeke had forbidden him to leave the house. On a school night? she repeated, raising her eyebrows. 'You must be joking.'

He had snuck out when she had returned to her work. American music. How could he pass this up? Kees agreed to cover for him in case Moeke came upstairs to check on him.

Willem's heart pounded to the drumbeat, and his foot tapped to the rhythm. Moeke was far from his mind. He had never seen such an upbeat band before. The men playing the trumpets were brown-skinned and looked very exotic. The saxophone player, a white man, wore owl glasses and looked more like a medical student than a band member. He wore a suit with a red polka-dotted bow tie. Willem dug out a packet of cigarettes from his trouser pocket, took one out using his lips, and searched for his lighter. The bartender held a flame to the tip of his cigarette.

'Dankjewel,' Willem said, breathing out smoke. 'Where're they from?'

'New York City,' the barman said, picking up a glass, washing it on the brushes in his sink, and adding it to the stack of glasses on the grid.

'The beat is...'

The bartender had moved away to the other end of the bar to take another order. Willem turned back towards the stage, drumming along on his knees. A slower song started, the muted trumpet playing a slow tune accompanied by more trumpets and a saxophone, and the drums' slow rhythm like marbles falling and rolling on tiles. The strings of the double bass veered up in a lovely tune. A trumpet took over the narrative, telling a story in notes, syllables of music rising to a climax and followed by a lonely and sad saxophone pushing along slowly, slowly following a slow rhythm like an obese man trudging up a hill. Willem swayed his head to the tune, closing his eyes and imagining himself playing along on the piano. Another song began, and he opened his eyes.

He saw a young woman on the dance floor with a heart-shaped face. She had blond hair with sculptured curls like movie stars. Her lips were rose red, and a pleated skirt swung around her like a harmonica, folding and spreading out on the beat of her feet. She twisted her hips to the music as her feet alternated fast and slow steps around the dance floor. Her partner danced as if the music had taken possession of his feet. He could tap his feet faster than you could see his heels and toes move as he turned and twisted around her, guiding her with his movement, lifting her onto his back, her undergarments exposed. No one seemed to notice as they clapped along. He flipped her back to the ground. She landed on both feet and did that twisting thing all over again.

Willem had never seen dancing like this. And the beat picked up even faster. How could anybody dance to this? But, oh, how they could. More people got onto the dance floor and danced. And a girl on stage, dressed in a white satin gown, floated to the microphone and sang. 'All right, I see... it's true; I can't get enough of you...'

A man cut into the dancing couple on the floor, and the girl danced away with her new partner. Willem enjoyed looking at all the lovely movements, watching all this happiness as the war outside became unreal – music like this was out of his world. He knew America was the place to be all along, but now he heard the music in real life and not over some scratchy radio, he was convinced he had a future across the Atlantic. He took another pull from his cigarette. Kees and Ab should have come along. He smiled; he liked the idea of twin older brothers. He had always liked Ab.

The man with the beautiful steps walked over to the other end of the bar and ordered a drink from the bartender. Willem gulped his beer, a pull from his cigarette, and slid over to the man. The bartender served the man a small glass of Jonge Jenever and a draught beer.

The man took a sip, pulled a bitter face, and washed it down with the draught.

'Where did you learn to dance like that?' Willem said.

'A Jonge and a beer works wonders with your feet.'

'And those girls. They're... amazing.'

The man laughed and shoved the rest of his Jonge over to Willem. 'Try it.' He drank his beer and walked back to the floor.

Willem emptied the Jonge, his throat burning from the alcohol. He pulled a worse face, coughed, and washed it down with his beer, emptying the glass in one swallow like the man had done. Warmth swept over him. His heart pounded with excitement. Was it the alcohol? He walked over to the band and waved his hand, gesturing for the saxophone player to come over to him. The saxophone player sat to the side, swaying to the music, and pointed to himself to make sure Willem meant him. The man got up, holding his saxophone by the throat.

He bent over towards Willem, bringing his ear close to Willem's mouth. Willem shouted that he wanted to play the piano. He pointed to a shiny black instrument standing vacant on the stage.

The man laughed and shouted, 'How old are you?'

Willem decided in a split second to lie. He should be younger, not older, and said he was fifteen, thinking being so young might make him a novelty like the bearded lady singing at the fair. It worked. The man laughed again and gestured for him to climb onto the stage. The other band members saw him talking to the saxophonist. When the saxophonist motioned that he wanted to say something into the microphone, the woman sped up the words. She laughed at her joke, singing faster and faster with the band speeding after her as if they, too, were hurrying to hear what the saxophonist had to say. The woman waved her hand as if giving up and said into the microphone, 'It's all yours.' She turned her back on him, crossing her arms in mocked agitation but still smiling. She bowed to the audience and moved to the back of the stage.

Once the crowd died down, the saxophonist said, 'Well,' into the microphone. 'It seems we have a piano player in the room, after all. But does the lad know the words of 'Eve'nings in Cadiz,'' he said, turning to Willem.

Willem hesitated.

'Come on. You know the words, don't you?'

'You want me to sing?' Willem asked. 'But I'm a piano player.'

'Singing is the easiest, and if you pass the test, the piano is all yours.' The saxophonist gestured towards the piano.

The band started to play, and moving a little to the beat, Willem tried to find the moment to start. After three restarts, he leaned forward towards the microphone. 'Grab,' he whispered. People laughed. Willem continued, a little louder, 'Your coat and take a chance...'

'Sing up,' the saxophonist shouted.

'Sing up, sing up, sing up,' the audience chanted.

'One lovely evening—' Willem tried louder.

'Louder!'

'I asked you to dance—'

'Lower.'

'Lower?'

'Louder and lower,' the saxophonist shouted again, lowering his voice, the words gurgling and twisting in his throat.

Willem was getting the hang of it. 'Under a veil of leaves,' he sang in a low voice. Willem noticed people were dancing to his singing and the band playing. He smiled, loving this, and twisted his hips to the beat, sliding his feet over the floor and bobbing his head to the music.

'On southern trees,' he sang. He was probably jumbling the words now, but nobody seemed to notice or care. The trumpets took over, and he felt so fine. He swayed to the music. 'Da-a-arling, in my dre-e-eams,' he sang, 'those love e-e-eve'nings in Cadiz.' The audience clapped. Willem took a bow and started to climb down, forgetting about playing the piano. The saxophonist took his arm. 'Do you know any other songs? Your fine singing voice sounds as dark as an American blues singer.'

'A blues singer?'

'Your voice can go so low,' he said, his voice as low as he could make it.

'I know Doodle Doodle Doo.'

'Can you play the piano and sing at the same time?'

Willem smiled. He could try. He hunched his shoulders and took place behind the piano. The woman in the satin dress lowered the microphone towards his face. He didn't want to sit down, not yet, so he slid it back up and, swaying and dancing, played the keys. This felt like Heaven. He hadn't had as much fun in years. After the song, even the bartender came towards the stage, clapping wildly and wolf-whistling.

'You know what, when you grow up, come to America, and we'll have a job for you,' the saxophonist said.

'Really?'

'Guys like you don't grow on trees. A drink?' He gestured, holding an imaginary glass in his hand.

'Yeah, please,' Willem said.

'By the way, what's your name?'

'Willem Mandemaker.'

'What, Mandemaker?' he asked, laughing, twisting the syllables. 'Sounds like double Dutch to me. Change that tongue twister into a simple Billy, why don't you? Billy Boy, short and sweet. So, how are you enjoying your stay here at this grand Hotel des Pays-Bas?'

'Pis Bak,' Willem laughed. 'We call it Pis Bak.'

'I heard about that. A urinal, you Dutch are crazy.'

'The name sounds so to us,' Willem laughed. 'When we say: Pays-Bas.'

The saxophonist laughed so loud his eyes brimmed with tears.

Willem hesitated. He noticed the dance floor had emptied, and most people had gone home or had returned to their rooms. 'I better get back home myself,' he said.

'Ah, you're not staying here? Hasn't Cinderboy overstayed his party with the curfew starting soon? When the clock strikes twelve, no pumpkin will take you home in a flash of lightning. Plenty of rats, though, out on the streets. They're called the SD, we're told. You better stay away from them. Why don't you stay with us until the curfew ends?'

'We're getting room service. Do you want something to eat?' the girl in the satin dress asked.

Willem hesitated. Moeke would worry. But only if she discovered his empty bed.

'You'll never make it. I don't know where you live, but if it ain't next door, you ain't gonna make the curfew,' the saxophonist said.

Willem nodded. 'I'll stay so,' he said.

'Right,' the saxophonist said, 'might as well get acquainted if we're gonna spend the night together,' shaking Willem's hand. 'My name is Nick, by the way, and that's Sonny, Bobby, Mike, Fred, and the gall is Gail.' Each shook his hand. 'Howdy. So, where did you learn to sing like that?' Sonny asked. 'You sound like the brother I never had – dark chocolate, my favourite colour,' he said, lowering his voice to tremble. He heaved the enormous double bass onto his back.

'Can I help?' Willem asked.

'Ah, shucks.'

'Strong as an ox,' Nick said. 'Here, take my saxophone.' Nick handed Willem the case with the saxophone inside, turned to the bartender, and ordered a bottle of that Dutch gin stuff.

The bartender handed him a brown ceramic bottle of Jonge Jenever. 'Will you be playing tomorrow?' the bartender asked.

'Yeah, we're here for the rest of the week,' Nick said. 'We'll stir this place up some more. Help the folks forget there's a war going on. You know, Billy Boy, we have an important job here, and it's not easy,' he said, winking his right eye. A cigarette hung from his lip, the ash tumbling down his shirt. 'Not easy at all, with all these black guys along.'

They all laughed.

'Black guys?' Willem asked.

'Ze Germs, ze no like no colour. What was the word they use – Zwartze?'

Everyone was in stitches.

'But they're my best friends?' he said, scrunching Sonny's hair.

They entered the lift, closing the cage door behind them. With the double bass huddled against the mesh, they squashed up against each other. Gail sang, 'Heaven,' and hummed a song Willem had heard on the radio before the war. 'That's what I see—'

'Yeah, sure. Say,' said Sonny. 'How many is this cage supposed to hold?'

'Every time you're here with me. In your eyes, I see heaven,' Gail continued.

'Eight, it says,' Mike replied.

'Eight, seven of us, Billie Boy there and Sonny's friend,' pointing at the double bass.

'Oops,' Sonny said, laughing; his voice sounded high-pitched and rolled in his throat. 'Ah, but he stands pretty still.'

'Heaven—' Gail continued.

The cable pulling the lift groaned.

'Well, Gail, you better stop singing, or the damn cable might snap, and you'll find yourself in heaven,' Sonny said.

'Ah, she's not going to heaven when there's so much more fun to be got down below where it's hot,' Nick said. 'Hey, this could be a song,' he said and sang, 'There's so much more fun – to be got – in the so-u-uuth – where it's hot.'

They all laughed. 'Ah, Nick, maybe leave the songwriting to Sonny?'

They arrived on the fourth floor, and Nick opened the gate, holding the cigarette between his teeth. Willem felt the lift veer as everyone stepped onto the landing. He was the last to leave.

'So, Billy,' Nick said, as he produced a key with a monstrous brass key hanger from his pocket, 'don't be too shocked by our humble dwellings.' He twisted the key in the lock, and the door slid open. 'After you,' Nick said, and Willem entered hesitantly. The room had three beds, all turned down and made up with light blue sheets and moss-green blankets, the flowery bedspread only covering the end of the bed. The curtains matched the floral pattern of the bedspread. There was a dressing table by the window, with a white and golden baroque design, full of uncorked Jenever bottles. On the stool in front of the dressing table stood a gramophone player. There was an oil painting of a saddled black horse with two white and black dogs hanging on the wall.

Nick took the saxophone from Willem's hands and laid it on the bed. He walked over to the bar – a drink cabinet with bottles of alcohol – and set out five glasses. He lifted the ceramic jug to his mouth to uncork the neck with his teeth. He poured gin into each glass.

'We'll have to share; we haven't borrowed enough glasses from the restaurant downstairs. What time is it?'

Gail was about to put a record on the gramophone and turned her wrist towards her, still holding the record.

'It's late. Okay, one song, and then I'll be turning in.'

'Turning in what, me?'

'Dance?' Gail said, holding out her hand to Nick.

'Oh baby,' Nick said, lighting a cigarette between his lips. 'I'm dead tired.'

'Dance?' she repeated, reaching for Willem this time.

Willem looked at the hand.

'Don't be bashful. Dance with the lady,' Nick mumbled.

Gail laughed, 'Is Jimmy Lunceford known over here?'

Willem took her hand, his face crimson. 'I don't know...'

The others hung out on the armchairs, and Sonny lay on the bed. Everyone smoked except Willem. Everybody had removed their jackets, unbuttoned their shirts, and wore clean white vests. Willem swayed with Gail to the music, a slow rhythm unlike what he had seen in the downstairs cafe. It wasn't any dance. At least not one he had learned in dancing lessons at Dance School Wensink on Park Street, where he had been taking ballroom dancing lessons since he started secondary school four years ago.

Willem loved it. He could have danced all night. Gail smelled so lovely, a scent he didn't know. When his eyes became heavy, Gail said she was tired too and wanted to go to bed.

'Good night, darling,' she said to Nick, bending down to kiss him. He reached up, returning her kisses. She left the room.

Willem sank to the floor, resting his head on the couch behind him. Fred beside him had already fallen asleep.

After Gail had been gone for about four or five minutes, a wild knocking sounded on the door. Nick got up, sighing, lumbered to the door, and looked through the spy hole. He opened the door. It was Gail again, and she came barging back into the room.

'What's the matter, honey? You'll wake the whole hotel making a racket like that.'

'Did you see today's evening paper?' she asked, her face white and biting her bottom lip.

She shoved the newspaper into his hands. 'It's Dutch... Billy read this?'

Willem took the newspaper from Nick.

Gail said, 'Japan, England... VS – VS is Dutch for the US, isn't it Bill? Orlogue means war, right?'

Willem looked at the newspaper headline. He translated: 'Japan at war with US and England.'

'What? How can that be?' Nick roared.

'Do you know Pearl Harbour?' Willem asked.

'Yeah?'

'Japan attacked it, sank US warships, and killed loads of soldiers. Now America has declared war on Japan.'

'What?' Nick said. Gail took back the newspaper and tried to read the words. 'What time is it?' she asked.

Nick woke the others. 'We have to get back to the States as soon as possible.'

'What about the gig?'

'There's a war on. Come on, let's get packing.'

'Can I come with you?' Willem asked.

They left after curfew lifted, at four in the morning, and promised Willem if he ever made it to the States, they would have a job for him.

Nick's last words had been, 'We'll see you in The States, Billy Boy?'

Willem had said he would be there, and that was a promise he would keep.

Pap braked, coming to a squeaking halt. Willem jumped from fright and braked, too.

'I think you'll be fine from here on,' Pap said.

Willem stared at him.

'It's so damn cold, and you don't seem to hear a word I'm saying. I might as well return home.'

'I heard every word...' Willem lied, but all he had heard was the squeak of their bikes.

'You'll be fine,' his father said, thumping Willem's shoulder with his mittened hand. He shook off his glove and held out his bare hand. Willem clenched his glove between his teeth, pulling it off as well. They shook hands like businessmen do. His father turned his bike around and got back on. He said, 'Best of luck, son,' and pedalled back towards the city, crouching forward into the wind. Willem watched him shrink and finally merge into a trembling wall of snow-flakes. Once his father had disappeared, Willem got back on his bike, swallowed, and resumed his journey, pushing himself forward. Next stop, America, he thought.

CHAPTER NINE

Kees

Kees dropped the silver bird Moeke had given him the first night he arrived at his new home into his pocket and glanced around his bedroom; how he loved this room at the back of the house. From his window he could see all the neighbours' private gardens and his family's land jutting out into the distance. He loved going on long walks through the fields situated like an oasis in the middle of the city, where it was possible not to meet a single soul outside his family all day.

He turned his gaze from the window, and lifted his latest puppet, a skeleton, from the desk, slid a nail between his lips, and took the hammer in his right hand as he tried to decide where to hang this one. He contemplated the cabinet on the far wall; Moeke and Nienke had put it there when he was four so he could see it as he lay in his bed. He remembered how his eyes traced the beauty of the details, and sometimes he couldn't resist getting out of bed, although Moeke had forbidden him to and tiptoeing to rearrange his collection, moving his latest find to the front. One of his unique objects was a porcelain bowl with a mermaid sitting on a ceramic water fountain. The top was a little chipped, but the mermaid was still intact. Her tail curled around the stand, lifting a shell-shaped bowl from a wave on the base. He'd try to imagine everything about it: the country it came from, the spicy smells of the food cooked there; he felt the salty sea breeze in his nostrils and the wind ruffle his hair as if he were standing on the deck travelling to an exotic country. As he fell asleep, he dreamed of leaving

70

home when he'd be old enough. Kees thought he was adventurous when he was a boy.

Turning into a teenager, his taste for collecting changed to all kinds of animals, bones, and skulls; and dead ancestors, father's father, dead as well, and the fathers before him, all dead. The fact of dying fascinated him, and he tried to get his head around the infinity of time after a human being died: the ceaselessness of death.

Petronella did not understand how his interest shifted from ocean memorabilia to skulls and ancestors. She also did not comprehend what ancestors and skulls had to do with one another, but she instructed Nienke and Mrs de Vries to indulge him. If he sterilised the bones in the kitchen, he was allowed to work on them in his bedroom. When his room had taken on a dusty, sweet odour, Moeke said to keep his windows open for at least an hour a day; other than that, Mrs de Vries or Nienke were not to curtail him in his desire to collect bones and carve skeletons from them.

He liked to reassemble tiny rabbit bones so they would look like miniature human beings. He would carve skulls from a cow's ilium or tibia, supplied by the abattoir near the banks of the Nether Rhine just a few streets away.

Mrs de Vries and Nienke could not hold their tongues. They complained that a vile smell saturated the kitchen when Kees sterilised his bones. Of course they smelled of bones – that's what they were.

They put clothes pegs on their noses and made fun of each other's appearance, asking what his lordship would think of next to keep him occupied. Willem, too, complained about the smell seeping into his room which was above the kitchen. His windows were located on the same inner yard as the kitchen, and when his windows were closed, the scent still drifted through the cracks into his bedroom. Willem would complain to Kees, saying, yours is on the Steeg where the stink can't reach. Finally, when Corrie complained, Moeke moved Kees to the garden shed and gave him a petroleum burner, a brass pot, and many instruments to work on his sculptures.

Kees remembered how inspired he was at first with his new private workspace. He was embarking on a new project, which excited him and made his skin tingle. He believed he could create a fantasy that would come alive if everything was done in a precise order. When finished, he would exhibit his works of art to his family. Oh, how amazed they would be.

He found a box on one of his treasure hunts, a beautiful smooth mahogany box with brass fittings and an ornamental key. Inside the box were five compartments. He had asked the school carpenter to replace the two outer compartments with fitted glass. Kees sanded the edges of the glass to slide them in and out without cutting himself. On the lid, the carpenter fitted a large plate to cover the whole top, and Kees's heart leapt at the beauty of the box. Kees took it home and inside it he arranged the biggest miniature skeleton. It had proper adult proportions: legs crossed like a tiny Jesus on a cross, and arms and intricate hands spread out from its body; each segment of the ribcage, vertebral column, fibula, phalanges, and other bones in their specific positions secured with scientific needles like authentic specimens, except the arms and hands. They needed something else, which he still needed to discover.

He looked for something colourful, something of beauty, and when his mother came home from one of her bargain hunts, a silk shawl tied over her elegant curls, he knew what he lacked. Later on, when everyone had gone down to dinner, he cut two large squares from the shawl, fumbling them into his pocket before rushing into the dining room. After dinner, he returned to his shed and cut two magnificent wings from them with tiny nail scissors. The wings were as exquisite as a butterfly's. It perfected the illusion he was creating. He knew this was going to be his best project yet. Pricking the wings in place underneath the arms and hands, and subsequently each little bone, his fairies had finally reached completion.

He could not contain himself. How real everything looked. Trying to keep from laughing while his lips formed a broad smile, he stroked his fringe from his eyes. Yes, this is what he had wanted to accomplish: fairies so real they could fly. Bursting with pride, he took his box to his mother. Moeke knew he had made something extraordinary and got up from her hobby table, dropping her embroidery to admire his craftsmanship. She didn't mention a word about her ruined shawl. 'Sometimes,' she said, hushing Punica, 'an artist needs to take liberties.'

Kees believed his sculptures possessed the ability to leave their display boxes. That was the reason he always fastened them securely to their cardboard backings. But now, being eighteen, Kees had stopped believing in fairies, and the silver bird's heart had stopped beating. The puppets he made were just childish fantasies and were lifeless, regardless of the work he put in them.

Kees glanced around his room. He must stop his mind from wandering, or he'll never decide where to hang his latest skeleton. Pap cleared his throat behind him. Kees turned to face him. While lowering the skeletal fairy, he took the nail from his mouth and stepped down from the chair, letting his hands hang by his sides so as not to attract more attention to the bundle of strings and tiny bones he was holding.

'What is that?' Cornelis asked.

Kees thought for a minute. He held up his creation for his father to see the work he had put into it.

'It's a puppet,' Kees said.

Cornelis reached out and touched it. 'Are you still carving these... objects?' he asked, pulling back his hand and wiping it on his trousers. 'Have you gone mad?' Cornelis asked. 'How long have you been working on this?'

'A month,' Kees answered.

'I meant on this?' Cornelis said, gesturing across the room with his arm and hand, 'All these, these... insane objects?' He walked to the door and called out onto the landing, 'Petronella! Petronella, please come and see what your stepson has been up to!'

He returned to the room, blowing air through his teeth and patting his sides. Kees stood aside, his face crimson, staring at his feet.

'What is the matter?' Petronella appeared at the door. She wore a silk scarf with roses and poppies tied around her neck. The colours complemented her green jumper and cream skirt. 'I'm writing an important letter, so please don't disturb me,' Petronella said.

'Are you aware your son has gone quite mad?'

'Mad,' she said, trying to fake a smile. 'Do we have to speak about this now, with Kees leaving us in a few hours?'

'Your eldest stepson is making – fairies. Fairies, for God's sake.'

'He's been making them all his life. Don't pretend you didn't know about this.'

'He's eighteen. He should hang out with his friends. Chasing girls—'

'Going to war,' Petronella added. She fixed a smile on her face. 'Darling,' she said. 'Can't you give him a lovely send-off on his last day at home?' She turned to Kees, 'Is Ab ready? You're both all packed?'

'He's in the bathroom,' Kees said.

'I'm happy he'll be with you, and you won't be alone out there. Such a good plan you two concocted.' She forced a smile. 'I'll just finish my letter. Maybe your father can go downstairs and make some sandwiches for your journey. Come along, I'll help you in a minute, Cornelis.'

Ab entered the bedroom from the en suite, holding a towel and wiping a line of shaving cream from underneath his nose. He looked at Pap but remained silent.

Pap squeezed his lips into a strained smile and backed out of the room. 'I'll leave you two to it. What time will you be leaving? I'll get the wheelbarrow out for the luggage so we won't have to carry it across town.'

'Moeke has arranged for someone. A car to take us.'

'Right. I've never ridden in a car before. That's very generous of whoever it was.'

'Pap, Punica is coming, and with the luggage. I don't think there will be room for more,' Kees said. 'Sorry. Moeke arranged it yesterday.'

Pap said, 'I'll see you downstairs.'

Kees watched Pap close the door behind him. When he had gone, Ab raised his eyebrows and smiled. He returned to the bathroom.

Kees remembered his father at the meeting in Musis Sacrum. He was the most complex person to gauge – one minute domineering, the next minute crawling with insecurities and going red. No wonder Moeke's family detested him. Kees sighed, embarrassed by his thoughts.

In his mind's eye, he saw his father cueing beside him at the concert hall, and he remembered his surprise when he noticed everyone was wearing a Nazi uniform. 'A Nazi meeting?' he had asked his father. 'Does Moeke know you've brought me here?'

The hall should have opened at a quarter to six. But with the sheer number of people showing up for the event, they opened the doors three quarters of an hour early so everyone was seated before the prominent speakers arrived. Cornelis and Kees were lucky to find seats near the podium. The hall filled up quickly; the balconies were packed, and more people stood at the back of the hall. The Nazis had decorated the stage with banners bearing swastikas. On the podium, chairs stood in a semi-circle around a lectern with a microphone. Kees looked around the hall. 'We should have brought Ab with us,' he said. He'd know what to make of this spectacle. Kees didn't.

Everyone's excitement whipped up Kees's mood. As the meeting progressed, he realised he had a future; even if that future didn't include his immediate return to university or his studies, he could give his life a new twist.

With the rising excitement around him, men and boys, ordinary folks without ambition but dressed in imposing uniforms, Kees realised that it was possible to achieve anything. Reichskommissar Seyss-Inquart wanted brave men to fight Bolshevism and free the Russian children from Stalin. Kees could go to Russia. His childhood dreams materialised in his mind's eye as the evening passed – he had always wanted to travel to Russia. Find his little silver bird's origins – maybe find the ice maiden. Perhaps it was all meant to be. Kees smiled; he could discover a magic that always surrounded him and uncover the secrets of his soul.

For the first time since the Nazis invaded his hometown, he didn't feel scared of them. Not at all. Look at them, their excitement. He, too, could do this. He could do this. And it would be much better than sitting in the shed feeling sorry for himself after being expelled from university for being unable to pay the fees; this was like... 'Pap, the excitement – the energy. I feel as if there's no war on... as if we can do what we want... start a new...' He couldn't think of the word. 'Direction? Did you see the plumber in a black uniform at the entrance, showing everyone their seats?'

Kees felt a spark of possibility – the energy erupted into a bolt of electricity as Reichskommissar Seyss-Inquart retreated, marching through the centre aisle towards the double doors. Everyone got up shouting 'Heil Hitler!', their arms raised in the Hitler salute. Kees joined them, realising it was the first time he shouted, 'Heil'. He joined in the chant at the top of his lungs.

Kees was caught up in the moment, which lasted one hour and fifteen minutes and ended as abruptly as it had started when he put his name down on the form to enlist. He wasn't like his father; he was like Moeke, even though she wasn't his biological mother. How could Kees become a Nazi when everything they stood for he opposed with all his heart? He hated the war; he hated the way Nazis used violence, and most of all, he hated the way they treated Jewish people, telling them what they could and could not do. Kees asked for the form back, but no one listened. And, when he tried to reach for it over the makeshift counter and started screaming for it, they had him removed from the hall. They threw him out onto the street. His father stood red-faced and did nothing to help his son. The plumber of all people who had fixed their toilet was the one who threw him onto the cobbles and kicked him as he lay confused, trying to make sense of what had happened.

His father stood there and did nothing while a teenage boy bent down and thumped his stomach. Kees lay huddled and moaned from the pain. Finally, after twenty minutes, he pushed himself up off the ground and walked home alone. Moeke was heartbroken when she found out, and breaking her heart had also broken Kees's heart.

Kees stood at the door opening of the bathroom. 'Do you think I've... we've made a mistake.' – Kees rubbed his face and groaned – 'I mean, you enlisting as well? I think I've made a God damn awful mistake, and the worst thing is I should never have got you involved.'

'Come on, pull yourself together, man.'

'Ever since I've enlisted, I have had a terrible feeling in the pit of my stomach. I think I've made a terrible mistake. I haven't had a proper night's sleep since I put my name down. My palms become sweaty every time I think of it. God, what have I got you into?' Kees's heart was racing; he was lying again; he knew all along what he had got Ab into. He knew the moment he mentioned it on the bench in the woods, and he hated himself for it. 'This might be the end of us. If we walk through that door, we might not be returning. Maybe you should make a run for it; you still can. Leave this place. Go somewhere where Jews can live in peace.'

'That's fear talking. Come on, pull yourself together. You'll be excited once we're on the train, trust me. We promised each other we wouldn't look back, remember?'

Ab put on Cornelis's old tweed jacket and wrapped a scarf around his neck. He pulled his little suitcase off the bed. His suitcase was filled with second-hand clothes Moeke had found for him. 'Let's get out of here. Get on that train and keep our eyes fixed on the future.'

Punica waited on the road to watch for the car to pick them up. When it entered Kerk Street, she ran into the house, calling Kees and Ab to come. Corrie was all excited, as if Kees was going on a holiday. And Blackie was hopping along, yapping, not understanding what was going on. Corrie asked Kees to bring back a present for her. He said he would and tried to wink while plastering a brave smile on his face. 'Don't worry about Blackie,' Corrie said to Ab. 'I'll look after him until you get back.' She offered to carry Ab's suitcase, but he refused and said he wanted to take it himself. Mrs de Vries and Nienke got their handkerchiefs out and dabbed their tears when they walked behind the boys through the vestibule and approached the car.

Pap looked baffled when he saw his father-in-law's car stop in front of the house and the chauffeur getting out. The chauffeur opened the boot for the suitcases. The boys lifted them into the boot, and Pap wanted to close it, but the chauffeur waved his hand. He would do it, not letting Pap touch the car. Moeke left the house dressed exquisitely, as always. She carried the letter she had written in her hand and slid it into her handbag while she and Punica got into the back seat. Kees turned to shake his father's hand. Kees tried to smile and turned and shoved in after them. Pap patted Ab on the back and opened the front door for him, but the chauffeur again took over from him and closed the door after Ab got in. Ab wound his window down to wave. Pap stepped back a few paces and joined Mrs de Vries and Nienke on the pavement, standing behind Corrie, resting his hands on her shoulders. The chauffeur tipped his cap, ran around the car, got behind the steering wheel, and started the engine. Blackie began to bark again but stayed by the women standing on the pavement. Cornelis lifted Corrie into his arms and turned to the house with her. Corrie roared for her father to put her down.

'I want to wave goodbye!'

When the car pulled away, they heard her screaming for Pap to put her down.

'I wish I had brought her with me now,' Moeke said.

Kees and Ab waved through the opened windows. Mrs de Vries and Nienke waved their handkerchiefs.

Although it was busy for a Monday morning, they arrived at the station well on time. Kees looked at his watch and swallowed. Punica hooked her arm in Ab's and walked with him into the station. Moeke got out her purse and gave Punica a few cents to buy gevulde koeken for the boys. Moeke said she wanted to speak to Kees alone for a few moments, so Ab offered to accompany Punica.

Kees dug the envelope containing his orders out from his pocket. They were to report on Platform 2b. Moeke took his arm. 'The others will catch up,' she said. 'Now, I finally have you to myself.' They walked through the hall towards the platform.

'We have had little chance to talk since Ab moved in,' Kees said. 'Was there something particular you wanted to discuss?'

Moeke squeezed her lips; her eyes were sad. 'Where are they sending you for training?' she asked.

'Senheim in the Alsace. Never heard of it, either,' he said when Moeke looked at him. They climbed the stairs to the platform. 'I think I'll be there for two months,' he said, 'and then travel by train and boat to a place called Omemel in Poland.'

The station's curved corrugated roof filled up with smoke from the train, ready for departure. Moeke sighed, trying to catch her breath. 'I haven't slept very well,' she said. She watched other parents with their sons climb the stairs behind her. No one seemed to realise where they were going – young, smiling faces surrounded by older, proud ones.

'A mother raises her sons with all the love in the world, and when the world takes her sons from her, there's nothing she can do about it,' Moeke said.

'Moeke, I'm coming back to you. Don't worry about me.'

The train was waiting. The locomotive puffed quietly impatient breaths of steam into the air. It was getting ready to leap towards Germany. Someone had written on the side of the train; We're going to Russia to take Stalin home, in big chalky letters.

'Kees... did Ab ever talk about his family?'

'No,' he said. 'They're working in Germany somewhere.'

'Did he tell you that?'

'God, where is he?' Kees said, looking at his watch.

'They're not in Germany.'

'You know where they are?'

Moeke opened her handbag, taking out the letter. Holding it in her hand, she pulled him into an embrace. 'You've always been my special one,' she whispered.

He rechecked his watch. 'Where is Ab? He's not having second thoughts?'

'Of course not,' Moeke mumbled, looking over her shoulder. The platform was crowded with young men pushing and pulling each other to get on the train.

'Where's Ab?' Kees repeated. 'What if he's changed his mind? What if he is at this minute running away from the station?'

The train whistle shrieked, and Kees jumped.

'All aboard!' the conductor called out.

Kees embraced Moeke once again. 'Boarding now,' the conductor said to him. Kees turned and took the first of the four metal steps.

The conductor laughed and urged him on, slamming the door shut behind him. Kees shuffled through the train to find a vacant seat. He put his suitcase on the overhead rack and opened the window, searching the crowd for Ab's face. Moeke had walked along with him and now stood by the opened window beneath him. Her gaze also searched for Ab and Punica. She turned to Kees.

'You'll be fine,' she called out as the train shifted on the tracks. 'You're strong. You'll be fine.'

'Moeke!' Kees called out, hearing the panic in his voice. 'What will I do?'

'You'll be okay,' she called after him. 'Stay strong... Do you have the bird?' she called out. 'Don't let the bird—'

'It's in my pocket.'

'Don't forget—' she shouted from the top of her lungs. But Kees couldn't catch her words. He saw her fold an envelope and put it back into her handbag.

Was the letter meant for Ab? Kees sat down. His eyes were prickly and brimming with tears. He tried to hide his face from the other men and took out a packet of cigarettes. Shoving one between his lips, he searched for his matches. He found the box in his trouser pocket and lit one. The smell of burning phosphor hung in the air as he sucked the smoke into his lungs. Men were still coming into the compartment, looking for vacant seats. They all adhered to the same ritual; they shoved the case overhead, sat down, and shook hands with the other passengers. Kees ignored them and looked out over the city, the distance between the houses growing and fields taking over as the train slid over the land. The landscape he loved so much now galloped away.

He heard the door open once more behind him and slammed shut. Someone thumped the back of his seat and the metal rack with a suitcase. He slid Kees's luggage to the side, put his on, and turned to sit down. Kees wasn't in the mood to get acquainted. As he glanced up to tell whoever it was to move on— 'You made it,' he said.

'Did you think I'd let you face Stalin alone?' Ab said.

CHAPTER TEN

Punica

Punica had made a Star of David from some scraps of sunny orange material she found in Moeke's sewing box. She pinned it on the left breast pocket of her raincoat. She missed Ab. He had sent her a letter in which he wrote they were settling in, becoming good Nazis (she laughed out loud, knowing he was only joking) and that they would be leaving for Russia soon. I miss you, he wrote. The words made her heart skip. She wanted to tell him how much she missed him, and about the new rule the Nazis had thought up – the compulsory Star of David the Jews now had to wear – and about what she was going to do about it. But she decided not to.

The word Nazi had become a taboo word in the Mandemaker household. If anyone mentioned it, it brought Moeke to tears and Papa to anger, and somewhere in between, Punica had made up her mind about the whole business. The compulsory Star of David and the J stamped onto the Jewish identity cards made Jews seem like lower people, and she would not stand for it. She wondered if her friends would be brave enough to wear their stars to school. They planned to do this together, convinced if everyone joined in, they would help their Jewish friends who had been expelled from school.

As she cycled, her star flopped like a daffodil in the wind. Peter had pointed out that the material was too flimsy, but the colour was almost right. She would have bought the real thing if she'd had the money. But at four cents apiece and the additional textile coupon from the ration book, she knew Moeke couldn't afford it.

81

On the road, people turned to stare at her. Someone shouted, well done, and you take after your mother. Most people looked confused or surprised when they saw the star flopping in the wind. Everyone knew her older half-brothers had left to serve Hitler. The gossip about them spread through the city like a virus. Seeing those faces on the road, she knew people wondered what was happening in the Mandemaker household. Were they collaborators, or were they part of the resistance? Or the women were against fascism and the men pro-Nazis. She wanted to tell them nothing was black or white. Willem slept snuggled up with one of his instruments, dreaming of going to America. He was trying to find a way there; Punica wanted to shout this at them. But she had to agree; a Nazi school seemed, even for him, a strange step in the wrong direction. And Kees. Well, Kees. No one knew what went on in his mind. She sighed.

She missed Ab the most. She hoped his decision to become a Nazi would keep him safe from the work camps. Word spread that they were terrible places where people starved to death. Ab had tried to convince her he had only enlisted for Kees's sake. Kees isn't as strong as your family thinks, Ab had said. He's vulnerable. Punica knew Kees was weak, and his weakness could get them both killed.

She worried about Ab so much she wanted to talk to someone about it. He was always on her mind, and every time his name was on the tip of her tongue, she bit her lip to stop herself from saying anything. She knew what Moeke would say: he's too old for you. But the age difference between them was only four years. What are four years if she were eighteen?

She parked her bicycle in the school shed behind the red brick building. The star pinned onto her breast pocket had rolled into a weird yellow shape, so she smoothed the creases out. Her fellow students noticed and stopped talking, nudging each other. And soon, everyone stared at her in silence. Punica wondered where her friends were and ignored everyone else. She remembered their laughter when the five of them, gathering in her bedroom, tried to figure out how one of those stars looked. When they had figured it out, they cut triangles from the material and arranged them into stars; they tried to decide whether to sew or pin the thing onto their coats. The boys wanted to use a safety pin and the girls wanted to sew it on. It would look neater, but ultimately, they decided the safety pin would work best for everyone.

Punica glanced at her watch. Although it was time for the first bell, there was still no sign of the others. One girl broke the silence and walked up to Punica.

'What do you think you are doing?' she asked.

Punica swallowed. 'Nothing,' she said, looking away from her.

Not wanting to face the teacher alone, she fumbled with the safety pin to remove the star to go to her classroom. Her friend, Annie appeared smiling as she held her star on her breast to stop it from flopping and folding on the lapel of her coat. 'We should have sewed them on,' she said and sighed.

'Oh God, I thought no one was coming,' Punica said, leaving the safety pin where it was. 'You should have seen all the people on the streets as I cycled past them. They acted as if I had pinned my heart onto my coat. Some even bowed their heads to me and said I took after my mother's side of the family.'

'People made way for me too. And one man shook my hand and said I made my parents proud.'

'Did you tell them?'

'My parents? No. You?'

Punica shook her head.

Peter showed up, his star sewn with tiny blanket stitches to his tweed jacket pocket. His star looked almost real. Punica and Annie shared a smile he caught.

'Looks very professional there, Peter,' Punica said. 'Your mother's handiwork?'

When Peter nodded, Punica added, 'We should have asked her to do all of them.'

'My mother said it looked messy, so she sewed it on my jacket while I ate breakfast.' He glanced at the crowd. Everyone was staring at them. 'Have we become the in-crowd? Someone on the tram even got up for me and gave me his seat. I think I'll keep the star on my jacket from now on.'

'I might do the same,' Annie said.

Punica wondered if she was joking or meant it. She was never this brave.

'So, where are the others?' Peter asked.

Wouter and Michael raced down the entrance lane on their bikes, ringing their bicycle bells and speeding past them without slowing down. The school bell rang, and they jumped off their bikes and launched them into the already-parked ones. Metal clanked into metal. They took their stars from their pockets and pinned them to their jacket pockets.

'Well, here we go,' Peter said as they linked their arms. 'All for one and one for all.' They laughed.

Once in the door, they split into two groups. Wouter and Michael had mathematics and Peter, Annie, and Punica had chemistry. They did their special handshake using only their pinkies, and each parted and said they'd see the other at the first break in the school canteen. 'With our stars still pinned to our clothes,' they laughed, 'no matter what.' As Punica walked up the stairs, she saw a few older pupils from the fifth-year wearing stars as well. She'd thought she'd had an original idea. They greeted each other while passing. She enjoyed the new status. Older students never greeted their juniors at school.

They hung their coats by the door and transferred the stars to their jumpers. They entered the lab; Mr de Wit noticed the stars. He got up from his stool to shake their hands, taking his time. Punica hoped Mr de Wit might say something about their protest. But he didn't. He said, 'Good morning. Quickly, people find your seats,' while shaking Peter's hand.

Peter sat two rows further back from the girls. Richard, who sat next to Peter, moved to the empty seat in the front row. When Mr de Wit asked him why he wasn't sitting in his seat, he said, 'He wasn't sharing no desk with no Jew, real or pretend.' Mr de Wit didn't even correct his grammar.

Besides Richard refusing to sit next to Peter, the lesson went without issue. As they tidied up and returned their books to their schoolbags, men of the Sicherheitsdienst showed up at the classroom door. Mr de Wit told the students to quiet down and return to their seats for a minute. He strolled to the door, offering his hand to shake theirs.

'Kriminalsekretär Schwarzwald!' the leader shouted at Mr de Wit, the hand stretched out in a Hitler salute.

Mr de Wit self-consciously raised his hand in the same manner, returning the salute, but there was no power in it. His arm bent at the elbow and returned to his side too soon, so the greeting seemed more of a nonchalant wave of the hand.

'I hear you have terrorists amongst your students,' the man in uniform said.

'I'm sure you must be mistaken. My students are children.'

'You,' the Nazi shouted, pointing at Annie, 'Come here,' as if ordering a dog to come. 'And you!' he roared, pointing at Punica, 'and you' – at Peter – 'Follow me.'

'We can settle this in a civilised manner,' Mr de Wit said. 'Children, remove those floppy flowery things from your clothes.'

'Sit down,' the commander shouted at Mr de Wit. 'Sit down before I lose my temper! You've had all morning to attend to the problem presented to you, and you did nothing. NOTHING. Walk!' he shouted to the teenagers. 'Raus!' he roared, shoving a bat into their legs and making them scramble out. 'And collect your coats on your way down. You'll need them. I'll see you in the entrance hall.'

Once in the corridor, Punica, Annie, and Peter put on their coats and jackets. They shuffled along the corridor and watched with growing anxiety what was happening around them. The men from the Sicherheitsdienst pulled open the doors to the other classrooms and searched them for protesters. Punica took Peter's hand. Doors slammed throughout the building, and loud marching boots made the floor tremble.

'What will happen to us?' Annie whispered.

Neither Peter nor Punica attempted to answer her.

When they reached the stairs, they saw older students walking down with two SD men holding machine guns behind them. The men gestured for Punica and Annie to get in line with them. And as the Nazis herded them down the stairs, they saw the other students rounded up in the entrance hall. Blood drained from their faces.

Punica glanced through the open doors at two more armed SD men and a lorry parked outside the school entrance. She wished she had told her mother about the protest and the stars.

'Sir... sir,' she slurred, her face stiff with fear. 'Sir,' she said, raising her voice. 'We're not Jewish.'

Kriminalsekretär Schwarzwald reappeared, descending the grand staircase, his men following him. She recognised him now. The scar on his eyebrow. He was the SD man at Ab's house. He had a meaner look now and no emotion in his eyes. He looked like a different person. But he had let her go once before.

'Sir,' Punica said, this time directing her question to Kriminalsekretär Schwarzwald. Peter squeezed her hand as if to tell her to shut up. Schwarzwald walked around the pupils and stopped by Punica. 'Yes?!' he shouted, staring at her for a long moment.

'Do you remember? We've met—'

'Raus!' he shouted. 'RAUS!' He turned to the doors.

'Do you remember the dog? Your daughter—'

He spun around and slapped her face hard. She raised her hands to her face, her eyes brimming with tears.

Stunned, she looked at him between her spread fingers. No one had hit her before. The others, including her friends, walked through the doors, and she watched them driven like terrified sheep out into the sun-speckled lane flanked by hazels and birches losing their bark in giant white curls. They walked into the silence on this bright spring morning. She couldn't follow them; she couldn't even move. Her feet felt like they were stuck to the granite floor. The lorry waited for them, the engine churning; the driver lowered the back latch, and she watched armed men force her friends to climb up into the darkness. Everything seemed unreal as Punica watched from the entrance hall. The men poked them with the barrels of their machine guns, and her friends were terrified and stumbling, trying to climb into the truck. Kriminalsekretär Schwarzwald stood a few metres away from Punica, keeping an eye on his men as they carried out their duties. The last student disappeared behind the black canvas cover on the back. The man with the scar turned, and his eyes caught the sun, making them devilish. He stared at Punica for a minute. Her heart rammed into her ribs, shaking her, and she found it hard to stay standing still. He walked towards her.

'I remember now,' he whispered, bending his head close to her. 'Fluffy?'

She nodded.

'Where's Fluffy now?' he asked.

'A... at... at home.'

'Are you telling me the truth?'

She nodded.

'And you want to go to him? See if he's all right, don't you?'

She stared at him.

'Maybe take him for a walk?'

She nodded again.

'My dearest Fraulein,' he said, smiling, the way he had at Ab's house when he talked of his daughter.

She relaxed, realising it had all been to teach them a lesson. Of course, he knew they were only secondary school students. She returned his smile.

'You know what, since I'm in such a good mood, with the sun shining. I'll give you a choice, a simple choice. You may choose to return to your lovely mother if you tell me who the ringleader is?'

'Will you release my friends?'

'Yes.'

She thought for a moment or two.

'Was it the boy, Peter?'

'It was all my idea,' she said, her voice breaking.

He observed her as she confessed her crime, and his face appeared like a father's, a doting father's, but when she had finished recounting to him how they had created the stars, his expression altered.

'Raus!' he shouted.

Punica jumped. 'I... I...' she said. 'I'm so sorry, but we're only teenagers.'

'Raus!' he screamed.

Punica ran like a drunk toward the truck. Her face throbbed from shame. What a fool she was. One man helped her up the step. He closed the latch and clicked it into the lock. He struck the metal twice to let the driver know the last was in, and the truck moved. Punica lost her balance and fell onto an empty bench. As she tried to climb back onto her feet, she noticed the lorry wasn't even half full. She and Annie were the only girls. The others, about eight of them, were boys. Shuffling and half falling into the students, she tried to reach her friends in the far corner. The engine roared as the driver changed gears, gathering speed and pulling out onto the road, making her fall over again. Her knee grazed on the rough wooden bench and started to bleed.

Everyone was silent, their cheeks vibrating on the engine's movement and the bumps in the road. After what felt like a long time, Punica checked her watch and realised they had been travelling for an hour. She nudged Peter. 'Where do you think they are taking us?' she said.

'I could be home now if it weren't for your plans,' Annie sneered at Punica.

Peter squeezed Annie's knees, hushing her. 'We'll be fine,' he said. 'We're only teenagers. What can they do to us?'

'I'm so scared,' Annie said. 'I can hardly breathe.'

'Should we remove the stars from our clothes?' Punica wondered out loud.

A boy sat beside Peter and removed his star from his jacket pocket. He screwed it into a little ball in his hand. The others took off their stars. Annie pulled at hers, but her fingers were stiff with fear, and she panicked and couldn't get the safety pin out of her cardigan. She tugged it, ripping the knitting. Peter calmed her and removed the star for her. He used the safety pin to unpick the sewing on his jacket, pulled out the thread, and started sawing it between his teeth. Finally, he ripped it off. One of the older boys didn't remove his star. His chiselled face concentrated on the canvas behind Punica's head. Punica searched his eyes. She touched his knee, and when his eyes looked straight at her, she gestured to show she had removed her star. 'Shall I help you?' she asked, leaning towards him. 'Please, take it off,' she said.

But the boy refocused on the canvas behind her head and ignored her.

She checked her watch once more.

'We've left the city ages ago,' she whispered to Peter.

Peter squeezed her hand. 'We're teenagers,' he repeated. 'They're trying to scare us, driving us around the countryside to deliver us back to school.'

'Do you think so?'

Annie trembled. Punica removed her raincoat and jumper and pushed them into Annie's hands. 'We'll be fine,' she said. 'We're only secondary school students.' She took Annie's star from her hand, collected the stars from the surrounding teenagers and pushed her hand through the opening below the canvas, scattering the stars like blossoms in the wind.

The lorry came to an abrupt standstill, and the teenagers fell into each other. The driver got out and slammed the door, and they heard boots march toward the latch, which fell with a loud thump that vibrated across the floor. 'Get out!' the driver ordered the students.

Punica dared not ask where they were, but they certainly weren't back at school. She jumped from the lorry onto the muddy ground and stumbled, falling onto her sore knee. Groaning from pain, she pushed herself back into a standing position. Mud covered her hands. She glanced around as she tried to work out where they were. Was it a work camp? Trees surrounded them. The road was a dirt path, less than a country road. They faced a large iron gate, and behind it was a compound fenced off with barbed wire more than two metres high. Beside her stood a wooden tower, like a hunting tower but taller and more prominent. On either side of the gate, an SS man held a machine gun. They didn't look like human beings. A man appeared at the door of a wooden prefab building. He stood at the top of the wooden stairs and ordered the guards to open the gate for their new guests.

The men with the machine guns herded the terrified students into the compound like animals. They ordered girls to the left and the boys to the right. They had to line up and wait until the Lagerkommandant decided what to do with them.

The Lagerkommandant left the prefab, skipping down the stairs and whistling as he walked along the barbed wire path and entered the compound.

'Welcome to our Rose Garden at Polizeiliches Durchgangslager Amersfoort,' the Lagerkommandant said.

Punica glanced around her. Massive bundles of barbed wire surrounded her.

'What's going to happen?' she whispered, leaning over to Peter.

'Ruhe!'

'My colleague, Lagerführer Dieter, will take total responsibility for you. Most of you have removed those pathetic stars from your clothes already. Good... good. But if you haven't yet removed them, please leave the stars on your clothes. It will make no difference to your stay here.'

The teenagers looked at one another.

'Heil Hitler!' he bellowed.

The students stared at him.

He walked to the older boy who would not remove his star and bellowed into his face, 'Heil Hitler!'

The boy ignored him.

Two or three teenagers mumbled, 'Heil Hitler,' waving a feeble arm.

'Well?' he bellowed into the boy's face, spittle hitting his chin.

The others shouted, 'Heil.' But the boy remained silent.

The Lagerführer walked along the lines and bellowed at each student.

And when each student bellowed back 'Heil,' the commandant smiled and returned to the boy. 'Well?' he roared, his face not five centimetres from the boy's face. He raised his baton above the boy's head and hit him across the face. The boy cried louder than anyone, 'Heil Hitler,' back into the Lagerführer's face.

The Lagerführer stepped back a few metres.

'Again,' he shouted.

He stood before the students and waved both hands as if directing an orchestra.

All the students shouted, 'Heil Hitler,' but the boy again remained silent.

'Again,' he shouted.

'Heil Hitler,' they all called.

'Louder!'

'Heil Hitler!'

The Lagerführer stopped by the boy, who had not removed his star. 'Well?!' he shouted.

The boy was taller than the German and looked over his head at the treetops. 'Well!' the Lagerführer repeated. The boy stared into the distance. Tears ran down his cheeks.

The Lagerführer again took out the club from its holder and hit the boy across the head with it. Blood seeped from his mouth, and he spat out a tooth.

Annie scrunched her eyes shut, lifting her shoulders to her ears as if closing herself off from what was happening around her.

'Boys, here!' the Lagerkommandant shouted, showing them where to line up. The Lagerführer was still hitting the boy, who lay scrunched on the ground.

The boys did what Lagerkommandant demanded – the two girls hugging each other stood aside.

The Lagerkommandant ordered the boys to undress. Men like skeletons, keeping their heads low and dressed in filthy clothes, hurried into the compound carrying a small table and two baskets. They brought them to the Lagerkommandant. A man in uniform took his place at the table and opened a ledger.

'Report to my colleagues at the post,' the Lagerkommandant yelled, gesturing to the tables. 'Give your name, date of birth, place of residence, and so on,' he shouted, twisting a finger through the air. 'Take off your clothes without emptying your pockets and put everything into the baskets. My colleagues will give you a number.

Attach the number to your uniforms. It will be your identification number. From now on, you have no name. Do you understand?'

'Heil Hitler!' the teenagers shouted.

The Lagerkommandant smiled.

Punica looked at Peter, who was undressing, dropping his clothes by his feet. Do they have to do this with us here watching them? 'Annie,' she whispered, 'Will we have to undress too and run naked across the yard?'

'I don't know,' Annie said, sobbing.

The skeletal men collected the clothes. Others gave the boys old Dutch army uniforms, filthy from former wearers, army trousers, a jacket, cotton rags for socks, and wooden clogs. The boys pulled the rags over their heads. Nothing fitted; the clothes were either too big or too small. Each received two squares of material bearing numbers to sew onto their trousers and jackets. They also gave them a red triangle, which they had to sew onto the uniform. Punica saw that the skeletal men collecting the boys' things wore green ones and wondered what the colours meant.

'Take these damsels to their quarters; they need their beauty sleep,' the Lagerkommandant said.

Punica laid her arm around Annie's shoulders and turned to the women in SS uniforms who had been watching them. They gave the girls red triangles and ordered them to follow them.

They entered a stone building with thick walls. The women in Nazi uniforms and evil eyes directed them to their cell – a small room with two bunks and two single beds by the outer wall. The floor was grey concrete, with whitewashed walls and a window too high to see through. Four women sat playing cards on the two single beds underneath the window. They looked up at them as the Nazis shoved Punica and Annie in. The girls shuffled in and flinched when the door rammed shut behind them. They stood by the door, unsure of their new surroundings, and stared at the floor.

'Shall we help you two?' A woman sitting on the bed with her back against the wall asked. She smiled. 'I meant sew those triangles onto your clothes?'

The girls gawked at them, unable to answer. A bell sounded, and the cell doors were unlocked, opened, and slammed against the wall.

'What's happening?' Punica cried.

'Time for dinner,' one woman said. 'We'll do it later.'

The girls followed the women back to the Rose Garden. Punica hoped this would all turn out to be a horrible joke. They got in line with the other prisoners, and the men lined up to the right. The Lagerführer called out each name. The boys had to respond by calling out their numbers, and the Lagerführer counted and checked the prisoners against a register. When the numbers didn't correspond with the list, each boy was called to the front. The boy who would not remove his star had made a mistake. Seeing the number upside down on his breast, he had mistaken the nine for a six. His face, already swollen and bleeding, received yet another beating.

The boy fell to the ground and screamed in pain. Punica clasped her hands on her ears. Annie slid her arm around Punica's waist. But the women from their cell urged her to stay in line, so she pulled back.

The boy stopped crying and lay limp in the mud. His face was unrecognisable and covered in blood. A woman in a nurse's uniform came out and ordered two men to pick up the boy and take him away. She walked through the lines, glaring at the boys from their school. She had a lollypop stick with her and ordered one or two to open their mouths as she pressed the stick onto their tongues. Peter, too, had to open his mouth. She selected him and two others to come with her. Punica watched Peter hurrying along; his demeanour had changed in those few hours. He hunched his shoulders, keeping his head low as he rushed by. Not looking up at the girls, he followed the nurse.

The starving men gave the remaining prisoners a quarter of a slice of German rye bread with a bit of butter and a smear of jam, and the Lagerführer ordered them back to their cells.

The door slammed shut behind them, making Annie jump from fright. Punica shuffled to the lower bunk and sat down, raising the bread to her lips. She hadn't eaten since breakfast but wasn't hungry. Annie sat beside her, holding the bread on her lap. The old lady wiggled between the girls and laid her hands on each girl's arm. 'I know it's hard, but it gets easier once you've got used to the routine.' The others returned to the bed where they had played cards and sat down, picking up the cards to continue their game.

The older woman wore a chequered woollen skirt and a thick lemon-yellow cardigan. She squeezed Punica's shoulder and smiled. 'Trust me,' she mumbled. But her smile wasn't happy. It was a commiserative smile you'd give a loved one at a funeral.

Punica tried to return the smile but couldn't, so she nodded, unable to speak.

'You can call me Oma,' the woman said. She wore her grey hair in a neat bun at the back of her head. The other women were much younger. Punica heard the army boots thumping in the corridor and looked up, startled at the door, her knees shaking.

'Don't worry,' Oma said. 'They are in the watchtower – they wear heavy boots that stump the floor and seem much closer than they are. You'll get used to it.'

'How long do you think they can keep us here?'

Machine-gun fire rumbled outside their wall, and Punica jumped from fright. The woman didn't react to the noise outside. She hunched her shoulders, answering Punica's question. 'Why were you arrested?'

'We... wore a Star of David on our clothes even though we aren't Jewish.'

The woman smiled, squeezing her lips, and her eyes became teary. 'After dark, the searchlight flashes along the walls every few seconds. Ignore it.'

'When will we get out?' Punica whispered.

'No one knows,' one woman answered.

'But we did nothing wrong.'

'Come, sit here... play cards with us?'

'What will happen to the boy from our school? The one they beat up?' Punica said, wiping away tears. 'Will they kill him?'

'He's safe enough. The nurse wouldn't have taken him if there was no hope for him. She runs the sickbay.'

'But she took Peter as well.'

'He's lucky. Sometimes, our White Angel selects healthy boys. The Nazis listen to her, and she knows how to keep them out of her hospital. They're so afraid of catching diphtheria. She tells them her patients have it.'

One of the younger women got up and walked over to the girls. She sat on her haunches at their feet, holding their knees. She said, 'You must do everything they order you to do, no matter what it is. Do it, and keep your head low. Don't look them straight in the eyes, or they'll find something to punish you for. And you must eat everything they give you, even scraps. You'll need food to keep up your strength. You will get out of here.'

'I wish I had never pinned that stupid yellow star to my clothes. I thought I was doing the right thing, but...'

'They expelled our Jewish friends from our school last September,' Annie said.

'I did it for my friend,' Punica said with tears in her eyes, 'My friend, he is Jewish. His father was a dentist – a distinguished older gentleman, respected by all before the invasion. I couldn't stand by and pretend those new laws were normal. How can everyone stand by and let them bully our friends and neighbours? I'm so sorry, Annie, for pulling you into this.'

'People are afraid. And fear is a bad advisor,' Oma said, 'but as I always say, bravery is an even worse one.'

'But we're only fourteen. The boy they kicked was sixteen, maybe seventeen, but not much older. He was in my brother's class—'

'Sweety,' the woman said to Punica. 'These are strange times.'

'Why are you here?' Annie asked.

'I work for a bank that distributed ration cards, and about a month ago, the resistance robbed our offices. The Nazis wouldn't believe it wasn't an inside job, so now my daughter, Marie and I are here, while my sons and their father are in the men's quarters.'

'But you are an old woman?'

The woman smiled, not in the slightest offended.

'They don't care about age, dearie,' she said.

'And we're here because two SD men wanted to take us out on a date, and we refused,' one of the younger women said.

'But how can that be legal?' Punica asked.

'They said we were anti-German. A neighbour heard us talking in the garden and reported us to the Nazis. All lies. They had the time of their lives as they wrote their false reports.'

'Come, join us at cards?' Marie said.

'No, thank you,' Punica said. She kicked off her shoes and rolled onto her back. She stared at the mattress above her. 'I'm so tired.'

Annie lay beside her and wrapped her arms around Punica. Their pillow became cold and damp with silent tears. It smelled of urine. Punica thought of Moeke as she listened to the women playing cards. What would she be thinking? Punica tried to picture her eating dinner with Corrie, Nienke, and Mrs de Vries. But in her heart, she knew Moeke would be frantic with worry.

The moon ended the day, and the searchlight entered through the tiny square window. It slid over the walls as if chasing them until it snapped back into the darkness.

CHAPTER ELEVEN

Willem

Willem's new school, a former psychiatric sanatorium for the wealthy insane named Koningsheide – King's Heath – with its herbal garden, cricket fields, and tennis courts, was on a large woodland area with hills, lakes, and moors. With thick layers of snow accumulating on the roofs and pathways, Willem entered a fairytale land. If only Moeke had come with him. If she saw this, she would congratulate him on his success – this significant life-changing achievement – and forget her anger about him going behind her back.

Willem had been one of forty boys selected out of five hundred and eighty candidates. He made the local newspapers, and the bullying and ridiculing at his old school stopped. The basket weavers' boy, a phrase the lawyers' and surgeons' sons taunted him with, had become the golden boy they now envied. If only Moeke and Punica shared his excitement.

Red banners with swastikas flanked the entrance doors. They seemed to open on their own accord as Willem approached. He parked his bike alongside a long row of tangled bicycles and walked up to the door, straightening his clothes and unwinding his scarf. He pulled off his knitted hat and entered a white, oval hallway with black doors around its circumference. On the wall hung a two-meter-high oil painting of the Führer. Hitler stared into oblivion somewhere in the sky, on his lips a faint smile; he looked proud and regal.

Two German boys entered. They raised their right arms and shouted, 'Heil!'

Willem shouted, 'Hooray!'

'Heil!' the one on the left repeated with angry eyes. 'Heil!'

Willem raised his arm again and shouted, 'Heil!' taking the same angry demeanour as the German boys, realising he should have switched the hat to his left hand. The cold burned on his cheeks. He stuffed the hat in his pocket and repeated the Hitler greeting, getting it right. It was the first time he had made a Hitler salute. He had only waved his hand the other times, at the entrance examinations. But he supposed he must put aside his pride and assimilate with the outsiders. Not that he was against greeting the others with Heil Hitler. That wasn't it. He thought they should welcome him in Dutch and not German. He was in Holland. Moeke always said foreigners are guests in our country, and as guests, they should adapt to our ways. But he supposed he could change and not make a big deal out of it.

They directed him to a young man in an adjoining room, standing behind a makeshift counter with boxes of books and shelves full of neatly folded clothes.

He handed Willem a sack that looked like a mailbag.

The boy said, 'Let me guess?'

Willem looked at him with a puzzled face.

'Your size? A forty-six?'

The young man busied himself, pulling out seven shirts and five jackets, five pairs of trousers, seven pairs of underpants, seven vests, a belt and leather boots and shoes, which Willem put into his sack, and when it was full, the young man handed him a little sword for his belt. He said, 'You're in dorm number four on the second floor. You must change into your uniform and make your bed with the sheets supplied in your dorm. Don't dawdle; your Zugführer expects you in the grand hall for lunch at precisely twelve-fifteen.'

'The grand hall?' Willem hesitated.

'Through there, second right. You can't miss it. Heil Hitler!'

The dining room was painted in a vanilla hue and had high arched windows that let the sun reach the back wall in rectangles of light. The German and Dutch boys were to alternate at the long oak tables.

Maids, girls a little older than Willem but not much older, served a bowl of vegetable soup with noodles and meatballs the size of tennis balls.

The boy sitting next to Willem asked him in German what Zug he was in, and Willem thought the boy must mean unity. He smiled. He was getting the hang of the unfamiliar names for everything and said, 'Fifth.'

The maid served him a slice of rye bread lavished in butter. She had plaited hair in a German hairstyle, the plaits fastened across her head like hairbands.

'You changed school in your last year?' the German boy said.

'Jawohl,' Willem replied in his best German. One year here, and he'd be off to study music at the conservatoire of his choosing, as promised in the newspaper article.

The boy stared at him, and Willem realised he was smiling. He wiped the smile from his face and ate.

After lunch, they were to report for roll call by the flag post at the entrance. Willem followed the German boys he had eaten lunch with but soon was told he should line up with the Dutch boys, so he rushed red-faced across the snow-cleared concrete to the other side. The boys stood in a wide circle around the flagpole while a line of teachers, or Zugführers, as they were called, assembled on the marble steps by the entrance. A senior teacher dressed in an imposing uniform with colourful medals took his position at the front. The boys bellowed the Nazi salute across the countryside, repeating it four times.

One of the younger boys raised the flag, and everyone took on the Nazi pose with outstretched arms and hands.

They sang a song once the flag flapped in the wind at the top of the pole. 'Du bist nichts. Dein Volk ist alles.' Although Willem did not know the words, he enjoyed the melody. It sounded like a march.

'Jungmänner, Wilkommen in Königsheide. I am Unterrichtsleiter Herr Naumann,' the senior teacher shouted. 'I welcome you to our beautiful school in Schaarsbergen on this great day. You have been chosen from many applicants to become our next generation of outstanding leaders. You will excel at every given task, and when you leave this elite institution, you will show the Germanic people how powerful and brave you are and what excellent characters you have developed.'

Willem's heart pounded in anticipation.

'You will be an example of what our great nation can achieve. You will become our next generation of fine leaders. Heil!'

'Heil! Heil! Heil!' the boys all chanted, raising their outstretched arms in salute.

Unterrichtsleiter Herr Naumann raised both arms and made downward motions to quieten the boys.

'We Germans, who alone on this earth show respect for animals, shall also respect our human beasts. Like a farmer cleanses his fields of weeds so his crops can thrive, we too must cleanse our people of mutations and weeds and once again become the Germanic Herrenmenschen we once were. And you, my dear Jungmänner, will be the ones whom everyone will expect to save our great culture. Only five to ten per cent of our nation,' he continued, 'the best of the best, are born to be our leaders. You are that five per cent, the hope for our future. The golden boys. Do not fail our people's trust in you. A true soldier never asks why. Only ask what you can do for your country to achieve victory. You will always obey our Führer's commands, even to the death. We are prepared to pay the ultimate prize. Our great nation shall conquer the world.'

'Heil! Heil! Heil!'

Once again, the officer raised his hands to let the commander speak.

'Your Zugführer will now take you to your classrooms and inform you of your task. Your time here will be tough, and we expect excellence, but only through iron discipline can we once again become the great nation we once were and win back the respect of our European neighbours.'

'Heil! Heil! Heil! Heil! Heil!' the boys chanted at the top of their lungs.

Herr Naumann smiled, turned to the door, and marched into the hall. The remaining teachers waited as each boy shouted his name and place of residence. A torrent of names ensued, and once the boy next to him had called out his place of residence, Willem screeched out with a voice a little too high, 'Wilhelmus Mandemaker, Arnhem.' The Zugführer nodded, and Willem, happy he didn't stammer, listened to the other boys calling out their names. How far everyone had travelled to be here. He was the only one from Arnhem. A waspy teenager with enormous eyes and mousy hair came from Den Helder, a town on the other side of the country. He was shorter than the others and wore glasses. The boy noticed Willem looking at him. Their eyes met for a second; the boy looked away.

Willem glanced at his group. Three rows of boys stood behind him. He couldn't spot any German boys he had spoken with during lunch.

'Where have the Germans gone?' he whispered to the boy beside him.

But the boy grimaced as if he'd eaten a demon, and before Willem could ask him what was wrong, he heard shoes slapping the concrete. A man appeared before him, a Zugführer with greased hair and a block-shaped moustache like the Führer. He wore gold-rimmed spectacles, leaned into Willem's face, and roared, 'Quiet!' His breath smelled of a rotting mouse.

Willem swallowed and felt as if the bone of his throat caught on something.

'Follow me!' the man yelled, his gaze piercing Willem. He called out nine more names. The Zugführer kicked up his boot and turned, marching back inside like a stork with legs too long and thin for him to carry his plump body. The boys followed in single file.

They were to report to the gymnasium in five minutes, but were first to change into their sports attire. They all rushed upstairs, pulled a white vest and shorts from the wardrobe, changed, and pushing their arms through the bathrobe sleeves; they ran to the sports facilities. When they entered the gymnasium, Willem saw two boys boxing in the ring, and others were boxing punching bags in twos along the wall. The windows near the ceiling were white with swirling snowflakes, and the sky was dark blue and beautiful. A strange, soft light illuminated the gym. Willem didn't know where to go, but the coach had spotted him and whistled for him to come to him. He stopped the fight in the ring, and the two boys moved apart. The coach stood between them as Willem walked up to the ring.

'I saw you during the exams,' he said. 'You showed a blazing bravura,' the coach added.

'Beginner's luck,' Willem replied.

'Right, take over from Klaus,' he said, gesturing to a boy in the ring.

Willem climbed between the ropes into the ring, took off his bathrobe, and hung it with his towel over the rope in the corner of the boxing ring. The coach laughed at him and told him never, and he meant never, hang your gear over the turnbuckle of a boxing ring. You'll never know what your opponent will do during a fight. 'Do you know he could strangle you with a towel or smother you with the bathrobe?' he said. The other boys roared with laughter. Willem tried to laugh, too, but he felt ridiculed and shamed. He knew he would have to prove himself and win his first match to make new friends here. So, bending over the ropes, he threw his stuff on the row of chairs nearest the ring and got ready to show them he wasn't a pushover.

The coach handed him a boxing glove, and once Willem had pulled it over his fist, he tied the laces. The coach pulled the other over Willem's right hand and let another boy do the laces.

Willem thanked him and started with stretches and crouches, the way the coach at his entrance exam had started the exams – to warm up for a boxing match – with all the boys copying what the coach did. His opponent was taller and looked more muscular, but Willem wasn't scared. It only improved his chances of showing those nitwits with laughing faces how strong he was.

The coach gestured for the boys to pay attention.

The boys quietened down.

Willem sized the boy he was to fight, standing opposite him.

'Good, but not great,' the coach said to him. 'Remember,' he said. 'It's all up here' – he touched the boy's forehead – 'and not here,' he said, jabbing his upper arm 'or here,' jabbing his chest. The boy nodded and walked to the ropes. He crouched and got out of the ring.

'Right, who's next?' the coach called out. 'Rudy, up here.'

The boy with glasses climbed into the ring.

'I can't fight him,' Willem mumbled.

'And why not?' the coach shouted.

'He's...' a dwarf, he wanted to say, but reconsidered and said, 'He's wearing glasses.'

Rudy took off his glasses and handed them to the coach, who passed them to Herr Naumann, standing outside the ring.

'Right, on the count of three,' the coach said, 'I blow the whistle. Ready?'

Willem nodded. The boy, Rudy, nodded, too.

Willem received a jab against his chin as soon as the whistle sounded. He stumbled backwards. Rudy stepped forward and gave him an uppercut followed by a cross, and Willem lost his balance and landed on his backside in a sitting position. He got up fast and started jabbing Rudy, switching from his left fist to his right, punching Rudy on the jaw, against the nose, and the ears twice. He gave him one almighty punch against his forehead. Rudy's eyebrow bled. Willem stopped fighting, but the coach's whistle did not sound. Willem glanced at the audience for a split second to understand what was happening around him. The boys had gathered around the ring and were shouting and showing how Willem should fight – showing him different moves – and telling him to finish Rudy off. Willem gave Rudy an uppercut. He wanted him to stop fighting so both could leave the ring unharmed. He gave him one more jab, one more to get Rudy to stop boxing him. Rudy fell to the floor. Willem moved to the far corner as the coach bent over Rudy and counted.

Willem felt bad. Everyone was whistling and cheering and seemed to be on his side instead of someone they already knew. They wanted him to finish Rudy off, shouting and showing him how to fight. He glanced at the coach, still counting, and at Rudy, struggling to get up. Why was everyone for him, while Rudy was the weaker opponent? Moeke had always taught him to stick up for the more vulnerable boys, but here it seemed to be the other way around. Willem looked at Rudy, hoping he would stay down and finish the fight. Up Rudy got and, standing opposite Willem, facing him, he seemed drunk as he swayed and stumbled on his feet. Willem caught him in his arms and pretended to fight, pretending to punch Rudy. Pretending the distance was too small to use any force. The coach blew his whistle to end this round.

'Are you all right?' Willem whispered before letting go. The coach whistled again, pulling them apart and sending them to their corners.

Two boys took care of Willem. One raised a beaker of water to Willem's lips. He drank a few sips and coughed. The other boy massaged his calves. Willem looked at Rudy. He was also struggling with the water and looked stunned, his eyes staring at the floor. Willem wondered if he should stop.

The whistle sounded; the second round. Willem got up. He watched Rudy shuffle to the centre of the ring. Willem threw him a punch and missed Rudy's face. He tried to make it look real, as if aiming for his temple but missing it, but it was all an act. How could he go on punching a boy so much smaller than himself? Willem rammed Rudy's shoulder, more pushing it than punching. He made sure it looked authentic enough, using as little force as possible. Rudy stumbled but regained his position and punched Willem on the chin. It wasn't hard, but Willem's lip tore, and he tasted blood in his mouth. He felt his chin and neck become wet. They both were bleeding; Rudy was still bleeding from his eyebrow, the blood streaming down the side of his face – blood and sweat saturated Willem's vest. Rudy struggled to see Willem. He turned his face to let the blood drip down away from his eyes.

Willem clenched him one more time.

'Give up,' Willem whispered. 'Damn you.'

'You give up,' Rudy mumbled.

The coach pulled them apart, but they soon fell into a clinch again.

'GIVE UP!' Willem shouted. The surrounding boys roared. No one seemed to hear what they were yelling at each other. Rudy screamed, 'NO!' And jabbed Willem with one almighty punch into his jaw.

Willem fell onto his backside and tumbled backwards, his head pounding the floor. His teeth locked into each other, his lower front teeth nearly pulling the upper four out. He stared at the ceiling. The rings suspended above him, the snow gathering on the windowsills outside. He wanted to stop. He had to stop, but those boys were urging him to get up, cheering him on, so he raised his head and tried to push himself up off the floor and onto his feet. The coach wasn't even bent over him or counting how much time he still had to get up from the floor, and when he was back on his feet, he saw the coach raise Rudy's arm, declaring him the winner. Was this even fair? Willem had been the strongest; Rudy had struggled all the way through. But Rudy was the winner, and Willem had lost. One boy handed Willem his towel. He wiped his bloody face on it and saw Herr Naumann, who had been standing by the ring the whole time, give Rudy his glasses and patting him on the back. 'You're improving.'

'Thanks, Papa.'

CHAPTER TWELVE

Kees

Kees sat near a rabbit hole. If he sat still enough and waited long enough, he knew a rabbit would pop out, not be alarmed by his presence, and accept him, as the rabbit would have had the time to get used to his scent and be more hungry than afraid; it would run around his feet, hopping happily and graze the sparse grass. And if Kees were fast enough, he'd be able to seize it in one swift movement and twist its head, breaking its neck before it even knew it had died and gone to animal heaven.

Kees laid the rabbit on the soft, clean grass where he and Ab had made camp and pulled his sculpting knife from his pocket. He made an incision near the base of the neck and cut off its head and, subsequently, the tail and feet, working from the back of the animal to the front. He placed the knife with the cutting edge facing up in the hide and cut it over the stomach to its neck, making sure not to pierce the bowels and contaminate the meat. With his hand, he loosened the skin. He put the index and middle fingers of his left hand inside the skin and his right hand on the bottom half of the incision and pulled the top toward the neck and the bottom toward the tail; he twisted the skin to break it and smoothly pulled the fur off the rabbit. Making a small incision in its stomach, he opened the chest cavity and dug his finger into the spine; he scooped out its organs and intestines. He cut through the pelvic bone, making sure not to damage the colon. Toward the rectal section, he placed the knife and carefully removed any excrement still there.

Ab prepared a fire, making a nest of dry twigs he had collected during their march from the port of Königsberg. Most soldiers cooked their own meals; some had schlepped tins of beans from Germany. Only a few waited for the Tross to arrive with food.

The soldiers' main occupation was waiting for orders, waiting for transportation, and waiting for their food and coats. The Tross brought supplies and took injured and sick men back with them. They also delivered their warm winter coats for the night and returned to collect them in the morning before the camp was broken and the soldiers marched on.

Ab had turned into a great fire starter. He no longer needed matches, having learned which twigs to use to get a fire going within seconds. Kees had woven the rabbit carcass on a stick and was preparing it for Ab's fire. He looked forward to finishing up and watching the rabbit roast. Kees's feet were sore; the leather of his boots saturated from the melting snow and wet grass, the skin on his heels worn raw. After departing the most tedious and relaxing boat trip from Poland to Russia, they had marched for kilometres on end and would have reached exhaustion if it weren't for the pills.

Kees raised the rabbit above the fire. 'We should have brought salt and pepper,' he said and smiled.

'And a little grease,' Ab added. He stretched himself, lying on the rubber blanket by the warmth of the fire. 'And I'd love a woollen blanket and a pillow,' he said. 'Shall I gather more wood and build up the fire?'

Ab had been feeling out of sorts all day, regardless of the drugs he took at breakfast before they took off this morning. Two tablets every eight hours, but even so, he seemed exhausted. Kees wasn't tired at all. The lid-poppers did an incredible job with his body; he had never felt so energetic or happy. Wondering if happy was the right word, he was relieved that the stressed and worried feelings were gone, at least during the day. But those feelings haunted him the more during the night when he'd lie awake staring at the stars and wondering if Moeke, Punica, and Corrie were watching that same sky as he was from their bedroom windows. Sometimes, he even woke Ab to talk, unable to divert his feelings of panic, his heart galloping in his chest and his breath punching from his mouth. Kees was certain if Ab hadn't come with him, he would have been dead already.

The memory of a boy at training camp followed him constantly. He was only seventeen and had been so homesick he panicked one night and ran away. The next day, their commander had set up a search squad that tracked his footprints in the snow and found him lying in a foetal position, trying to hide in a forest bare of leaves. His former friends, two Germans, not much older than Kees or Ab, brought him back like slave hunters, their victim bleeding from the torture they had already inflicted on him. And Kees understood they were all slaves. Hitler's slaves. He realised they had signed their own death warrants the moment they enlisted. Kees wondered how far humans could go in dehumanising their species into worthless animals. And he wondered if other species killed their own like humans did if they had the power to do so. The world seemed so crazy. He pulled up his collar and hunched his shoulders, crossing his arms and wrapping them around his body. He shuffled closer to the fire and watched Ab's face sink away in sleep.

For a week, they had been marching. Kees set up camp on the periphery of the German SS camp. The others, the Germans, thought the Dutch recruits beneath them. They called them traitors and taunted them for joining the wrong army. Wasn't there a Dutch division for them? Kees wanted to explain that Seyss-Inquart promised them a Dutch division. They shouldn't even be in the SS. The Germans tried to lure Kees into a heated discussion. Ab touched his shoulder, and Kees understood he'd better shut up.

Since leaving the ship in Königsberg, the Tross has given them two tablets a day. No one knew what the pills were for, but they all took them, although hesitantly at first. They soon noticed changes. They could march maybe four hours without medication, but with medication, they could march half the night, sleep for only two hours, and still march on.

Kees noticed the side effects, too; he saw that kind and empathic men changed into evil monsters. His mind flicked back to the boy who tried to escape. Kees, Ab, and the other recruits stood in a circle around the flagpole when the boy's former friends brought him, dressed only in a shirt – his legs were bare, his feet as well – and told him to stand by the flagpole. The boy still had hope in his eyes, but Kees knew he'd be dead in three minutes. Kees closed his eyes. One shot echoed across the countryside. When he opened them, the boy lay motionless, bleeding out on the frozen concrete ground. Afterwards, no one talked about the boy's death, not even Ab, not even when he and Kees were alone. Kees thought talking about the dead boy would make it all too real. He assumed Ab had closed his eyes, as well.

The rabbit was coming along nicely, its flesh roasting to a crisp. Some boys further away worked together and killed a wild boar; the roasting meat smelled delicious. But Kees and Ab stayed away from the Germans. They were crazy. And the rabbit was enough food to sustain both of them. Kees wasn't that hungry, anyway.

Branches cracked behind Kees, and he jumped to his feet. He grabbed his rifle and aimed it into the woods expecting a boar. But it was a man, a scared stick of a man who seemed as much startled to have walked into an SS battalion as Kees was to come face to face with him. He was a Russian soldier who seemed to have lost his way. The man panicked, and spoke pleading words to him. Ab woke up and scrambled to his feet.

Kees lowered his voice, asking the Russian to quieten down; he didn't want to arouse the others yet. Kees wasn't in the mood for killing, not that he had killed anyone yet. He spoke in Russian, which he learned on those rainy afternoons when he and Ab studied the Russian version of Anna Karenina, deciphering the Russian words as they compared it to the Dutch version.

The Russian said he wasn't a soldier; he was a peasant. In the woods, he found the uniform on a dead soldier and exchanged his rags for it.

Ab held his rifle but wasn't aiming it very well. He looked at the man, forgetting everything he learned in training. 'He looks starving,' Ab said to Kees and asked the man in Russian if that was so.

The man nodded, eyes wide, staring at the SS men some fiftymetres behind Kees and Ab. He crouched down and started to walk backwards, retreating to safety.

Kees hesitated. Letting him get away wouldn't be the intelligent thing, but he didn't want to shoot another human being at point-blank range. And the man seemed unarmed. He might be speaking the truth. Breathing fast, he told the man to stop moving and raise his hands. To run into any Russian soldiers after just seven days of marching was unexpected. The others behind them started to stir. He heard them but kept his eyes on the Russian. Oberscharführer Schachner ordered them to stop the man from escaping.

Kees shouted, 'He isn't a soldier! He told us he took the uniform of a dead man.'

The Russian turned and ran, but Kees darted after him and tackled him even before he reached the forest. Kees kept him pinned face down on the ground. His knee pressing into the Russian's back, he searched him for hidden weapons. He had none on him. Kees pulled him back up to stand.

Oberscharführer Schachner said, 'Ask him where his company is.'

Kees asked him in Russian.

The Russian shook his head.

'He insists he is not a soldier,' Kees said.

Schachner told the soldier to kneel, which Kees translated.

But the Russian stayed standing, repeating several times; I am not a soldier. His terrified eyes pleading with Kees.

Schachner kicked the man in the knees, bending his leg the wrong way. The man screamed like an animal and lay twisting on the ground.

'You broke his knee,' Kees uttered, an already apparent fact for all to see.

The man's face contorted, his gaping mouth stretched to its maximum capacity, revealing rotten molars, but no sound came from his throat.

Schachner coolly raised his pistol and shot the man in the head as if switching off a light. He returned the pistol to its holder on his belt. A stream of blood squirted from the Russian's temple as the man sank into the long grass like a bundle of discarded clothes.

'He was a filthy Jew,' Schachner said.

Kees straightened his clothes and rubbed his forehead, his mind chaotic as he tried to make sense of what had happened and what his part in the Russian's death had been. He said in a panicked voice, 'How do you know? How do you know?'

Ab had returned to the fire, sitting on a log and staring into the flames. His arms were crossed as if hugging himself.

Schachner approached Kees and bent toward him, bringing his face close Kees's. He stared into his eyes. 'How dare you strike a tone like that to your superior?' Schachner shouted. He fidgeted for his pistol in the holder, his face turning red, finally got it out and raised the barrel to Kees's temple. Schachner's eyes turned wild. Kees hunched his shoulders, expecting the bullet to end his misery.

Schachner lowered his voice. 'You have very dark hair.' He seemed to contemplate something for a moment. 'I'll tell you what. I won't kill you just yet. Let's see how useful your ability to speak Russian will be. The Russian saved your life,' he sneered. He didn't mean the man lying dead at their feet.

'I am not a Jew,' Kees whispered.

After the Russian's death, Ab withdrew. He had trouble sleeping and refused to eat almost everything Kees foraged. No more than a week after the Russian died, Ab's health took a turn for the worse during the night. He started running a temperature and called out a couple of times in a fit of anguish. Kees lay beside him and tried to calm his friend but was exhausted by the fear he suffered throughout the day. He wondered if he had slept through some of Ab's nightmares and if the others had heard him. The following day, he propped Ab against a tree and folded his winter coat into a pillow to support his head. Ab seemed conscious of what was happening. He stared at the movement; the whites of his eyes were visible from fear. Kees fed him rabbit meat. He wanted to talk with Ab but wondered if he was up for a conversation.

Kees wanted to discuss running away and leaving their battalion, even though Schachner would hunt them and have them executed when found. But he feared it was only a matter of time before Schachner discovered their lies. During the day, Kees tried to pretend all was well. He sang their German battle songs along with stamina, his voice loud and making up for Ab's silence.

He watched Ab like a nurse, hoping with all his heart he would soon feel better, trying to make marching manageable for him, helping him rest when no one was looking. When he could, he would take Ab on his back and walk with him for as long as his back could handle it. The other Dutch lads told Kees he should report Ab to the Tross, so they'd take him to the hospital, but Kees was afraid. He feared that as soon as the medics took Ab away from him, they would catch on he was a Jew and have him killed like the Russian.

The men around Kees packed their gear and heaved their rucksacks onto their backs. Kees put Ab's heaviest equipment – his steel breadbox, tent canvas, rubber blanket, gasmask, and half of his ammunition – in with his gear when no one was looking. He added the foldable shovel under the leather strap on the side where his shovel hung to make Ab's rucksack lighter.

Kees heaved Ab up and let him adjust to the standing position. He thought he caught Schachner's eye, but Schachner turned towards the forest and ordered them to march. Kees ensured they were the last of their battalion so they could rest whenever Ab needed to and Schachner wouldn't notice. The only problem was catching up, but he had time, he told his nerves. They would be lost in the chaos as long as he made camp when the others were still busy preparing their meals; with the movement of the ones that went out to hunt and others searching for cold mountain streams to refill their flasks, no one would know who was coming or going. Kees fed Ab his Pervitin pills to help him find the energy he so lacked, and with the double dosage, he did seem to recover and could march sixty-five kilometres, but when the pills wore off, he relapsed into a half-conscious state. Ab asked Kees more than once what he had dreamed and seemed comforted by Kees's hallucinatory dreams of does and ice maidens. Ab said he saw her, too. She followed them through the forest.

Kees let it go. He built a fire and spread rubber blankets on the ground for Ab, covering him with their winter coats. 'Stay awake,' Kees implored Ab. 'I'll be away a little while to hunt for meat.' He stressed Ab needed to stay sharp. He didn't trust him to be quiet when he was sleeping. Ab had called out the weirdest things in the last week or so. Kees was afraid he'd give himself away in one of those tantrums, and if he did, Schachner would kill him without hesitation.

Kees had seen Schachner murder civilians many times during their march towards the Eastern Front; it gave him a sense of satisfaction – especially if he thought his victims were Jewish. He quenched the life from them as if squashing fleas between his fingernails. The Germans were joining in. Even his fellow Dutchmen were hanging Jews from electricity poles and posing with the dead as if taking holiday snapshots. What were they thinking? Were they planning on passing the photos around the dinner table when they returned home?

The tendency to murder seemed to increase with the dosage of those pills. One soldier, his eyes continually flicking around, taking in every movement, bragged he had murdered a whole family that day. He told them how he discovered the mother, the father, two kids, and a grandmother hiding in a shed. He set the entire thing on fire and boasted he had shot the family dog before he left.

Kees was still tending to his friend, who seemed to have recovered physically, but the cruelty surrounding them tormented Ab's mind. Ab had started to pray and sing the songs he had learned as a boy. He found comfort in the old Yiddish songs, and Kees often heard him murmur them under his breath.

The moment of death came unannounced,

as is usual in these events.

Schachner discovered Ab's secret. And as with the executed Russian, he did not ask for an explanation. He took his pistol from his belt and aimed it at Ab's temple, and just like he had killed the Russian, he pulled the trigger. Ab sank like a hunted deer to the ground, the wound in his head jetting blood. Kees aimed his rifle at Schachner and would undoubtedly have shot if Schachner had not reacted unexpectedly. He asked Kees if he, too, was prepared to die. Neither pulled the trigger. Kees knew he could not survive if he shot Schachner. The Germans would slaughter him. Kees wanted – needed – to survive. He told himself he must stay alive, even if only to tell everyone about all these murderous crimes, so he lowered his rifle to his side.

He remembered the little silver bird in his pocket and felt its pulse against his thigh. In his mind, he heard Corrie's voice.

Kees sank to his knees beside Ab's body and gently took his friend's hand in his, stroking the fingers as death froze the corpse. He took the sculpting knife from his pocket and spread Ab's left hand, his still-warm fingers on his lap. He felt Schachner's gaze on him as he checked if the blade was sharp enough. Schachner gasped as Kees sliced off the pinkie. Kees trembled from shock, clenching the finger in his shaking hand, his heart now at the back of his throat. He lifted Ab's hand to his lips; the wetness of blood smudged on his cheeks.

Schachner said something. Kees registered Schachner's words without listening – something about taking a trophy. During the few months Kees had been on the Eastern Front, he had seen the worst of human nature. Schachner would put this down to one of those acts of barbarism, and he cared little. His friend was dead, and his finger was the only thing Kees could take to save Ab's soul.

Schachner smiled; Kees had impressed him all right. 'How many fingers have you collected?' he asked Kees. Without waiting for an answer, Schachner returned his pistol to its holder and ordered the men to pack up.

Kees pulled a roll of bandages from his trouser pocket and wrapped Ab's finger in it. When the blood stopped seeping through the muslin, he cut the rest of the roll off with his knife and wrapped it in a clean handkerchief. He raised the finger to his lips one more time and kissed it; loose threads stuck to his dry lips; he lowered it into his inside pocket and closed the buttons of his jacket. Kees wanted it as close to his heart as possible. He wiped the knife on the moss, returned it to its leather holder, took out his foldable shuffle, and dug a grave.

CHAPTER THIRTEEN

Kees

Kees watched Oberscharführer Schachner through his riflescope. He clenched his jaws. Sand grated between his molars as he ducked lower. A shell screeched towards him and rammed into the ground, catapulting black crows of clay into the air. His ears rang. He wiped mud from his face. Schachner ran a few metres towards the Russian infantrymen and dropped to the ground, taking cover. Bullets sliced above his head. Kees saw the Germans from the edge of his gaze but held his eyes on Schachner. They got up, advanced a few metres, and dropped back to the ground, a chain of paper cut-outs, carrying guns, throwing shadows of dust. Kees lay waiting, his rifle aimed, his finger on the trigger, ready to shoot. His mind was calm. Calmer than it had been for weeks, months even, weighing Ab's life against Schachner's.

Kees felt the trigger pulse against his finger as if wanting him to squeeze it. He stared into the cloud of dust and smoke surrounding him, his brain empty. 'I'm sorry,' he whispered. 'I'm so sorry.' He touched his chest, and underneath his jacket, he kept Ab's finger close to his heart. The loud screeches of shelling softened as Kees tensed every muscle in his body and prayed for Willem to be safe. But he didn't pray to a God. There was no God in hell, only the devil. He had to find a way to persuade Willem to return to his old school in Arnhem. But how, when the Germans censured all his letters? Kees had met boys from the Reichsschule who told him everyone enlisted after graduation. It was expected, they said; compulsory.

But they wouldn't send children to this Russian hell, would they?

With a bolt of electricity running through his body, Kees realised Willem would graduate within the year, and he was seventeen. Half his company were seventeen-year-olds. Even the boy in training camp who tried to escape had been seventeen when they executed him.

Kees would write a letter to Moeke to fetch Willem home. His own death would be enough for a family to bear. Since Ab's murder, Kees knew he was living on borrowed time.

'Go home while you can,' he whispered, as if to Willem, clenching his teeth.

A fresh rain of shells dispersed around him, but most flew like a rainbow of lightning to strike the SS, who were taking cover behind him.

When the bombs grew silent, the Germans got up and ran to the river, keeping ten metres between them as they had learned in training camp so as not to deplete their numbers should a bomb hit the ground between them. Kees followed, and when he reached the pontoon bridge, a fresh supply of shells flew toward him.

'Take cover!' Schachner shouted.

Kees dropped to the ground. Bombs screeched and dug into the earth, spitting bars of soil and clay around him. He raised his hands to his helmet to shield himself. Images of dead soldiers, their helmets covered in bullet holes, in their eyes a horrible emptiness, came to mind. How could flesh protect his skull if steel could not? Exploding bombs dived into the Neva, spouting giant mushrooms of brown water into the air, and one hit the bridge. Dusk was crawling in from the forest. The hailstorm of bullets finally grew silent; the Russians seemed to have retreated for the night. Schachner ordered the Italians to repair the bridge. Kees rested a little; he knew Schachner wanted them across before daylight.

After midnight, Schachner pulled Kees's shoulder.

'Wake up, you lazy dog. You're the last to cross.'

So Kees got up, straightened his steel helmet, which had doubled as his pillow, and heaved his equipment onto his back. He wondered how he'd survived those weeks carrying Ab and the extra gear. He must have possessed the strength of the insane.

119

He stumbled across the bridge while the Italians, their tools scattered around them, repaired the damage. The Russians reopened fire, and a fresh hail of bullets nipped into the wooden deck around Kees. He ducked lower and nearly tripped over an arm as it reached for a handful of nails, but he regained his balance. He saw the Germans reach the riverbank in the flashing lights of exploding bombs. The Russians must have night vision; their bullets were searching their flesh like mosquitoes in summer. Kees still had a good twenty metres to go. Out of breath, he reached the other side and collapsed onto the soft shore to rest.

But, as soon as he hit the ground, he heard the command, 'Get up. The air is full of metal. Leave the riverbank now!'

An hour later, the fighting stopped. Kees could hardly see his hand before his face. Trying not to stumble, he followed the inky silhouettes of the Germans to where there was air. Schachner ordered them to dig foxholes in a clearing behind some houses for the night. The ground was too sandy, too loose, and it kept caving in. The others were lying behind shallow ridges–Kees lay in a dent in the earth and stared at the stars. The Tross hadn't delivered their coats yet. He wasn't cold; too much adrenaline was still pumping through his veins. He listened to the quietness of the land and the howling wolves in the distance.

Schachner sat by the wall, leaning his back against it. The moonlight lit him up with cold, colourless light. He looked tired and was smoking a cigarette. Kees watched him cautiously, his gaze on him, but his head turned the other way.

Beside Kees, someone else smoked a cigarette. Kees was aware of the motion of the cigarette being raised to the man's lips. The smoke wafted over Kees. He turned his eyes, not moving his head, and saw a youth his age watching him. He had a thin moustache like Clark Gable. The flames twitching from the burning houses flickered in his eyes. He gestured, asking Kees if he wanted a cigarette. Kees squeezed his lips and shook his head a little.

Since Schachner had murdered Ab, nobody had spoken to Kees, and he kept himself out of their conversations, marching silently alone with them and camping alone during the nights. He hated the

Germans as much as they hated him. Übermenschen – angsthazen – all cowards, he thought, every single one of them with their so-called Aryan superiority.

'Come on,' the soldier whispered. 'Take one,' he held the box of cigarettes out to Kees while leaning over towards him. He spoke Dutch with a thick German accent.

Kees's eyes turned to Schachner. His mouth was open. He was snoring while he held the cigarette, still lit, between his fingers. His hand rested on his leg.

'You're German?' Kees asked, cautiously keeping his voice low. 'But you speak Dutch?'

'Jawohl,' he said, smiling, tipping his helmet as if saluting Kees.

Kees wondered what he was doing, speaking Dutch to him, even speaking to him at all. Kees took the cigarette but had no intention of smoking it and said, 'You speak Dutch very well.'

'And Italian, French... even Russian... well, pretty good Russian. And more languages I came across during my travels in Europe.'

'Russian is a beautiful language, though,' Kees said, looking over at Schachner. 'I studied it at home before the war. I wanted to read Anna Karenina in its original language.'

'At university?'

'Nah, I did one year of medical school. It's Russian literature that I wanted to read in its original language. I have a thing for languages. They all seem to have the same common words and a few extra words you must memorise in order to say you can speak the language fluently.'

Kees wondered which books the soldier had read. Goosebumps prickled his arms. Maybe he was talking too much. He shouldn't be so open; it only made him look weak.

'My mother is Russian,' the soldier whispered and raised a finger to his lips. 'But don't tell Schachner, or he'll have me scouting behind enemy lines.'

Kees lit the cigarette and filled his lungs with smoke. That was a secret he was willing to keep. He knew the only thing keeping him alive was his ability to speak Russian.

'I'm Wolfgang, but you can call me Wolf,' the soldier said. 'What you said about languages is true.'

The nicotine danced through Kees's veins. It had been a while since he smoked.

'Kees,' he said, introducing himself.

'Keys? Well, the name can't get any more Hollands.'

'Case,' Kees repeated, correcting Wolf, 'as in suitcase. It's my father's Christian name, short for Cornelis. He gave my two half-sisters the same name as well, adding a's. He loves tradition and himself.'

'I take it you're not too fond of him?'

Kees shook his head. 'He uses his children to serve his own ambitions. Ambitions he's too cowardly to pursue himself.' Kees contemplated. 'I found out when it was too late. But I'll tell you about it some other time.'

'What's the story with the finger?'

'They told you?'

Wolf raised his eyebrows, a smile slowly building. 'Something that wild rarely stays a secret.'

Kees tried to decide if he wanted to scare Wolf off or keep the info to himself.

'Ab was my best friend,' he said.

Wolf snorted.

Kees glanced at Schachner; his cigarette had fallen to the ground. It hadn't set him on fire. He was always lucky, that man.

'Ab, you say? I heard about him all right. He mustn't have been in his right mind to sign up. How did he think he'd get away with it? Did he pass all the tests? Even the Aryan ones?'

'Well, that only goes to show,' Kees said.

They had been so naïve. Naïve. Was naïve the right word? Kees flicked the cigarette away and wrapped his arms around himself.

'You're from the same place as him, the Dutch guys tell me. Arnhem?'

'Yep,' Kees grunted.

'You're not crazy, are you?'

'Crazy?'

'The finger thing... do you still have it on you?'

Kees thought for a bit, and after a long pause, he said, 'We're all madmen out here.'

He gazed at the stars, the same stars Willem would look at in Schaarsbergen and the same Punica would stare at from her bedroom window, dreaming of Ab's return. He hadn't written about Ab's death yet, and he knew as long as he was serving on the Eastern Front, Schachner was keeping Ab's death a secret, too. If he had mentioned him in the long list of casualties, they would have ordered Kees to stand trial for fraud and faking a twin brother. Schachner must need him more than he realised.

He contemplated writing the letter to Punica right now; she would be waiting for a letter from either or both of them. Kees knew they had fallen in love, and even though she was only fifteen, she seemed so much older. Kees had seen them sneaking out after curfew into the garden and climbing the fence to the fields. The land had become a sanctuary since the war started, and he had wanted to follow them and tell them how inappropriate their friendship was. Kees sighed with relief that he had not interfered and had let Ab and Punica enjoy the freedom they found together. He never even let on to Ab that he knew. How Kees wished he had told Ab being his brother had been a dream come true. He thought about the time by the pool. Ab and Punica's faces as they listened to him telling them about his dreams of a mystical frozen forest and the doe. How weird they both must have thought he was.

Kees heard Wolf breathe deeply, his lips parting slightly as the air pushed from his lungs; he had fallen asleep. He contemplated if he should write the letter now while everyone slept. He saw the doe from his dreams, watching him from the side of the house. It sniffed Schachner's clothes and slowly turned her head and looked at him. Her eyes sparkled. Kees got up and walked towards her. He made soft, reassuring sounds and reached his hand to her, whispering for her not to be afraid of him; he meant her no wrong. She gazed at him. The moonlight glistered on her coat, growing brighter. Her body seemed to glow, and she shone so brightly that her shape became sharply outlined against the blackness of the night. Kees stared into the light and discerned a face, the beautiful face of a young girl watching him. Is she made of snow? He awoke, his face sweaty, his body shaking from the cold. The reality of his surroundings hit him hard, and he felt like crying. He got up and took a cigarette from the packet lying by Wolf; he lit it and sucked it as if his life depended on it. Was he ever getting out of this hellhole?

CHAPTER FOURTEEN

Willem

Willem had been at the school for no more than three months when, during morning assembly, Unterrichtsleiter Herr Naumann announced the Luftwaffe had requisitioned Koningsheide. All students were to report to Schloss Bensberg, a castle on the outskirts of Cologne in Germany.

On the last evening, some boys had planned a pillow fight, an international match between the German and Dutch boys. They were thrilled to learn that their music teacher, Mr Ros, would be the designated night watchman. Everyone knew Mr Ros as both kind and incapable of keeping order, so they asked him to referee the fight.

At 21.00 the boys stood armed with their pillows, dressed only in underpants and vests, ready to charge each other. Mr Ros stood between both teams, waiting for the dial to hit the twelve on his stopwatch. He held a hanky by its corner above their heads.

Willem stood in the Dutch team's front line, flanked by the biggest boy from his year, Tommie de Bruin. That afternoon, Tommie and Willem had sworn allegiance, as both were desperate to take revenge on those Schweinehunde. The night before, they had stolen a sandwich from the kitchen but were caught by Rudy. He had told his father on them, and both boys still felt the hot marks of their whipping across their buttocks.

Willem had learned not to underestimate the small boys. Those short Germans, he concluded, were the most vicious and unrelenting. He watched Rudy as he stood opposite him, lining up with the rest of the German boys.

A film of sweat formed on the back of Willem's neck. He clenched his pillow tighter, flexing the muscles in his jaw as he peered into Rudy's eyes. Rudy was flanked by one of the tallest and most robust boys on the German side. His name was Friedrich Höge; he was a fanatic Nazi from Munich with an intrinsic hatred of Jews and an aversion towards the Dutch boys who were, in his eyes, inferior to him. Willem hated him back as much; he would love to smash his brains in with his pillow. Willem pulled a face to intimidate him as he waited for Mr Ros to start the countdown.

'10...' Mr Ros said. '9... 8... 7... 6... 5... 4.... 3.... 2...'

'Charge!' Willem screamed at the top of his lungs and started beating Friedrich and punching Rudy at the same time. He didn't even see Mr Ros's face change to one of panic or him stumbling on legs too wobbly for him as he tried to get out of the line of fire. Willem beat with all his might, screaming all the way, shouting for backup, ramming into those two German idiots. And he wasn't even fighting for himself; he was fighting for Ab's family, who had disappeared into work camps in Germany, and for Ab, whom he considered his brother. When Ab moved in with them, Willem hadn't realised how far the German hatred for Jews went, but now he knew. The Nazis had passed yet another law. From now on, Gentiles were not permitted to have intimate relationships with Jews. And only this morning, he read about their latest humiliation: Jews weren't allowed to drive or take lifts in cars. Willem had to listen to these Germans continuously air their hatred for a religion – a religion, for God's sake. There was no way he would buy into their brainwashing propaganda tactics any longer.

He made a terrible mistake coming here and now had to live with it for as long as the war lasted. Anti-Semitism had started amongst Willem's new friends as a joke. Still, it was turning into a way of life for them, and they seemed to seize every opportunity to demean Jews to their faces, and afterwards, they'd all have a great laugh about their bold behaviour. Everyone seemed to have lost their ability to differentiate between right and wrong. Even his father, even the man who allowed him, even encouraged him to go to this school – a school for raising devils – and had no interest in what happened to the Jews as they watched the Germans force them onto trains bound for the work camps in Germany and Poland. God, how the teachers had tried to teach Willem to hate, and how he had learned it, but not for the people they had in mind. His pillow ripped, but he kept on ramming now, using his fists while clenching the empty pillowcase. Even if it were only this one time, he would win for his friends at home and his brother. His brother, who had left a short while ago, and Ab, who were now sleeping in the mud and the snow while their father sat by the fire wearing his woollen slippers, reading his Goddamn Nazi newspaper Storm. A lump formed in Willem's throat.

'For once,' he screamed, 'For once, I'm... I'm going... to... I'm going to... to... kill... you!'

A steel whistle screeched. He noticed his opponent had stopped punching him, but he didn't care and rammed his fist like a madman. Hands grabbed his back and yanked him off Rudy, who lay limp underneath him, his eyes bulging with terror. Three boys on his team shoved Willem against the wall. The whistle screeched again. Willem's front teeth hurt, his jaw was numb from the beating, and looking at those bloody faces around him, everyone panting from exertion, he wondered why they had stopped. They were so close to winning. His mouth filled up with blood, and he suppressed the urge to spit it out.

Naumann, dressed in his immaculate uniform, appeared between the boys, holding a whistle between his purple lips. His face was red as he peered at Willem from under his heavy, arrogant eyelids. Naumann turned his head slowly, taking seconds to take in the state of the room. Their gear was spread around them as if a minor explosion had occurred, and the dorm lay in ruins – mattresses pushed away from the beds and empty steel bed frames stacked and scattered along the walls – feathers twirling everywhere.

Herr Naumann turned to Mr Ros. 'How dare you let this happen on your watch.' His tone was loud and intimidating, like Hitler's during those famous speeches on the radio. 'I will not tolerate this behaviour, and least of all from a Zugführer.' Now, addressing the boys, he yelled, 'I expect you all outside IMMEDIATELY!'

He turned and marched out. Willem wiped the blood from his nose and swallowed. With blood-smeared cheeks, he looked at Tommie. Tommie's nose bled, and he smeared it across his cheeks and forehead. They looked at each other and smiled, spreading streaks of blood over their arms and upper legs, turning themselves into Apache warriors. They turned to follow the others down the stairs to the beetroot fields outside.

In rows of tens, Naumann summoned them to lie down in the freezing mud, stand up, lie down, stand up, lie down stand up lie down stand up lie down. Naumann bellowed at them across the echoing empty fields. When they thought they could go on no longer, they were ordered to jog along the perimeter of the cornfield, the mud sucking their feet into the depths until their muscles trembled from cold and exhaustion.

'Inside. Washed and dressed, I will see you in the hall in two minutes!' Naumann ordered.

The boys wiped their bare feet on the mat by the door and ran up the slippery stairs, turning the white steps to streaked brown ones. They all crammed into the showers, and after soaping their bodies and rinsing them clean, they ran naked across the landing to their rooms in search of presentable uniforms. They all made roll call just in time.

The boys stood in the hall, a semicircle of coldness, as Naumann read aloud from the rulebook. Slowly, exasperatingly slowly, he read every single rule out to them. Rudy stood in front of Willem, his legs trembling. When he collapsed, his head sounded like a sodden leather football as it landed on the marble floor tiles. Willem pulled his shoulders back and stood erect. He would show Naumann, whose son now lay unconscious at his feet, who was the Übermensch now and who was not. Even when milky sunlight shone onto the faded wallpaper behind Naumann and a new day was dawning, and Willem's knees shook, he still stayed upright.

Willem focused on a tree outside the window, struck by lightning a few nights ago, the top half bending back toward the ground. The leaves, now brown and dead, still clung to their branches and swept the grass. An owl settled on the stump, where its colours almost merged with the bark and the colour of the split wood. The owl's yellow eyes stared at Willem, and once Willem noticed those eyes, they could not be unseen.

Willem's legs shook, his knees giving way, but he would not let himself collapse to the floor. Rudy still lay unconscious, and Willem wondered, remembering the boxing ring, how Naumann could stand watching Rudy being beaten by a boy much more robust and a head taller than his son. Naumann had showed no emotion as he held his son's glasses in his outstretched hand. Willem hated the compassion and pity he now felt for Rudy. It had been easier when he loathed them all. Them against us. Rudy's face was as white as a tissue. His father did not even glance down at his son once.

All Willem wanted now was to escape. And escape he would. Appearing weak would not get him out of here. The owl's yellow eyes observed Willem as he tried to make a plan. The owl spread its wings and flapped them, and Willem watched the white fluff glitter in those first rays of sunshine, but the owl did not fly away. Show me your freedom, Willem thought. Fly away. Show me the animal world has not changed. But the owl remained there, sitting on the stump by the window, and stared at him. Sweat dripped down Willem's nose from his chin onto his uniform, the pea soup colour now dotted with dark green, but he stayed standing as Rudy lay unconscious at his feet.

At seven in the morning, Naumann finally ordered the cook and the kitchen maid to lift his son from the icy floor. They laid him on the kitchen table as if he was a corpse. The cook covered him with a blanket, but Willem could not see if it reached over his head. Naumann ordered the remaining boys standing to collect their gear and report back within ten minutes. And when they had returned with their backpacks hoisted onto their backs, they stumbled to the station in long, dreary lines.

The train arrived with a tunnel of steam following its chimney and came to a screeching halt. The boys boarded and quickly found their seats. The train pulled away, shaking and tearing through the countryside towards their next destination: Schloss Bensberg, where their education continued. One step closer to Russia, the start of Willem's plan to find his brother and bring him home. Willem finally allowed himself to fall into a comatose sleep for two hours.

His Zugführer de Zwart woke him as the train slowed when approaching Cologne station. From there, they travelled by tram to their new school, a massive white castle with five turret-topped towers, a hilltop fortress turned Reichsschule for Jungmannen. They arrived after lunch, but the boys were glad they could skip food. Sleep was what their bodies craved. In the afternoons, they were required to rest on their beds, still dressed in their uniforms and still wearing shoes. Usually an hour of boredom, but today, they all fell asleep when their heads touched the pillows.

An hour later, a fierce roar awakened them, and they were to report at 15:00 outside in the rain for the flag ceremony as was usual at a Reichsschule. After the German boys hoisted the flag, for probably the second or third time that day, a Geländespiel was planned to familiarise the boys from Holland with the woodlands and fields surrounding the Schloss. But Willem knew it was to test these new Dutch boys in action and determine the strongest and most likely to graduate.

This time, they put Willem into a different team than Tommie. The teams were mixed with boys from both nationalities. The Dutch and the Germans were to become one people. Naumann had informed them. Their home country had ceased to exist, and from now on, they were to refer to Holland as Westland. Willem cared little what names they used. All he cared about was finding an opportunity to escape, and winning would place him higher in the school's hierarchy and offer him more freedom.

The referee gave each boy a wooden stick to symbolise his soul. The boys stuck the stick inside their jacket breast pockets. Once they had lost their souls to their opponents, they were out of the game.

A farmer with a horse and cart took Willem and his team to the left side of the woods; Tommie's team went to the right. They got down on hands and knees and crept between the trees like commandoes. They crept through brambles and nettles and were so excited and running on adrenaline that they didn't feel the sting or the ripping of their skin on thorns sharp as fishhooks. Willem had played this game many times in Schaarsbergen and knew through experience that their legs would burn like hell later in the shower. And even then, they would bite their lips and ignore the sting as they listened to the weaklings moan for the Heimmutter to rub some vinegar on their red skin. No way could Willem show any weakness. Weakness would not help him escape to the Eastern Front.

It was getting dark, and Willem had four sticks in his belt. The souls of German boys he had 'slaughtered'. Feeling proud, he crept into a bramble bush to hide and prepare for a new offensive. Girls' soft voices sounded from above him. Willem recognised the distinct Amsterdam accent, peered through the branches, and discerned two girls clamped together, sitting on a branch about two metres above the ground. He listened closely to their whispering; they must not have seen him on the ground.

'How will we get out of here?' one said in a squeaky voice that sounded as young as his little sister Corrie.

'Quiet,' the other answered. 'I hear something.'

Willem tried to slow his breathing, swallowing back breaths to stay quiet.

'Is there someone down there?' the squeaky one whispered to the other.

'What are you two doing here?' Willem whispered, peering up. He could see their surprised faces through the branches.

'Who are you? Are you hiding from them as well?'

'Yes, but not because I'm Jewish.'

'Who says we are Jewish?'

'Why else would you two be up a tree?'

'I can't see you; it's so dark down there.'

'It's dangerous here. Don't you know where you are?'

'We know,' the older girl whispered. 'Shh, you be quiet,' she said as the little girl tried to say something, interrupting her. 'That's why

131

we're up here. Are you a Jungmann?'

'I am, but don't be afraid. I won't tell anyone you're Jewish. You do know everyone around here hates the likes of you?'

'We're not Jewish. Shh!' she said again to the younger girl, who tried to interrupt her. 'Be quiet. Let me do the talking. As soon as it gets dark enough, we're leaving,' she continued.

'Where are your parents?'

'We don't know. Mama said they were going to Germany.'

'We're not supposed to tell anyone,' the younger one said, interrupting the older one again.

'He knows anyway,' the older one said and continued. 'We didn't like the family they left us with, so we ran away to find our parents.'

'Listen, you must return to those people,' Willem said. 'Where do they live?'

'In a village near Leeuwarden. There's nothing there, only fields and sky—'

'We prefer Amsterdam,' the younger girl said in a squeaky voice.

'Go back to Leeuwarden—'

A branch cracked about ten metres away. The little girl gasped.

'Leave as soon as it is dark,' he whispered sternly.

He crawled from his hiding place. A fist landed on his ear, knocking him sideways, and as he fell to the ground, his eardrum folded double. A boy in uniform kicked him in the stomach, but he couldn't see who it was. He crumbled, pulling up his knees, trying to protect himself. The boy stood back and looked at him.

'Tommie?' Willem gasped. 'What are you doing?' he said, coughing, trying to catch his breath. 'We're friends, remember?'

'Give me your soul.'

'What? We're allies?'

Tommie sat on Willem's stomach, holding his hands pinned to the ground. Willem looked over Tommie's shoulders into the tree. The girls clenched the branches around them as if expecting to be shaken from the tree; their eyes bulged, and their mouths contorted. They were about the same age as Willem's sisters. They had raven black hair like Kees. Their dresses had torn hems. Their ankle socks were filthy, and their shoes, which looked expensive, had holes in their soles. They must have been walking for days.

'Come on,' Willem said to Tommie. 'It's a stupid game. Get off me. Let's go back, and I'll give you one of my captured souls, so it's a draw.'

Tommie let Willem go. Willem got to his feet and wiped the dead twigs from his clothes.

'How many souls have you got?' Tommie asked.

'Four.'

'That'll make mine nine,' Tommie said, 'counting yours. So, are you going to give them to me nicely, or do I have to knock the shit out of you?'

'God, what's wrong with you?' Willem put his finger into his ear and checked if his ear was bleeding. 'Let's get out of here.'

A broken branch fell between their feet. Tommie looked up, 'One of those owls, up there again,' he said, glancing up into the trees.

Without hesitating or even thinking, Willem grabbed what was closest to him, a branch about a metre in length and thick as a child's arm, and swung it, whacking Tommie across the temple with it. Tommie slumped on impact into a bundle on the ground. He lay unconscious by Willem's feet. Tommie had a nasty scrape across his face that bled. Willem sank to his haunches. 'Shit. Shit, shit, shit,' and looking at the wound, he raised his hands to his face. 'SHIT!' he groaned. He patted Tommie's cheeks, but he wasn't responding. Damn, he shrieked and bore his fist into the tree trunk. His knuckles were bleeding now as well.

'Are you all right?' the girl with the squeaky voice asked.

'Get out of here!' he whispered loudly, trying not to raise his voice. He opened Tommie's jacket, took the five sticks off him, and put them in his jacket. Willem pulled Tommie's arms to position his body and yanked him onto his back.

He stumbled through the woods to where the teachers were waiting for them to emerge. Everyone cheered as Willem appeared, hunching forward to keep Tommie from falling off his back.

Willem turned out to be the last one still alive in the game. He laid

Tommie at their feet, took all the sticks on him, and threw all nine onto the grass. The other boys cheered as Naumann declared Willem the winner. Nobody cared about Tommie. Instead, they patted Willem's back. 'So many souls,' said one of the boys. 'Amazing. No one had ever brought back so many souls before.' Naumann sent a boy to fetch the Heimmutter for Tommie. Willem watched Naumann march away and wondered about Rudy.

The German boys hoisted Willem onto their shoulders, and the others cheered as they ran along, singing the conqueror's song. Willem smiled.

CHAPTER FIFTEEN

Punica

Punica heard the doors of the cells along the corridor slam one after the other against the whitewashed walls behind them, and the Germans shout that all prisoners were to report to the Rose Garden. She pulled on her shoes; her pulse racing. Annie's face turned as white as the wall behind her, her eyes flashing over her friend but unable to focus. The aunts put on their shoes in a much more leisurely manner. They followed the girls into the corridor and onto the muddy paths outside. They entered the Rose Garden and got into neat lines, the women behind the girls. The boys were running to their positions, their heads bent down, their bodies slumped. They looked terrible. Skinny, filthy, and their clothes rags and stiff with dirt. Peter wore wooden clogs too big for him. They had shaved off his thick, wavy hair; his eyes were sunken; the skeletal bones of his skull were visible through the features of his face.

Punica noticed her skirt had started to slip down to her hips, and her socks refused to stay up, continually slipping down her skinny calves. Her underwear was wet. A fortnight had passed, and feeling dirty while wearing the same clothes, she washed her underwear every two days, alternating between her underpants and her slip so not both were wet and cold at the same time. There was no predicting when they would be driven out into the Rose Garden, so when the doors started banging along the corridor, she hurriedly slipped on her underpants even though they were still drenched. She hoped they would have been a little dryer, but she didn't want to walk out without underwear, even though her skirt now hung halfway down her shins.

Punica couldn't see the boy from school who had been so brave and who had been brutally beaten for getting his number wrong. She touched the girl next to her and asked her to swap places. She worked her way across the yard in this way, towards the boys and ended beside Peter. Peter looked askance at her, his eyes squinting as if expecting to be hit. She mumbled if the boy from the lorry was all right. He said nothing, keeping his head down, obviously too scared to answer her. An older boy from her school stood two places back, near the barbed wire. She swapped with the woman behind her.

He had been beaten since she last saw him. She noticed he had a nasty cut across his naked skull.

'Are you all right?' she whispered, standing next to him, keeping her head down.

He ignored her.

A door slammed. Punica looked toward the noise and saw a guard walk down the steps of a small building just at the entrance gates she had assumed was an office. He strode down the path and took the turn into the Rose Garden. Punica's eyes fixed on him. He marched to the women's Blockführer, who in turn marched to the Lagerführer. The Blockführer slammed her heels and raised her right arm, giving him the Hitler salute. The Lagerführer stopped shouting and turned his head towards the prisoners.

At that moment, the world stopped turning and grew silent. Even the birds stopped singing, and the leaves stopped rustling, but still, she could not hear what was being said. The Lagerführer glanced up to where Punica had been standing. His eyes slid over the women's and girls' faces, searching them for one particular face, it seemed. His gaze rested on hers for a second. He mumbled to his guard, who screamed her name, 'MARIA MANDEMAKER!'

A shock wave passed through her. She felt nauseous and nearly vomited her heart out onto the mud, but nothing came as her heart had lodged itself, throbbing wildly, in her throat. She looked at the aunts from her cell and Annie. What should she do? They kept their eyes on the ground before them. She knew in a place like this, she would be alone in the face of danger. Just like you die alone and are born alone. She straightened her shoulders, tucked in her tummy the way her mother had taught her, and walked out from her line. The boy from the lorry mumbled something as she left him behind her. He said, beware of Father Christmas. She turned to him, but he raised his shoulders and bowed as if ready to receive a whack across the head.

She moved toward the Lagerführer.

The Lagerführer shouted. 'Hurry!'

She sped up as the other prisoners made way for her, shuffling to the side as if she had become a pariah whose misfortune could spread like a virus and infect them. When she passed Peter, he reached out his hand and brushed her fingers. They linked hands for a second and quickly let go of each other again.

'Come here!'

She ran towards him.

'The Lagerkommandant wants you!'

The guard walloped her back to hurry her up, and she lost her balance and fell onto her hands and knees into the mud. The Lagerführer picked her up, pulling her arm. 'Come, come,' he said to the guard, 'That's no way to treat a girl, as you well know.'

The guard took her arm and pulled her along toward the office building. Punica stared at the windows. She always assumed the building was an office, but... what function did it have? Every corner of the camp seemed to harbour some torture chamber. Maybe they saw her move across the compound to find the brave boy? They might do the unthinkable to her. Her mother always warned her about it. The reason for never walking alone in the dark or finding herself singled out away from her friends when boys and men were involved. The lace curtains blocked any view of what was going on inside. Her throat was so dry she nearly choked. She tried to swallow but gasped and went into a coughing fit. The guard stopped walking, but only for a moment. He pushed her onto the steps. She landed on her knees. Clumps of mud trodden into the gritty wooden surface grated her skin.

'Ca... ca... can't I go back to my cell... please?' she stuttered. But the guard took no notice, lifted her by her arm, and forced her to take the first step. Her legs seemed to give way, and she stumbled like a puppet on a string, her feet twisting beneath her, and this time she fell against the door. The guard rammed it open, and it slammed against a coat stand.

Behind a desk sat the Lagerkommandant. The registration book with the prisoners' names lay open before him. She stared in disbelief, deciphering her name at the top along with Annie's, Peter's, and all her fellow schoolmates, the names upside down to her. She might have given them the wrong name. She might have said her name was Punica instead of Maria Cornelia, and they only found out now. Punica was her own chosen name. She hated Maria.

By the window stood a small desk where a woman with a thick plait across her head in a German-style typed voraciously. A woman gasped behind her. She realised the coat stand was a person. She bent her head forward and slightly turned to see who it was standing half-hidden behind the door. The woman lifted a handkerchief to her eyes and started to cry. Punica recognised the shoes first. Brown leather walking shoes, the coat, a lovely blue she so adored, and the pink rose scarf, and only after taking in all the details of the woman's clothes did she finally dare to glance at the face she had pictured every night before falling asleep and every morning when waking up. That beautiful face, with eyeliner, mascara, pink cheeks, and perfect lipstick on lips made for wearing lipstick.

'Moeke,' she whispered.

Her mother sobbed aloud as she took her daughter into her arms. 'How can this be?' she whispered. 'How can this be?'

'Your daughter has committed a terrorist act. Her treatment is the same as any other political prisoner.'

'But she is only a child,' Moeke blurted out. She seemed to realise something, and pulling her shoulders back, she said, 'Herr Commandant,' – she looked him straight in the eyes – 'my daughter has served her time. Don't you agree?'

Moeke sounded brave and dignified, but such a tone would only get her into trouble at this camp. Moeke's voice trembled, and Punica realised Moeke knew this herself. Punica tried again to swallow. During her short time in the prison camp, she learned that being brave got you killed. She hugged her mother, digging her face into her mother's fur collar as if clutching onto a life before this prison camp, when mothers could still fix every stupid mistake you made.

She wondered if her mother had been told what her crime was. She hadn't obeyed her about the star and had worn it anyway. Mr de Wit probably informed her after school what had happened.

The Lagerkommandant inclined his head to the guard, telling him Punica could return to the others. The guard grabbed Punica's arm and dragged her outside without closing the door.

'Your daughter has broken the law and is being punished,' the Lagerkommandant said. 'She is treated fairly, as you have seen. She may wear her own clothes and is not required to wear the prison uniform like everyone else.'

Punica screamed as the guard dragged her down the stairs, her legs giving way.

She looked back at her mother. 'Moeke, Moeke,' she pleaded.

Moeke got down on her knees. 'I beg you,' her mother said, 'to reconsider. My daughter is only fifteen.'

Punica had heard it all before. Her teachers had tried to convince the SD to release the students. She had been the last one in the hall and heard everything, but the Germans were relentless.

She screamed louder still, her voice rasping her throat as the guard pulled her further away from her mother. She screamed so the entire world heard what was happening in the prison camp. But everyone knew what was happening. There was no wall built around the complex, only barbed wire fencing, so everyone travelling the road witnessed the starving prisoners and the Nazis armed with machine guns, forcing them to dig a two metres deep trench into the forest floor. A trench solely to keep them occupied, and they called it the shooting range because they shot prisoners daily for not working hard enough. Everyone living in the surrounding houses had seen everything and heard the bullets being fired, and no one did anything for them.

The guard dragged Punica back to the Rose Garden, and this time, it seemed all the worse, not only because they would make an example out of her. The man with the bat they called Father Christmas would bludgeon her to death. She would not survive. She was not like the boys, their faces all bloody and swollen but still standing with hope in their eyes, and she knew the White Angel would not come for her.

When the Blockführer dragged her into the gate to the Rose Garden, something remarkable happened. The Lagerkommandant bellowed from his office doorway: Return the prisoner!

She saw her mother walking down the steps towards her. The Lagerkommandant ordered the Blockführer to return to her duties.

Moeke took Punica into her arms and shuffled with her, holding her tightly toward the camp's gates, and when the guards opened the gates for them, she ushered her out onto the road, still embracing her. The faceless guards slammed the gates behind them and locked them with chains. A sound Punica would never forget.

Punica turned to the Lagerkommandant, looking at her from his office door. She watched him in disbelief, unable to adjust to this new reality. Or was she dreaming? She envisioned this so many times these past weeks, but had lost hope of it ever happening. The Lagerkommandant turned and went back to his desk. The secretary closed the door. The guards in the Rose Garden shouted at the prisoners. The prisoners shuffled like chained slaves in wooden clogs over the muddy ground to their cells. In the distance, machine-gun fire rattled, and another life ended on the shooting range in this hell on Earth called Polizeiliches Durchgangslager Amersfoort.

She turned to her mother, unable to speak. She was too stunned to realise she was on the right side of the barbed wire fence.

'Try to walk, darling,' Moeke said.

CHAPTER SIXTEEN

Kees

Kees and Wolf remained silent while they waited for the fighting to start. The soldiers lay on their stomachs, side by side, hiding behind mounts of earth and uprooted trees. Their rifles aimed at the invisible enemy on the horizon. Schachner walked between the soldiers. Kees studied his face. All the lines on it seemed to meet between his eyebrows above his nose. His eyes followed the same angle, the outer corners slanting down, the inner corners higher up. His eyelids hung over his eyes like an old man's eyelids, but he wasn't much older than his regiment. Kees guessed somewhere in his mid-twenties. The corners of his lips pulled downwards as well. An arch of wrinkles on his forehead extended and plunged towards his earlobes.

Kees reached for his pillbox in his inside pocket and clicked the metal lid open. He had only six pills left, barely enough for three days. He raised the box to his mouth and emptied it. The pills melted on his tongue and filled him with warmth.

'How many have you taken today?' Wolf asked.

Kees closed his eyes. 'I... I don't — I just, I... I need them.'

His tongue almost folded itself double at the back of his mouth. He couldn't take it anymore. All he wanted was to go home. He thought of Ab. The truth broke his heart. He fought in a war alien to him. Not that Schachner would consider letting him return home, even if he knew what was going on with Kees's mind. So many of his comrades used more drugs than prescribed to help them get through the hell of each day, so why wouldn't he?

When still a child, Moeke had told him the story of a Russian girl made of snow and ice, her heart frozen within her chest. The girl's greatest fear was finding her true love because true love would warm her heart and melt her from the inside out. Even at six, Kees wondered what was worse – a heart of ice without feelings or falling in love and dying for it? Although the story had faded over time, it had crept back into his thoughts at the strangest times in the last year or so.

He remembered Moeke's shocked face when she learned he had enlisted in the SS. She had been so disappointed with him. He remembered Ab's words: 'Let's find that ice maiden of yours, Sneg – what's her name?'

Flashes of Ab's face returned to his mind. Always the same ones, the moment Kees realised his friend was dead. Ab's eyes were empty of his soul. Kees stared into the distance. The horizon had disappeared; mist or smoke had erased it. In his mind's eye, he closed Ab's eyes and whispered aloud how sorry he was for his mistake. Ab should have stayed with Moeke in Arnhem.

A cloud of dust floated towards them, followed by a thunderous noise Kees could not place. Schachner ordered them to shoot a red star shell into the sky to warn their troops behind them to prepare for battle and imminent danger. A few minutes later, Schachner ordered a green shell to be fired, warning of the attack. Kees waited, his throat contracting from fear. The noise sounded like a herd of monstrous animals stampeding their way.

Schachner ordered them to open fire. Kees hesitated and closed his eyes. Ab's face appeared before him when he lay in Kees's arms, dying. He felt Ab's finger pulsate in his pocket.

The loud screeches of bullets softened. Kees squeezed his eyes shut and pulled the trigger. He saw the bullet eject from the barrel. It sliced through the air and he watched it enter Schachner's back. Schachner contracted and collapsed, face first, like a soulless monster of dust and earth, onto the ground; his blood steamed from his body and ate away the colour of his SS skull-and-bones coat.

'Schachner's been hit!' he heard. 'Mandemaker, over here.'

And Kees leopard crawled underneath the torrent of bullets towards them.

'Take him back to B Krad.'

Schachner groaned. His tongue was bloodless. The bullet must have missed his vital organs.

Kees lowered his forehead into the dust beside the wounded man, gasping, trying to think. God, he wanted this man dead.

'Put him on your back and start crawling!'

Kees took out the square of canvas he used for the nights to keep the cold off him and rolled Schachner on top of it. He knotted the corners across his right shoulder and underneath his left arm and crawled to where he thought the B Krad – a motorcycle with a sidecar – was most likely to be parked. Schachner moaned as Kees tried to keep him on his back.

'Those damn Russians,' Schachner groaned.

Kees ignored him and crawled. Kees could not tell how long he'd been crawling: his mind sped through memories and thoughts, and the battle sounds ebbed away.

A robin, its chest a wonderful red, landed before Kees and started to sing. Kees felt the sticky wetness slide down his neck into his coat; Schachner's blood had drenched him. He watched the robin's beak open, and the songs roll from its tongue, and Kees crawled from underneath the weight and looked at the now grey face and purple lips of the dying man. His mouth was trying to talk, his eyes knowing, but he had become powerless. Kees sat on his knees beside Schachner, looking at his eyes – those eyes now begging Kees to show mercy. Mercy, what is mercy? Letting this dog of a man live? Live so he could kill again.

Kees's neck felt cold, and he wiped the blood, his fingers turning a vibrant red. A lovely comparison to this empty grey world. He raised his fingers to his mouth and tasted the blood. It energised him, and he heaved Schachner back onto his back and found the strength to go on. He crawled into the forest, away from the sound of war and the B Krad. And when he was out of sight, he unknotted the canvas and thrust Schachner off his back onto the ground. He hovered above the petrified German. Kees bent over him, pressed his finger on the saturated coat, and licked his fingers again.

Schachner looked at Kees, opening his mouth, but could only groan as if he no longer had a tongue. Kees stared at Schachner. He lowered his head, his ear close to Schachner's mouth, to decipher what he was trying to say, but he heard only sounds in warm breaths; not words but the gasps of a dying animal.

The hoarse shrieks of crows pierced the robin's song. Kees looked up and watched crows tear at the white sky. A crow behind him startled him, shouting a word Kees understood. A command. He turned back to Schachner and saw his face fill with terror. Kees reached for his sculpting knife and held it against Schachner's neck.

'Are you afraid?' he asked softly. And when no answer came, he repeated the words, 'Do you think Ab was afraid when you murdered him?'

Kees clasped the knife between his teeth and pulled at Schachner's coat, wanting to see the bullet wound. But the buttons wouldn't give, so he sliced the material with his knife. Schachner's skin was yellow, blood oozing from one single bullet hole, shit-brown. Kees laughed.

'The crows want me to kill you,' Kees said. 'They...' he whispered, pointing to the sky. 'They know who you are.'

Schachner nodded slightly, his eyes alert.

Kees pressed his knife slowly into the wound, pushing hard, putting his whole weight into it. The blood bubbled around his hand, and he knew he had reached the lungs, and pulling hard as the flesh tried to keep the knife in, he pulled out the blade.

'You are the dragon,' Kees whispered, pushing it back into the flesh. 'You are the dragon.'

Kees felt a cold sweat form on his face. He woke up with a gasp as if he'd been underwater and saw the Russian cavalry emerge from the dust, an army of maybe six hundred men on horseback dressed in long black coats and red shirts. On their heads, not steel helmets like the German army, but furry, floppy hats. They wore leather belts around their waists, and above their heads, they held old-fashioned swords with curved blades instead of rifles.

'God damn,' Kees said. 'God damn—'

Wolf shouted, 'Shashkas.'

The voice of the masses echoed across the horizon.

Schachner shouted, 'Fire!'

The scene resembled a children's book. Silence followed. Kees sweated, his riflescope fogging from his body heat. Killing Schachner had been a dream, a hallucinatory dream brought on by the drugs, but what was the scene unfolding before him?

Schachner repeated the order, a roar from deep inside his throat. Behind them, the rumble of artillery fire started. The grenades whistled over their heads, exploding between the galloping horses. The German infantry opened machinegun fire; their opponents became easy targets as bullets hacked into their horses and riders. The wondrous scene of confidence, colour, and courage changed into darkness and death. Their beautiful horses were mowed by metal and sank in a screaming panic to the ground. An endless stream of men kept coming, riding the labyrinths between the carcasses, brandishing their shashkas in fierce determination.

Panic-stricken horses, having lost their riders, ran between the carnage. Kees and Wolf ducked further into the soft sand to not be shot by the German soldiers firing from behind them.

Finally, the order was given, and the screeching missiles stopped. Kees saw a few, not many, maybe only twenty Cossacks still riding towards them. They leapt up between them and crossed the German lines, their swords held above their heads, their faces the pallor of wooden toy soldiers. Kees followed them with his eyes until they became invisible in the smoke and mist. He turned back to the carnage before him. Dead and wounded, screaming horses, men with half their faces blown off. Severed arms and legs lay scattered like macabre party decorations. Soldiers were trying to pull themselves from under their dead horses.

The dust settled and revealed a landscape of death and destruction as far as the eye could see. And the smell of burning flesh and a horrible, undefinable, sickening smell lodged inside Kees's nose.

He turned to Wolf. Had he imagined everything? Kees swallowed back bile.

Schachner got to his feet and paced between the rows of dead Russians, counting the casualties.

'Mandemaker,' he shouted. 'Ziegler, Schmidt, put those damn horses out of their misery.'

Kees pulled out his handgun and walked to the first horse on his path. It was lying on top of a soldier; the soldier's brains were splashed across the ground. He took the horse's head and looked deeply into its eyes. The brown eyes stared back at him. They reminded him of the doe's eyes from his dreams. He gazed deeply into them and saw a ghost, a girl as white as snow, appear in the shifting light behind the pupils.

'The ice maiden,' he whispered.

The horse's dark eyes followed Kees's movement. It wasn't wounded, not even a scrape. Its legs weren't broken; it must be just exhausted, but with Schachner watching him, he raised his pistol to the horse's head. He didn't want Schachner to become suspicious of his mental state. Kees needed his trust. He needed Schachner to think he was entirely under his command.

Kees positioned the barrel of his gun against the horse's temple, its artery pulsating against the metal, trying to keep his hand and arm steady. The horse looked at Kees. He imagined Schachner's face up against the barrel. He lowered his pistol, put it back in his holster, and coaxed the horse to get up. He pulled her mane and felt her legs as she struggled to get up. She stood before him, beautiful and unhurt. He took his gun back into his hand and pulled the trigger. The horse immediately bolted away from them. Kees watched her disappear into the atmosphere. He turned to a horse screeching in agony, a beautiful brown mare with a white flame across her face. Her hind leg had a large piece of bone sticking through the skin. He raised his hand, aiming his gun at her temple and glancing at Wolf further down, also raising his pistol to a horse's head and pulling the trigger. While thinking of only one thing, he must find more drugs, Kees pulled the trigger, silencing the screeching horse

When ambulances arrived and men and women in bloodied white

uniforms collected the wounded soldiers, Schachner ordered the troops to prepare to march on. Schachner wanted to be out of the clearing before dusk and to set up camp in the woods. Kees didn't speak as he prepared. Wolf stood beside him silently. On the command, they turned and marched into the vast countryside.

CHAPTER SEVENTEEN

Petronella

During the past two weeks, Petronella had been reviewing every detail of the day Punica disappeared. Could she somehow have prevented it? She was frantic with worry, and needed to think up a plan to find Punica and bring her home.

Petronella sat in her dressing gown at the breakfast table. A bowl of cold semolina stood before her; she held a cup of cold tea in both hands. Mrs de Vries stood by the counter, her back turned to Petronella, preparing a shopping list and checking the ration book for the coupons. She took the tin from the mantelpiece and checked if they had enough money to buy food. Petronella's income for her embroidery and furniture commissions had become scant. Cornelis spent the money he earned from the organisation doing various odd jobs on Jonge Jenever. Not that she wanted what she considered to be blood money from him.

Mrs de Vries interrupted the silence. 'I suppose I could ask a neighbour if they'd like to exchange some sugar coupons for cash. We can't afford sugar anyway,' she said, more to herself than to Petronella.

Corrie ate her pudding silently; she hadn't been to school since the day Punica didn't return home. Petronella was too afraid something would happen to the only child she had left at home.

Petronella's mind trailed back to the day Punica disappeared. She remembered when Punica didn't return for tea and then for dinner, an awful feeling started to creep up on her. When she couldn't take it any longer, she got up, put on her coat, and left the house, taking

Corrie with her to find out where Punica was.

Petronella hurried to Wouter's house to ask if he knew where she was. They often spent time together after school. Corrie was convinced the curtain moved on their front window, but no matter how many times Petronella rang the bell, the front door would not open. She went to Annie's house but regretted it as soon as Annie's mother appeared at the door. Annie had told her she would be at Punica's home doing homework together. So now she, too, was worried sick.

Petronella ran towards the school on Staten Lane. She prayed Punica had got detention once again. She prayed she would still be in there, but it was nearly dinnertime, and they had never kept Punica at school so late. She hurried towards the park. A sign at the entrance said: For Jews Prohibited. A shock pierced her gut. Punica hadn't done that star thing after Petronella had forbidden her to, had she? Oh, why was she so outspoken? Petronella ran as fast as her high heels allowed and approached the school. There were no bicycles in the forecourt, and the place looked deserted. Petronella rang the bell, and when no one answered it, she pulled and pulled continuously for what seemed a long while. Finally, one of the senior teachers opened the door. He was strangely timid and not the cheerful teacher she remembered him to be when Willem was in his class.

'Punica didn't come home—'

'You better come in,' he said.

Petronella shuffled into the great hall. Seven or eight teachers sat on the wooden seat by the wall, others stood silently with white faces.

'What's happened?' Petronella asked, her face stiff, dreading their answer.

'Eight pupils were arrested by the SD this morning and taken away.'

'Arrested for doing what?'

'They wore yellow stars—'

'I told her not to do it. Oh God... Where have they taken her?'

'We think the police station. But we don't know.'

'Were Wouter and Annie with her?'

'Annie was. Wouter and another friend initially wore the stars, too.

But their teacher told them to take them off during their lessons.'

'Why didn't anyone tell Punica to take it off?'

'Mrs Mandemaker, maybe your husband knows where his colleagues have taken your daughter?'

'His colleagues?' Petronella cried. She rushed out, nearly forgetting Corrie, who anxiously ran after her mother.

Annie's mother entered the school gate, but Petronella couldn't talk to her. She knew Annie was probably pulled into this by Punica. Punica was so strong-willed. She covered her mouth with a handkerchief and ran home.

Petronella waited, pacing the entire ground floor, skipping dinner and ignoring all Corrie's questions. An hour after Corrie's bedtime, Mrs de Vries put her to bed, and Nienke read her a bedtime story. After Corrie had climbed out of her bed for the third time, screaming at the top of the stairs. 'I want to know where Punica is. I'm not a child anymore, in case you're wondering!' Petronella went up to her and tried her best to sound cheerful. She read her yet another bedtime story and told her Papa would know where Punica was. Petronella promised Corrie that Papa would bring Punica home before curfew. She returned downstairs. To her horror, Cornelis still had not returned. His dinner plate was still waiting for him in the oven. Petronella had no idea where he was, but not knowing where the Nazis held Punica was unbearable.

She paced the drawing room, unable to sit, and at two minutes to midnight, finally, Cornelis's key sounded in the lock of the front door. It would be too late to do anything about fetching Punica home, even if he knew where she was.

Cornelis was stone drunk. She had to tell him the whole story three times, and when he repeated her questions like an idiot, unable to comprehend what she was telling him, she kicked him out onto the streets. 'Go to your friends,' she called after him, not caring if they arrested him. 'Find out where they are keeping your daughter!' she screamed. 'And don't dare return before you can tell me where she is.'

He hadn't been home since that night. He neither cares nor is capable of finding his daughter. How could a father send his sons into the devil's clutches? Petronella asked herself so many times, And now his daughter is God knows where. Every morning, she hoped Punica would reappear at her doorstep, and she cried herself to sleep every night, wondering where she was.

Cornelis finally sent word. Punica was in a prison camp in Amersfoort. Petronella rushed upstairs to change and entrusted Corrie to Mrs de Vries's care. 'Don't let her out of your sight,' she said. 'And if my husband returns to the house... Keep him away from Corrie.'

Petronella counted out the money for the train ticket to Amersfoort and two return tickets to Arnhem. She added extra cash for emergencies and put the rest of her money into the housekeeping tin on the kitchen mantelpiece. Mrs de Vries tried to convince her to take more, but Petronella wanted to make sure Mrs de Vries had enough money to keep the household going if they detained her. She embraced Corrie tightly, kissing her on her forehead. She kissed Mrs de Vries and Nienke on the cheek and left for the station.

Petronella had to change trains in Utrecht and find the right platform for her train to Amersfoort, which was more complicated than expected. The central hall was packed with travellers. The Nazis ordered Jews to form lines along the walls and checked people's identity cards randomly. They ordered everyone wearing Yellow Stars to join the queues.

Mrs de Vries had told Petronella about the extra trains, now used for taking the Jews to Germany. She couldn't believe Dutch railroad employees helped the Nazis. But now, seeing families towing their luggage, their eyes filled with fear as they held their children close, she knew everything Mrs de Vries had said was true.

A loud voice thundered from the speaker. Jews were to report at platform 2b, the voice shouted in German.

Petronella stopped and looked around her. She didn't know where to go. A conductor came her way, and she asked him for the platform number for the train to Amersfoort.

'Through there to the last platform,' the conductor said, pointing into a vast dark tunnel. 'The train should be waiting on the left-hand side, madam. Take the stairs to the left,' he added. 'And hurry,' he said, looking at his watch, 'It'll be leaving in a few minutes.'

Petronella ran up the stairs to the platform and rushed to get on board. The conductor's whistle screeched, and he slammed the door shut behind her. A few moments later, the train rumbled and slid over the rails, gathering speed, leaving the station behind. The next stop would be Amersfoort.

After about half an hour, she arrived at the station and climbed down the metal steps. 'Which way to the camp?' she asked and left the station. She walked towards the forested area on the city's outskirts. Petronella passed a bakery shop, exuding hot, sugary scents from its ovens. She wondered if she should buy a bun for Punica. She might be hungry. She stopped and went in.

The black and white tiled floor was polished and it shone in the sunlight. The bakery smelled sweet, too sweet for Petronella's taste, but she wanted something to raise Punica's spirits, and sugar always did the trick. She hoped Punica would understand that it took two weeks for Cornelis to find out where she was. But two weeks is such a long time.

Petronella was the only customer and faked a smile. 'So many to choose from,' she mumbled. 'Which one shall I take? It's for my daughter, you see.'

The woman smiled and told her to take her time.

'I think she... would love a pudding broodje. She pointed at the biggest one. The lady nodded and reached for it. She slid it into a paper bag and asked for two cents. Petronella felt for her purse and remembered she hadn't brought a pastry or bread coupon. She laid the money on the plate for coins. 'I'm sorry,' she said. 'I've forgotten my ration book.'

The woman looked at her. 'I can't sell it to you without the coupon,' she said.

'I have plenty of coupons at home.'

The woman took the bun out of the bag and returned it to the shelf on the display counter. 'I'm sorry,' she said.

Petronella's eyes brimmed with tears. 'The... the way,' Petronella hesitated, 'to the prison camp. Do I follow this road into the woods?'

She tried to keep her voice from faltering.

'It's quite a climb. But yes, follow the main road.'

'Good day,' Petronella said, turning to leave. She lowered her hands into her pockets and felt her gold cigarette case slip between her fingers as she left the shop. Petronella remembered her money on the plate standing on the counter. She returned and slid the coins back into her pocket, smiling awkwardly.

'I'm sorry,' the shop assistant repeated. 'I...'

Petronella waved her hand and closed the door behind her.

She needed to think up a plan, her mind trying different scenarios as she walked towards the camp. A girl of fifteen. A child. Children don't belong in prison camps, she repeated over and over in her mind.

A barbed wire fence surrounded two barracks built parallel to the road. She turned the corner. A hedge obstructed her view. At each corner of the camp, guards stood on watchtowers, helmets on, holding machine guns. Their heads followed her as she made her way along the road. Petronella crossed the lane to the high black camp gates made of iron and wood, and now she could see into the camp. To her right was a tiny building, a kind of gate lodge; behind that, more barracks, and in between the buildings, a muddy field surrounded by barbed wire. A lorry drove up behind her. She stepped aside onto the verge to let it pass. The black canvas on the back flopped open as the truck jolted over a hole in the road. The men sitting inside seemed to be in a trance. Their faces were white. Two guards opened the gate as it stopped, the brakes hissing. The front doors swung open, and three men in SS uniforms jumped out, cursing the mud on the road. Two walked to the back of the lorry, pulled the lever, lowered the hatch, and ordered everyone out. The other spotted Petronella as he leaned against the side of the truck and lit a cigarette. He watched her closely.

Men jumped out of the back and huddled together as they shuffled with terrified, bulging eyes. The guards herded them with bats through the gates and into a labyrinth of barbed wire paths.

Petronella asked the guard standing watch by the gate in her best German if she may speak to the Camp Commandant. It was a matter concerning her daughter, who she believed was imprisoned at the camp. Machine gunfire rattled in the woods, and she jumped

'Madam?' the guard smoking by the lorry called out in Dutch. 'What are you doing here?'

'I... I... believe my daughter is here.'

'Go home. This is no place for the likes of you,' he said in Dutch.

'I'm not going anywhere without my daughter,' Petronella said, turning back to the guard.

'If your daughter is here, she won't be leaving anytime soon,' the guard said.

'She's a teenager... fifteen.'

'A group of teenage terrorists was brought in two weeks ago.'

'Yes, one of them is my daughter,' Petronella replied, relieved she had come to the right place. 'I want to see her.'

The guard laughed. 'Run along to the office there, and they will help you further.'

Petronella's shoes sank into the mud. Pulling them loose, she climbed the filthy wooden steps and knocked politely on the door.

'Herein!'

She slowly opened the door to find the Camp Commandant sitting behind a desk, writing on some papers with a black fountain pen. His SS cap lay to his left, and the skull and bones faced her. Petronella straightened her shoulders, took a deep breath, and pranced in.

'Good afternoon,' she said. 'I am Mrs Man—'

He raised his hand without looking at her to stop her from talking. Frowning, he concentrated on his writing.

Petronella closed her mouth. A young woman sat at a desk with her back to the door. She was dressed in a Nazi uniform, SS, and was painting her nails bright red. The office smelled of acetate and sweat. The secretary didn't look up either. A sheet of paper stuck out of the typewriter.

She glanced around the tiny room. Two windows, one on the back wall and one on the side, had net curtains. Beside the woman's desk stood two filing cabinets. The man's desk stood in the centre of the room, facing the door. Someone had painted a mural of the camp's layout on the wall to her right. Polizeiliches Durchgangslager Amersfoort, it said on a red banner. She counted the barracks, getting up to twelve before—

'Yes?' the man said.

'Pardon me, Herr Commandant,' she said in German. 'I believe my daughter is imprisoned here by mistake.'

'Name,' he said.

'Punica. I mean Maria Mandemaker,' Petronella said. 'Punica is her pet name. She is only fifteen. She had got into a little trouble at school but has always been a good girl.'

He looked up at her, laying his pen down on the papers.

Petronella stared back, not knowing which was the better option: looking away or showing strength. He stared at her for one long second. 'I... I...' she stammered, trying to think of something to say.

He sighed deeply and called his secretary to bring him the prisoners' book. She got up, took out a thick book with her fingertips from a drawer of one of the filing cabinets, and strolled over, blowing the nails of her free hand.

'When was she arrested?'

'Arrested?' Petronella gasped. 'Two weeks ago, on Monday.'

He sighed once again. 'Date,' he said, annoyed.

'May the fourth,' she said.

He turned the pages to the fourth. 'Mandemaker?' he said. 'Can you spell the name?'

'M... A... N—'

'For God's sake... ah, here it is. Arrested for terrorism. She sabotaged our authority by wearing a Jüdische Stern although she is not Jewish.'

'She wasn't...'

He looked up, staring at her coldly.

'Sabotaging your authority. She was upset about her friend who had been expelled from university, and another friend got her to join their protest.'

His mouth tightened. 'So,' he said. 'Your daughter has a Jewish friend who was expelled from university? And he or she was the ringleader who tricked your naïve little daughter into joining a teenage

155

terrorist group? Which friend are we talking about?'

'Annie,' she said, thinking of Ab. He must remain a secret, or Kees would be arrested, too. Oh, her heart broke now. How could she incriminate Annie? Punica was very strong-willed. This whole star thing was probably her idea. She'd had these wild ideas from early childhood and always took the lead. This wasn't the first time she had got into trouble for her opinions, and it certainly wasn't the first time she had taken her obedient friends down with her.

'Annie, you say? Do you have a last name?'

'I'm sorry, I... it... slipped my mind. Something like... van de Heuvel.'

He bent over his desk towards her and peered at her shoes, walking shoes, royal blue coat, and silk scarf. He leaned back in his chair, the wood creaking under his weight. 'You don't know her surname?' he asked, his brow wrinkling. He lifted the fountain pen to his lips and bit the back end. 'Annie, you say. Could it be Annie Bergsma?'

Petronella turned crimson. 'No... Annie is quite a common name in Arnhem. But the Annie I'm talking about, her last name is van de Heuvel.'

'I'll humour you.' He nudged his head to the secretary, who got up and left the office.
'Even though you are a terrible mother.'

She nodded.

'How many children do you have?' he asked, his voice sounding less stern, almost amicable.

'I have four — five,' she said.

The secretary returned. 'She's coming,' she said, sitting back at her desk.

He laughed, 'So how many, exactly?'

'I have two children,' she said, her back becoming sweaty. 'My husband had three from a previous marriage, which I raised as my own.'

'Fair enough,' he said.

Petronella turned crimson. Feet drummed on the wooden steps outside the door. She flinched when the door swung open against her.

'Ah, finally,' he said. 'Here she is. Das Mädel.'

Punica walked in toward the desk. Her head bent towards the floor. Petronella gasped when her daughter appeared before her. Punica's clothes were filthy. Her legs and hands were covered in mud, but most of all, she had become so thin her skirt hung limply on her hips. Her cheeks had thumb marks, and a fresh red hand-shaped blotch was across her face as if she had recently been slapped.

'Moeke,' Punica whispered and ran into her mother's embrace.

'Darling,' she grabbed her daughter into a tight hug.

'Now you've seen she is fine,' he said. 'Take her back,' he ordered the guard who had brought her.

'No, Moeke, don't let them take me. No, Moeke, I promise I'll be good.'

'Please,' Petronella pleaded. 'I promise she will do nothing to harm the Third Reich ever again.'

The guard pulled Punica from her mother's arms.

'Take. Her. Back!' the Commandant said, returning to his writing.

Punica screamed while the guard dragged her like an animal down the stairs and onto the muddy concrete path.

'Please, Herr Commandant,' Petronella said. She got down on her knees. 'Please, I beg you... please,' she pleaded. She lowered her hand into her pocket and took out a gold-coloured cigarette case. Tears dropped from her eyes as she clicked the lid open; it contained photographs, not cigarettes. Petronella looked through them and took a photo of Kees and Ab, both wearing their uniforms and grinning into the lens. She hated that photograph – the boys wearing their SS uniforms with the skull and bones – but loved those two boys so much that she always kept it with her. She flicked through the rest of the photographs, searching for Willem's picture, him wearing the Reichsschule uniform. He had sent it to her from Germany. His friends had taken it after he had won the Geländesspiel. 'My oldest boys are fighting in Russia,' she whispered. 'My youngest son is at the Reichscchule in Bensberg in Germany. The blond boy... my eldest boys are missing in action,' she said.

The Commandant stood up from behind his desk.

'Two boys, I've lost two already. I beg you.'

He took the photograph of Ab and Kees from Petronella's hand and studied their faces. He reached out his hand for Willem's and studied that, too. He placed it on top of Kees's and returned it to Petronella.

'Schutz,' he shouted. The guard stopped. 'Let her go.' He turned to Petronella, 'I suggest you take better care of her.' He sat back down behind his desk as she scrambled down the steps. 'Thank you,' she sobbed. The secretary walked to the door.

Petronella walked out into the sunshine. The door closed behind her. Punica ran to her on wobbly legs and fell into her mother's arms. Petronella gasped, embraced Punica, and tried to walk with her, not letting her out of her arms. She ushered her through the gate before anyone changed the Commandant's mind.

'You're out,' she whispered.

But Punica dug her face into her mother's coat.

'Come now,' Petronella said. 'We have to get home.'

She put her arm around Punica's waist to support her and returned to the road. Machine gun fire echoed in the woods; Punica's body grew rigid, and her legs wobbly. But Petronella kept her up, holding her with two hands now, and finally, they turned onto the road, where ordinary people were going about their business, pretending life was untouched by war.

People stared and made way for them. It was as if everyone knew where they had been. No one talked to them, but all showed pity in their eyes. They passed the bakery. The woman who would not sell her the bun sat on the windowsill in the sunshine. She was smoking a cigarette. When she raised the cigarette to take another puff, her gaze met Petronella's. Her arm froze, holding the cigarette in mid-air, as she stared at them, her mouth slightly open. She flicked the cigarette away and rushed into the shop. A moment later, she reappeared, running after them, holding out a paper bag.

'But I don't have the coupon,' Petronella said.

The woman waved her hand, dismissing the coupon. She tried to smile as her eyes glazed with tears.

158

Punica accepted the bun solemnly.

'You're afraid to let them out of your sight these days,' she said. 'I have one the same age. You sit with them at the breakfast table, hoping and praying they come back to you for dinner.'

An army truck rumbled on the road. The woman turned and rushed back inside.

CHAPTER EIGHTEEN

Kees

The moment he read the letter, everything started to fall apart. He had lost compassion for others with every surprising word Moeke had written. He burned the paper the letter had been written on as if burning the words, but the words could not be erased. Why not tell him everything before he even got on the damn train? Why afterwards, when nothing could be done to change the course of events?

The night he enlisted after returning with his father from Musis Sacrum, she'd acted so strangely. She must have known Ab's secret then, and if Kees had known what had happened to Ab's family, he could have run away with him. They were young; they would have had a chance together. He could have dealt with it. Ab must have felt so lonely in his pain.

'Let's find that ice maiden of yours,' Ab had said. 'Sneg—what's her name?'

How could Moeke hold her tongue for so long? Even the letter hadn't touched the surface of the danger hidden beneath her words.

When Ab appeared on the train, Kees laughed out loud and grabbed Ab's shoulder while shaking his hand, not letting go for a long while. Ab, his Jewish friend, had been courageous enough to join the SS and come with him to fight on the Eastern Front. Two friends out on an adventure, they thought. Kees should have sensed the distress Ab was going through. But he didn't. He had no clue what was going on in Ab's life.

Kees took the pillbox from his inside pocket and clicked the metal lid to open it. A weight pressed on his arm as he took out a pill and placed it on his tongue. He stared at a hand on his sleeve, not comprehending. His eyes traced the hand to the sleeve to the shoulder to Wolf's face and stared at him. Wolf's gaze seemed to ask him to return the pill to the box.

'We're required to take these,' Kees mumbled. 'They prescribe us Pervitin to keep us going. They gave me a fresh batch, just this morning.' Kees shook all the contents into his mouth and closed the lid.

'How many were in that box?' Wolf asked. 'They were supposed to last you a week.'

'Lay off me,' he said. 'God damn me!'

Kees lifted his helmet from his head and rubbed his skull hard. He took a deep breath and trembled a moment as if to shake off a horrible memory. He laid the helmet on his lap and once more took the box from his pocket. But it was empty, of course. His throat contracted from thirst, and he coughed. The smell of something unimaginable wafted towards them from the battlefield. Kees scrunched his eyes as it shifted like a shroud over his face. 'How can you stand this place?' he said. 'Without the eye-poppers?'

Wolf watched him without answering.

'I think I'm losing it. Man, I'm losing my mind. And there's nothing I can do about it,' Kees said, hitting his skull with his fists.

'Ease off the drugs,' Wolf said.

'The pills are the only things keeping my mind inside my head.'

Schachner shouted for Kees. Kees hesitated and didn't answer, not sure if it was real or hallucinatory.

Schachner's voice repeated his name. Failing to answer his command, Schachner marched up to Kees and stood red-faced at his feet, kicking the soles of his boots.

Kees got off the ground and stood between tufts of dead grass poking through the snow. Schachner's eyes were such a light blue; they seemed almost inhuman, piercing into him like metal daggers gouging out his thoughts.

'Sieg Heil,' Kees shouted, doing the Hitler salute.

Schachner returned with a forward wave motion. He reached for

161

Kees's chin, held it tightly, turned his head slantwise, and stared into his eyes. 'You and Ziegler are scouting today,' he said. 'Find a route through the forest, and mark where the Russians are on the map.'

Wolf got off the ground and stood to attention, shoulder to shoulder with Kees.

'Bring back one, if possible, without arousing the others,' Schachner said and marched off.

Kees looked sideways at Wolf. His eyebrows pulled low. 'One what? A Russian?' he said.

'I don't want to scout today,' Wolf moaned.

Kees packed up his gear, ignoring Wolf. He heaved everything onto his back, and Wolf did the same. They marched in single file through the labyrinth of rotting bodies lying on the battlefield. The Tross had removed the German casualties and the wounded Russians. But the dead Russians lay scattered between the dead horses and were dusted by sugary snow, crystal flakes caught between eyelashes and hair. A metal sharp wind swept in from the north. They marched towards the forest. An endless hum of sawing sounded in the distance. The Russians were preparing a route for transporting tanks and heavy artillery. The forest sank into darkness as the sun turned orange and slid behind the horizon. Kees glanced back. Tiny flashes of evening light reflected in Wolf's eyes. He seemed frightened.

'Take the pills,' Kees whispered. 'It'll make it easier.'

Wolf grunted.

'Look, you don't have to come with me. I'm fine on my own. Hide here till morning and tell Schachner you lost me.'

'Trying to get rid of me?'

Kees sighed.

'Orders are orders,' Wolf said.

Twigs cracked, and Kees reached out to Wolf to stop him from moving. He froze. Kees gestured towards where the sounds came from, some thirty metres away. They sank to their haunches and crouched low, scanning the forest.

The rustling shuffled towards them. Kees raised his rifle and aimed, and Wolf followed his example. Two Russians appeared from the growth. They stopped not even a metre away from them. Kees's sight blurred; his legs trembled, his hands too. He was thankful he was sitting on frozen moss and not on crackly, dry leaves and branches. He tried to slow his breathing so they wouldn't discover him. One nearly touched Kees's knees. Kees bent backwards towards Wolf to avoid contact. The Russians were scouting just as Kees and Wolf were. The Russians stopped moving, took out cigarettes, and lit them. Taking deep puffs without saying a word, they crept away and disappeared behind the dwarf Siberian pines. Wolf took out his pillbox, changed his mind, put it back, took out a cigarette, and lit it. Treading through darkness was like treading molasses. Kees told Wolf to stay put and get a couple of hours of sleep. Clouds obstructed the moonlight, and they did not know whether they were even heading for the river any longer. Their feet sank through the forest floor, and the effort of pulling them free was sapping their strength. 'Let's make camp here,' Kees said. He unrolled his tent canvas. His legs were heavy, and so were his arms. Despite the pills, he was exhausted. He spread the canvas and covered himself with his rubber blanket. He leaned his head against his backpack and pulled the blanket over his face. His body sank through the snow and mud as the forest sucked him into its womb.

Kees pictured the garden at home to calm his thoughts, the sun peeping through the horse chestnut leaves in summer, light dancing between branches. To stop his head from spinning, he closed his eyes and listened to the trees moaning in the wind. He tried to imagine the summer warmth and Arnhem, the scent of grass just mown, the fragrance of the lilacs on the breeze. Mrs de Vries's cooking wafted through the opened French windows. The sweetness of red cabbage flavoured with cinnamon and apple, sour gherkins and boiled potatoes, and spiced haché meat with cloves and onion gravy. His stomach rumbled. He wondered if his stomach was the only part of him that remained human.

Was it the yearning for a house that was keeping him alive rather than love for his family? Humans were so complicated. He hated the beast-man he had become. The emptiness of his heart reminded him of his father's attitude towards his children. He wished he was brave enough to cut the parts that resembled his father from his body.

Kees listened to the wolves howling in the distance. Why were they here when they could go anywhere on Earth? He supposed they would stay where there was plenty of food and enough dead to scavenge. Animals choose the easiest way, while humans prefer the most difficult.

The doe appeared at his feet. He must be dreaming. She stood quietly, watching him. He stared, his body stiff and unable to move. He wanted to say something but couldn't make his voice leave his throat.

Wolf shook his arm. 'Wake up,' he whispered. 'You're having a nightmare.'

The doe appeared again as soon as Wolf let go of his arm. Kees raised his hand to her snout, but she bolted off. He woke with a start, shaking. He pulled the rubber blanket and the tent canvas closer and waited for morning.

When he opened his eyes, it was daylight. The sun glittered on the fresh snow and lit his face with yellow light. Pine needles and dead curly leaves hung from old spiderwebs. A silhouette loomed up, a deer sniffing long dead grass spiking through a sheet of snow. Her jaws moved as she watched him. Kees checked Wolf to see if he could see her, but he was asleep. The doe slinked into the misty shadows. Her eyes glimmered as she watched him from between the trees.

Kees got up, gathered his gear, and followed the doe for three-quarters of an hour. A river meandered between the trees and smelled of fresh tea and metallic snow. Kees listened for human presence. He heard a gunshot in the distance, sending a flock of crows into the sky. The mushy, half-frozen water rolled by. The doe stood on the bank and lowered her head to drink. He wanted to show her something and searched his inner pockets for Ab's finger. He took the tiny parcel out of his pocket, raised it to his lips, and kissed it. 'Look,' he whispered. 'With this, I can find my friend.' The doe looked at him. She lowered her head and drank some more.

He returned the finger to its hiding place. His chest itched, and he pulled his vest from his skin, seeing fleas scramble into the folds of his clothes. He stared at the river, removed his jacket, pulled his braces from his shoulders, lowered his trousers to his knees, and sat on the snowy sand to remove his boots.

He waded out, and wild ducks waddled after him. The doe stood at the water's edge, watching him. Kees lowered his face underneath the surface of the water.

'Come in,' he whispered, raising his head.

The doe looked at him, twitching her nose. Kees walked backwards until the water reached his groin, and he felt the coolness on his buttocks. He turned and dived, splitting the thin layer of ice on the surface, pushing his body lower into the dark depths. Ab swam underwater towards him. Kees raised his knees to his chin and somersaulted over and over again. The water fingered his face, stubbing into his nose, his ears, his crevices; tiny bubbles escaped his lips and rolled over his cheeks, along his eyelids, tickling him, until disappearing into the mirrored world above him. His skin was a cool turquoise now, like Ab's, like a ghost's; he returned to the surface, his shaven head breaking the layer of ice anew. In the distance, purple clouds rumbled and twisted, kneading like dough. The wind unleashed its fury beyond the forest, but where Kees was, it caused only a slight change in the air. The water protected him from the war, raging only a few kilometres away, where he should be, finding that lonely Russian to take back to Schachner like a trophy. Ab was beneath the water's surface, and Kees smiled.

Kees returned to the bitter coldness down below. Ab swam away, and Kees wanted to follow him but lacked the strength. He needed air. He craved air. His body floated back up. A cold sheet slid over his back, clinging to him like a wet garment. He shivered and raised his head above the surface.

He swam, slicing his way towards the shore. When his fingers scratched the sandy bank beneath him, he slid onto his back to check if Ab had followed him and come to the surface, but the water was smooth like a frosted mirror. Kees took in the view for one last time; the hills and the trees in the distance, their blue sleepiness sprinkled by snow and fading into the morning mist on the horizon. Bombs exploded in the distance. A ripple passed underneath him.

'Pretend,' he told himself, 'pretend the war is just a passing thunderstorm.'

He got up and turned towards his clothes. Ab was waiting for him.

He closed his eyes. He knew he was going crazy. At least he still knew what was real. He squeezed his eyes shut for a moment and then opened them. He was alone. He ran to his clothes, shivering, and pulled his vest over his head, but as he pushed his arms through the armholes, he caught a flicker of movement from the corner of his eye. A Russian soldier? He crouched, grabbing his rifle from the ground. His senses sharpened, and the forest quietened to silence, the air dense as he tried to breathe. He listened but heard only silence. Crouching, he grabbed the rest of his uniform and crawled between the saplings to hide and wait. But there was nothing. He pulled on his socks, the rest of his clothes, and his army boots. He hid his rucksack between the pine and spruce.

Another flicker of light, as if the sun had caught a closing windowpane. Kees ducked deeper between the pine branches and dead needles, scraps of bark stuck to his clothes. A woman strolled from behind the trees. She was close by, a young woman with black hair, dressed in an embroidered white coat, her shoulders wrapped in a flowery shawl trimmed with rabbit fur. Across her back, she wore an archer's bow. She picked up a rabbit and pulled an arrow out of its neck. Oblivious to Kees's presence, she returned the arrow to her quiver hanging from her belt. She seemed unreal in a place like this, the battlefield with its littered corpses and skeletons so close. The rabbit swung from her hand at her side as she ran soundlessly and disappeared between the birch trees.

CHAPTER NINETEEN

Willem

Willem had won the Geländespielen on his first day at Bensberg and now belonged to the best boys. During morning assembly, Herr Naumann called out his name as the boys stood around the flagpole. Naumann told everyone Willem would be leaving them for a month. He had won an apprenticeship at the Deutsche Maschinenfabrik in Duisburg. Naumann said Willem was the only Dutch boy to get into the new scheme. He articulated the words as if giving a Sunday sermon. Naumann told them it was an honour to be sent out into the Reich to help the war effort, and it would be a fantastic opportunity for Willem to climb the hierarchical ladder of the Third Reich and fulfil his ambitions. At the end of his speech, Naumann congratulated Willem and told the Jungmannen to salute their winner. They shouted Heil Hitler three times, raising their straightened arms.

Herr Naumann said Willem could choose his partner from the runners-up and read their names. Willem interrupted him, calling out that he had decided on Tommie. The boys turned toward him.

Herr Naumann noted only students from the list were eligible. Since Tommie had failed in the Geländespiel and was still recuperating in hospital, he was not eligible or suitable for opportunities meant for the best of the best students.

'Might I speak to you in private, Herr Naumann?' Willem asked.

A collective gasp moved around the circle of boys. Naumann smiled; he seemed impressed with Willem's boldness and said Willem may accompany him to his office. Naumann saluted the Nazi flag, kicked his heels, and marched into the building. Willem did the same and followed him inside.

Herr Naumann entered his office and sat behind a wooden desk. The Fuhrer's eyes followed Willem as he entered. Willem closed the door behind him, repeated the Nazi salute, and stood to attention before the Unterrichtsleiter. The room smelled of cologne and dusty books. The wooden panelling made the room dark, although a weak sun shone through the two large partitioned windows to the left. On either side of the Fuhrer's portrait, a red and white flag bearing a black swastika hung from the ceiling. Two skulls lay on a bookshelf. Beside it stood a photograph of a woman with blonde hair smiling into the lens. She had a movie-star hairstyle, flat on top and curly on the shoulders. Willem didn't see any photographs of Rudy.

'Well?' Herr Naumann said.

'I wish Tommie to accompany me,' Willem said.

Pausing for a moment or two, Herr Naumann opened his mouth to talk, but Willem interrupted him.

'Tommie is a talented boxer,' Willem said. 'And he won both the fencing and the horseback riding competitions. Tommie dared to dive from the highest diving board. And he's the best marksman in our class in both archery and rifle shooting categories. And he won all the Geländespielen when we were on the same team. He's as good as me and should be my partner.'

'Well...' Naumann said.

'I want Tommie, and if he's not allowed to accompany me, I won't go either.'

'You won't go?' Naumann repeated.

'No, Herr Naumann,' Willem said.

Naumann grunted. 'You are the best student at our school,' he said. 'And I've already let the factory in Duisburg know you are coming. A Dutch boy. I cannot send anyone else. None of the Dutch boys come close to what you've achieved. Tommie has lost his drive since he arrived here.' Naumann got up and walked towards the window. He stood there, his back to Willem for a few moments. 'Can you tell me why?'

168

Jungmannen marched in the corridor, and the murmur of voices seeped through the wall.

'One of the German boys struck him,' Willem said. He needed to think, anticipating the next question, for Naumann was sure to ask.

As Willem tried to think up the name of a boy he hated the most, Naumann said, 'I will put Tommie's name down. But,' he added, 'on one condition. Tommie will be your responsibility.' He stared at Willem. 'A chain is only as strong as its weakest link. I think with this deal, you will learn the best lesson of all. If your friend is a weed, you need to work twice as hard to blossom, or you may decide to exterminate him from your garden altogether.'

'A weed?' Willem said, his voice rising.

'I know my students. I know their strengths, and I know their weaknesses. Tommie is harmless but not up to the standards of Reichsschule. You will learn to choose your friends more wisely; some build you up, and some hold you back. You must discard those that hold you back.'

Discard, Willem thought. Discard and exterminate?

'You may go,' Naumann said.

'Dankjewel,' Willem said in Dutch. Then: 'Heil Hitler,' correcting himself. He turned and marched out of the room.

When Willem told Tommie they were going to the city, he expected Tommie to be ecstatic, but he wasn't. He wanted to return home to his family, Tommie said. His father would never let him come back as a failure. 'You're certain it was one of the German boys who struck me in the woods?'

'You're joking?'

'Someone tried to kill me,' he said. 'Remember?'

Willem forced a chuckle. 'No one tried to kill you. Someone needed to win for reasons obscure to us normal Nazis. Next time, you'll wallop some unsuspecting guy across the head yourself to win his soul. That's what we good Nazis do.'

'I've lost interest in becoming a good Nazi. Whatever a good Nazi means, anyway,' Tommie said. 'Everything is always over the top, marching until we vomit, standing to attention until we collapse, riding a galloping horse until we fall off. Why can't we slow down to think about what we are doing for once?'

'Why not come with me and enjoy yourself for once,' Willem said. And when Tommie shook his head, Willem said, 'Mr Ros is coming with us. No more bullying by the German boys or Zugführers, and imagine what we could do on those long evenings in a city like Duisburg. Cabaret, dancing, girls, beer, beer, dancing, girls. Girls?' he repeated louder, nudging Tommie's arm with his elbow as he raised his eyebrows and smiled. Tommie's expression didn't change. Willem said, 'You better get used to the idea because you're coming with me whether you like it or not. After all the trouble I went to. Jeez, I thought you'd be happy.'

Tommie stared at him in disgust.

Willem added, 'I'm not leaving you here to be kicked around by those rotten Germans. Remember what happened to Rudy? It'll be the death of you.'

'Rudy was a rotten German himself,' Tommie said.

Willem was happy he had got Tommie's name on the list; his conscience had been at him after he had knocked him out. It meant they were even, and Tommie was the only one he trusted to watch his back among the school's crazy Nazi fanatics.

Willem cringed when he remembered the sound of Tommie's skull on impact as he struck him. He didn't understand why he had done it. Willem had visited Tommie daily in sickbay and had felt sorry for him for missing the bombing of Cologne. 'Ninety minutes of non-stop explosions,' he told him. 'Every five seconds, a British aeroplane dropped a load onto the city.'

He told Tommie how he and a few of his new friends had climbed into the tower, seated as if in a royal box, and watched a surreal fireworks display while smoking American cigarettes. 'Twelve thousand fires coloured the sky red above the city of Cologne,' he said. 'It was in the newspapers,' Willem added as if Tommie had asked how he knew it was twelve thousand fires. He told Tommie how he and his fellow elitists had witnessed the carnage two days later when they went to the opera. The Nazis had swept the pavements clean of debris while the rest of the city lay in ruin. The old town suffered irretrievable damage, he added, 'But something has to give to make room for the new.'

Tommie seemed more interested in the opera. 'Der fliegende Holländer,' he repeated when Willem told him.

'Yes, the Flying Dutchman. Have you remembered anything about what happened?' Willem asked. A question he repeated almost every day since the incident.

'No, nothing. The doctor said it was a normal reaction and that my memory would return to me in a few months. The brain erases everything to protect us from psychological trauma,' Tommie said. 'I remember I won five souls. One of those Germans must have taken them while I was unconscious. But what gets me the most is that he can't own up to nearly killing me. Why doesn't he tell me he is sorry so we can move on?'

'No point in looking back,' Willem said. 'Let's look at what the future has in store for us. We're going to be apprentices in a real-life factory in Duisburg.' He didn't wait for Tommie to reply and rushed to add: 'I will be glad to get away from this place. Meet girls. Dancing and boozing. This place is becoming surreal. Did they tell you about the boys from the first Zug who were playing cowboys and Indians last night?'

'Yeah, yeah, they built a campfire on the ballroom floor and almost burned the place down. The nurses told me.'

'You should have seen those boys. War paint on their faces and feathers in their hair, stark naked except for a belt and two towels, one over their private parts on the front and one over their behinds.' Willem laughed out loud. 'If I hadn't come along and kicked the fire out, God knows what might have happened.'

'You pop up at all the right moments to save the day, don't you?' Tommie said.

'Well, no—' Willem started to say.

Tommie had turned his back to Willem and jerked his head. His stitches caught on the pillowcase. 'I'm going to sleep now,' he muttered.

'Cheer up. Think of the fun we'll have away from the Zugführers.'

'I can't wait,' Tommie said, sighing.

The nurse walked in. 'Time for your nap,' she said.

'Right, I'll see you later.' Willem got up. 'When will the doctor remove his stitches?' he asked, turning to the nurse.

'Any day now,' she said, pulling a thermometer from her apron. 'Now, turn onto your stomach,' she said to Tommie.

Before they knew it, they were on the train to Duisburg. A welcoming committee met them at the station; a woman dressed in a Nazi uniform and her driver, a boy of about eighteen with white hair and red eyes. He must be new to the city, as she had to give him directions. She took them to an old draughty warehouse, and a room filled with about twenty bunk beds. Down the corridor was a shower and toilet room with filthy cracked floor tiles, and an overpowering smell of urine and faeces greeted them. Everything was old and makeshift, and they had to share the building with workers from different countries within the Reich, but it meant freedom from their Zugführers and liberty from their bedtime curfew. They could go anywhere after work, visit theatres and cinemas, bars and strip clubs, and wherever they wanted to go, they could go. Their chaperone, Mr Ros, enjoyed his early evenings and many books, which meant they would finally taste the fruits of life teenage boys so craved.

Tommie had recuperated astonishingly well. The scar on the side of his face was red but healing without infection, so hopefully, leave no permanent disfigurement. They completed simple enough tasks in the office during the day and the nights were theirs. Tommie seemed to forget about the attack in the woods and relaxed enough to enjoy his newfound freedom.

One evening, Willem discovered he had left his wallet in his work pants. He kept his work clothes in his locker at the factory. The communal showers there were warm and cleaned daily, and Mr Ros had a key to the factory so they could wash there. Willem needed his allowance. Without the money, they would have to stay in the dorm without beer, girls, or any form of entertainment.

The boys knew Mr Ros was a sucker for family, reminding them to write to their mothers. So, Willem persuaded Mr Ros by telling him his stepmother's birthday was that day, and he needed the money to pay for a telegram to send his greetings. Mr Ros pulled out his wallet to lend Willem the money. But Willem waved his hand, saying his stepmother told him never to borrow money for anything. Before you know it, you're over your head in debt. Mr Ros agreed with this sentiment, so he removed his slippers and pulled on his leather shoes. He walked with the boys to the factory's side gate. Once he had unlocked the padlock, he ushered them in and followed them. But his key did not fit the lock on the door to the washroom. Willem said it might fit the backdoor into the factory, and from there, they could take the route they were familiar with from the office.

'Why not just take the money?' Mr Ros said. 'You don't have to pay me back. It'll be a gift.'

The cost of a telegram would not cover what Willem had planned for the night, so he walked ahead and pretended not to hear Mr Ros's objections, with Tommie also pretending, and following close behind.

The factory resembled a space station from a science fiction book during the day, but it grew beyond anything they could imagine at night. They walked around the massive building like tiny alien beings. The wind bellowed, and a constant mechanical clicking echoed through the deserted building. Willem was in awe of the magnificence and scale, the moon shining onto pipes as wide as trains and conveyor belts reaching beyond ten-story buildings into the dark, starry sky.

They heard a sound, like an animal's cry, as if in pain, and Willem swung his flashlight around, aiming it at the noise. He searched the shadows. The beam slid over the giant contraptions suspended above their heads. Convinced something was lurking in the shadows, he crept into the darkness. Mr Ros followed him. Tommie stayed on the path where the pavement lights projected a series of misty triangles onto the ground.

Willem and Mr Ros heard another sound and turned towards it. Tommie gasped, 'Over there,' he whispered, pointing. 'Willem!' he whispered. 'Over there!'

Metal sparkled in the light, and Willem discerned a cage as it loomed from the darkness. Willem saw eyes flash in the light from his torch. He moved closer and saw many cautious eyes. And closer still, he discerned men caged like wild animals, faces watching him from behind the metal mesh. Willem waved his flashlight over them and counted ten, maybe fifteen men trapped in a cage made of chicken wire not much bigger than three by three metres. The roof was a woven tapestry of barbed wire. The people stared at Willem with bulging, suspicious eyes, their whites visible. They wore rags, their heads shaven, and some huddled together for warmth.

'Who are you?' Willem asked.

No one answered him.

Willem moved closer. Mr Ros remained at a distance, watching them as he rubbed his head. His mouth hung open as if he wanted to say something but couldn't decide what.

As Willem approached, the caged people huddled together and scrambled into the far corner, trying to hide behind each other.

'I won't hurt you,' Willem whispered. 'We are unarmed.'

'Do you have water?' a man asked.

Willem walked to the cage and shone his light on each face. The prisoners peered back at him.

Mr Ros's footsteps clacked behind him. 'My God,' he whispered. 'What happened to them...? Who locked you up?'

Someone mumbled in Russian. Willem had heard Kees talk with Ab enough times to recognise the language.

'They brought us here and forced us to work for them,' a Dutchman said.

'Were you deported from Holland?' Willem asked.

'They arrested us in February for going on strike. My colleague and I are from Amsterdam.'

'But this is slavery,' Willem mumbled. 'Mr Ros, we need to do something. Can we inform Herr Naumann?'

'Come away,' Mr Ros said, pushing Willem back to Tommie and towards the gates. 'We need to get out of here before someone sees us.'

'But they need food and water,' Willem said.

'Water,' the voices mumbled. 'Give us water!'

Mr Ros grabbed Willem's arm. 'No!' he whispered. 'We need to return to our beds. Now!' he said, suppressing his trembling voice.

'But they're thirsty.'

Mr Ros pushed Willem along before him. Tommie rushed before them and was the first to reach the gate. Willem realised Tommie had changed since he struck him across the face in the woods. He didn't even try to persuade Mr Ros to get water for the prisoners.

Mr Ros forced Willem onto the road, told him to stand by Tommie, and fidgeted the key into the gate lock. He told the boys never to tell anyone, 'And I mean anyone,' he stressed, 'about what you have witnessed here tonight.'

Willem knew what he had sensed since his first day at the Reichsschule – those bright futures were all lies. The Reichsschule was another part of the engine that kept churning within the Third Reich, eating away at what it was to be human. He would not be a part of it. He would not enlist in the SS to be sent to the Eastern Front like his predecessors and become cannon fodder. Willem worked harder than ever during the day and couldn't wait to lie in bed at night to plan his getaway. He was going to Russia to find his brother and leave this place for good, and he was taking Tommie with him.

They returned to Bensberg, and Willem grabbed the first opportunity. Naumann sought volunteers to work as farmhands in Warthegau. Willem put Tommie and his name at the top of the list, and this time, Tommie did not protest.

'Fresh air and working on the land might mean no more headaches, no more ringing in my ear,' Tommie said, hoping aloud.

'You will be fine again,' Willem assured him.

He didn't tell Tommie that Warthegau was near Danzig; from there, they'd take a boat to Libau. 'We'll sit out the war on the land – beautiful stretches of vast countryside and sunshine. You'll be your old self in no time. And after the war, we'll return home in one piece. Heroism is for idiots who end up in cages.' A quick false smile appeared on Willem's face as he raised his finger to his lips, 'But don't tell anyone I said so.'

Tommie looked at him. 'I don't know,' he said. 'When my father finds out I've quitted school, he will murder me.'

'You can't stay here. Once you graduate,' Willem said. 'They'll send you to God knows where to kill – yes, kill people whom they consider Untermenschen. The sooner we're out of here, the better.' Willem slapped Tommie's back. 'Come on, pack your gear.'

CHAPTER TWENTY

Kees

Wolf was asleep when Kees returned. Kees got down on his haunches and squeezed his arm. Wolf flinched.

'We better get back,' Kees said.

He laid a hand on Wolf's face. Wolf pulled back, and Kees saw a few drops of melted ice clinging to the hair of his moustache. His face was red.

'Are you tired?' Kees asked.

Wolf tried to get up but fell back onto the ground.

'Have you slept on the snow?' Kees asked. 'Come on,' he whispered, pulling his arm. 'You better get up. We need to get back to our battalion.'

'What about orders?' Wolf mumbled.

'I've scouted as far as the river. There are no Russians that way. I think they're going south towards Moscow. Anyway, they're not here,' he said, lowering his backpack. He hadn't written notes on the map and must scribble something before they reach Schachner. His mind switched between thoughts, and he felt unnerved about seeing Ab after dawn, swimming beneath the skin of the water.

The frightened screech of a pursued animal, a hare, echoed through the empty forest. Kees jolted around and listened. A large animal, maybe a bear, was trudging between the trees, maybe fifty metres away.

'Get your gear together,' Kees whispered. The sounds of the forest closed in and grew louder around them. His mind churned with

177

thoughts. What was real, and what was fantasy? The girl was real. But the doe? The doe had been dominating his dreams since Arnhem and must be a fantasy. He wished he could talk to someone about this parallel world. He knew Wolf wouldn't listen to his muddled accounts. Kees had better keep his mouth shut; Schachner would shoot him for losing his mind. If he had discovered that Wolf's mother was Russian and that Wolf was more proficient in Russian than Kees, he would have been dead already.

These thoughts filled him with foreboding.

Was it Moeke who had kept him on the right side of the liminal between reality and fantasy? She had always listened to him and helped him decipher his prophetic dreams. Moeke kept him sane. God, why did he come here?

'Pack your stuff. We have to get out of here,' Kees said to Wolf.

Wolf stared at him.

'Are you burning up?' Kees asked. He reached out again to touch Wolf's face, but Wolf jerked back.

'What the hell?' Wolf said.

'Let's go. My past is catching up with me,' Kees said, watching swatches of snow tumble like sheepskins from the swaying treetops. Pine cones dotted the ground like spilt hand grenades. The tall trees creaked and moaned as they swayed. That animal screeched again. Wolf followed Kees's gaze into the trees.

'On warm summer evenings...' Kees whispered, realising he was talking out loud, he continued in his head. Those scented evenings, rose petals scattered on the breeze like snow. 'Yes, snow,' he said aloud. He continued in his thoughts again. How the petals caught Ab's hair, the pink matching the blond. He had watched those petals swirl and float lightly, fingering Ab's hair. He watched how Ab shook his head to free himself from the blossoms. How Kees missed Ab's laughter. The mere thought of him warmed his icy bones. The memory of the journey to Sennheim and Ab's smile as he placed his suitcase on the overhead rack on the train. Another memory floated into his mind, and he didn't realise it at first. Ab and Punica were climbing the fence into the fields. A vision of them running out in the middle of the night, the cool blue moonlight catching them. The coincidence of him seeing them from the hallway window after discovering Ab's empty bed. The ticking of his alarm clock had awoken him – the ticking. The ticking awoke him, and he remembered Punica's muffled laughter as she jumped into Ab's arms. He imagined the fields behind his family home on Kerk Street. Watching Punica and Ab climb the gate. Ab wanted to help her down, and she dropped into his arms. He twirled her with her feet up off the ground. They laughed, not out loud, but he could decipher their body language by the way she plopped her head onto Ab's shoulder. Kees felt a jealousy twist in his gut when he saw them. Why hadn't Ab awoken him so he could accompany them, break curfew together, and go on an illegal midnight walk? How many times before had they crept out together behind his back? What were they doing out there in the darkest of the night?

His sister was beautiful and happy and very self-assured, and Ab needed her. He was alone, his family gone. But Kees wasn't prepared to let him ruin everything in his absence. He had to come to Russia with him. Ab had no business fooling around with his sister. She was only fifteen. Kees had never mentioned seeing them together at night, not even to Moeke, not even on their last day at the station when Ab and Punica had disappeared.

Kees stood by his backpack and reached into his coat for the letter Moeke had sent him, but pulled back. The letter he had burned. Kees remembered what Moeke had written word for word, but its unwritten meaning haunted him.

Wolf thumped his arm to warn him to get down on his haunches. Kees remained standing with Wolf low by his knees. Wolf boxed the back of his knee, and Kees sank to the ground. Wolf raised his finger to his lips. Kees saw the finger shiver. He knew it; Wolf was running a temperature. Kees heard the snow contract and a branch snap as he wanted to look up. It was coming towards them. Wolf's frightened eyes grew wide, and finally, Kees understood. Russians surrounded them. Wolf gasped; he was finding it hard to keep his breathing low. Shiny drops of sweat covered his upper lip and nose. It reminded Kees of Ab's face when he knew he would be killed. His shoulders shook uncontrollably. Their comrades stood around him. No one tried to help Ab when Schachner pulled the trigger and shot him through his ear.

The Russians moved away, disappearing between the trees. Seconds later, approaching feet loomed from the silence once more. One Russian had straggled behind, and before they could react, they stood face to face with him. His eyes were wide, as bewildered by the sudden encounter as they were. Kees jumped at him and stabbed his sculpting knife into his throat, twisting it, pushing it. The Russian gargled. Air escaped the lacerations in his windpipe. His flesh sucked the blade.

The Russians ran and shouted for their comrade.

Kees dropped the Russian to the ground.

'Run for it,' he whispered to Wolf, sliding his knife back into his pocket.

Wolf jumped up and ran towards the river. The Russians opened fire and shot him in the back. Kees dived behind pine trees, his clothes drenched in blood. The metallic smell made him sick. He tiger-crawled in search of cover, expecting a bullet to slice into his flesh as he tried to get away. A fallen tree blocked his course, black with rot, its branches bare and broken with a large cavity inside. He writhed in, but his legs didn't fit, so he pulled his rucksack up to hide them. Three or four Russians crept around the tree, darting their rifles at every sound around them, but not at Kees. Did they not see the trail of blood on the snow? Kees saw their faces, but they glanced over him, not acknowledging his presence. One sank onto his haunches, looking into the tree. Kees stared back, watching the Russian's face, his green eyes looking at him. The Russian pierced his rifle into the hollow, poking Kees's stomach and his chest. The Russian got up and called out to his comrades.

'Did he get away?'

'I got him good. Three shots in the back. The devil always takes back its gifts,' someone shouted back to him.

Kees heard laughter, the Russians making a joke out of Wolf's death like the Germans did when they strung the Russians up, not wanting to waste their bullets on them.

CHAPTER TWENTY-ONE

Petronella

Petronella tried to find her way through Utrecht Central Station. The main hall and the tunnels were packed with Nazis and people wearing the Star of David. There was a never-ending stream of trains coming and going. She wondered why the Germans wanted so many people. Older men and women, and mothers with babies and infants? Over the intercom, a tinny German voice ordered the passengers going to Germany to queue in the tunnel to platform 2b.

A Jewish woman stopped Petronella when she tried to pass her. 'Will you take my baby?' she begged.

Petronella's mouth dropped open. What was she supposed to answer? How could a mother give her baby to a random stranger at a railway station? The little girl smiled through her tears. She was wonderfully dressed in an expensive woollen coat and white leather baby shoes with a satin bow and a little pearl button at the side. Petronella remembered Kees and Willem as toddlers and knew she would love this baby, too. But could she go through losing yet another child when the mother returned? Petronella wanted to say no thank you as if offered a biscuit, but an NSB man caught the woman by her collar and pushed her back in line, the baby nearly falling from her arms. Petronella hesitated. Her heart was pounding within her rib cage as she tried to decide what to do. She shuffled towards the woman, but an officer pushed her aside. 'Move along,' he shouted as he passed her. He was huge, taller than anyone she had ever seen. Petronella lowered her hand around Punica's waist and pulled her away from the Jews.

Punica shuffled beside Petronella as if she were a robot. Petronella looked at her daughter's face. Her heart was breaking for her daughter, but also for the baby she should have taken with her. 'Punica, please say something?' Petronella pleaded, missing the chatty, carefree teenager she had always been. 'I should have taken the baby,' Petronella whispered. She looked back at the Jewish people lining up. 'Oh,' she said, half crying and in shock, 'I don't know what to do. Should I go after her and get the baby?' A woman shuffling behind her moved closer and said softly, 'You can't save the world. Get your daughter home.' Did she know the woman? Petronella glanced over her shoulder. The tunnel was packed with faces, but no one seemed to see her.

Petronella wrapped her arm around her daughter's shoulders and ushered her through the stream of people. Punica stared at the stars on the clothes of the queueing Jewish people to the side. Her face was white and emotionless.

'They're Jews,' she said. 'That's their crime... their only crime.'

The ceiling rumbled, and the lights flickered on and off. A train arrived overhead. The Nazis moved the Jewish people along and up the stairs. They struggled with suitcases and children too tired to walk. Petronella saw the woman with the baby at the top of the stairs turning the corner, the child playing with her mother's fur collar.

The tunnel to the platform for the train to Arnhem had emptied. A woman's high heels tattered on the tiled floor behind them. Her perfume wafted on the draught. Petronella raised her scarf over her mouth and nose.

On the platform, Petronella found her way to the waiting room with Punica. Their train would not depart for half an hour yet. The waiting room smelled of crispy newspapers and stale coffee. Petronella changed her mind, turned, and ushered Punica out in front of her. They would wait out in the fresh air. She took a seat beside a lady dressed in a mink coat, letting Punica sit between them.

'Would you like to eat your bun now?' Petronella asked Punica. Punica regarded the rusty rails, not answering her. Birds pecked at breadcrumbs between the gravel.

Petronella checked the metal clock hanging from the ceiling, the seconds ticking away until it reached twelve. There, the dial stuck to the Roman numerals. It trembled briefly, pulled loose, and ticked on as before. Finally, the train to Arnhem arrived, and they boarded. Petronella found two vacant red velvet seats by the window.

Petronella watched the wet countryside slide past. When the fields gave way to woodlands, she knew she was almost home. Yellow light grabbed at their faces as the evening sun followed them through the trees. She looked at Punica's reflection in the window, her eyes so far away. She took her hand and held it with both of hers. 'It won't be long now,' she whispered, bringing her face close to Punica's. 'Darling...?'

Punica shook her head slowly, her eyes staring into the distance. She held the paper bag containing the bun on her lap. She rolled the paper up, smoothed the creases, then re-rolled it and smoothed them out again.

'Still not hungry,' Petronella whispered in Punica's ear. 'No matter, we'll be home soon.'

Once at Arnhem station, fellow passengers noticed how weak Punica was and helped her climb down the few steps onto the platform. Petronella convinced them she would manage. But on the stairs, Punica stumbled. A man in a long black coat, wearing a hat and holding a briefcase, helped to catch her and stop her from falling down the stone steps. He took her to a bench, and Petronella let Punica rest for a little while. She thanked the man and tried to convince him to leave them. Petronella said help was on the way. He went reluctantly, as if he doubted her words. When he was out of sight, she moved Punica to another free bench in the station hall. It had rained again. She waited for it to stop, but the clouds only darkened, so Petronella crouched before Punica and urged her daughter to climb onto her back.

Petronella wobbled with her daughter's weight over the square where the trams stopped. The bell rattled, warning pedestrians that the tram was leaving the station. Her heel slipped on the iron tram rails, and she stumbled. Petronella's heart galloped when she saw the tram approach her. The tram came to a screeching stop. The driver swung the doors open. 'Madam?' he called out. 'Please?' He held out his hand as he leaned out of the door. He gestured for her to board the tram.

She shook her head. She had spent everything on the train tickets and hadn't the money for the fare. He hopped down the few steps, walked onto the road to her, and lifted Punica off her back.

'I have no money,' Petronella pleaded, keeping her voice low so the other passengers on the tram could not hear her. She tried her best not to cry.

'Please,' he said. 'Your daughter is too heavy for you; you can't carry her all the way home. Please, let me help you. Your father helped me years ago when he was our mayor. You would be doing me a favour in letting me help you.'

Petronella swallowed away her tears. Her father had been the one she had always turned to as a child; he had always helped her. How she must have hurt him when she turned her back on him so many years ago to marry Cornelis.

The tram stopped on Market Square, and Petronella was getting ready to help Punica from her seat when the tram driver stopped a man getting out and asked him to carry the girl. But Petronella assured both men she could manage. She was coaxing Punica to leave the seat and walk with her. All these good people offered to help her. She had married a collaborator and an idiot and a traitor and felt so ashamed realising it now. Her husband hadn't lifted one finger to get his daughter out of the clutches of his colleagues. One brief letter she had received from him in a fortnight, with just one sentence that told her quite soberly without feeling where Punica was imprisoned.

The man helped her despite her protests. Once the tram had departed, he asked her where she lived. 'No... no thank you. I can manage. It is only a short walk now,' she assured him.

After taking frequent rests to let Punica sit on a bench or the edge of the pavement for a few moments, they finally rounded Eusebius Cathedral and entered Kerk Street. The windows of her house were alight with yellow light, and the curtains were not yet drawn. Tears prickled her eyes. As soon as she fumbled her key into the front door, Nienke pulled it open. 'They're here!' she called to the kitchen. 'Punica is... home!'

Blackie was ecstatic, yelping and jumping up on Punica's knees, wagging the stub of his tail wildly.

'Thank God, thank God!' Mrs de Vries called out, running into the hallway. She pulled Punica into a hug. 'How thin you've become.' Mrs De Vries sobbed. She hugged Petronella too.

'She was in a dreadful place,' Petronella mumbled. She turned to Punica and laid her hand on her cheek. 'Darling, you are home now, safe and sound.'

Punica stared at the floor, not reacting to Mrs de Vries or Blackie. Petronella said, 'Mrs de Vries, do you have something warm for her to eat? Porridge maybe?'

Nienke touched Petronella's arm and tried to catch her eyes. She gestured towards the drawing room.

'What is it, Nienke?' Petronella asked.

'He's back,' she whispered. 'Mr Mandemaker is inside.'

'Where?'

'I have warm soup, sweetie,' Mrs de Vries said, wrapping her arm around Punica's shoulders. 'I've made a lovely vegetable soup for you, your favourite, with vermicelli and lots of potatoes.' She turned to the maid, 'Nienke, will you run a bath and fetch a clean nighty for Punica?'

'Will you be okay, Mrs Mandemaker?' Nienke asked, half turning to the stairs but hesitating.

'Where's Corrie?'

'She's in there with him. She was thrilled to see her father. I'm sorry. I couldn't keep her from him.'

Corrie had always been his favourite child.

Mrs de Vries closed the kitchen door behind Punica, and Nienke ran upstairs. Petronella stood in the hallway, exhausted. She removed her coat and hung it on the hook instead of the cedar hanger. She looked in the mirror. Her hair hung lank, her wet fringe plastered onto her forehead. Her clothes were creased and muddy from Punica's hands and knees. Petronella looked as if she had aged ten years in one day. She took the lipstick from her handbag and painted her lips bright red. Her skin looked sallow. She pushed up a few curls of her fringe, but it was useless. She straightened her jumper and strolled into the drawing room.

Cornelis was eating a roast chicken; the smell filled the room. Corrie sat on the rug at his knees, trying to catch some snippets as she watched the food enter her father's mouth. Corrie obviously longed for a bite, but wasn't getting anything.

'Moeke,' she shouted, jumping up. 'Did Punica have a good time? Where is she?' she asked, scanning the hallway.

'She's exhausted, darling,' Petronella said. 'Leave her a minute and tell me what you have been doing all day?'

She glanced at her husband, eating a chicken leg, holding it by the bone.

'We sell food coupons from our ration book to have money to buy the bare essentials,' Petronella said. 'And you come here eating a whole chicken and not sharing anything with your daughter?'

Cornelis broke off another leg, ignoring her remarks.

'We do have cutlery. And plates,' Petronella said. 'And what are you doing here?'

Corrie returned to her father and sat back on the floor by his feet.

'Corrie, come away from there now,' she said. 'Haven't you eaten? Mrs de Vries has vegetable soup.'

'I don't want vegetable soup,' Corrie said. 'I want chicken.'

Cornelis didn't acknowledge his daughter and continued eating, raising a few chips to his mouth and stuffing them in with his fingers.

'Papa says if I go away with him, he will give me an accordion, and we'll eat chicken every day.'

'A what... what? An accordion?'

Cornelis stopped eating, wrapping the food back into the paper. He picked a bit of chicken skin from between his two front teeth with the nail of his pinkie. 'I didn't say—'

'Corrie, please go to the kitchen.' Petronella turned to her husband. 'Cornelis, you haven't asked how Punica is?'

'Papa said— '

'Nothing,' Cornelis said, interrupting her. 'I said nothing' – turning to Petronella – 'I didn't promise her an instrument,' he said, smiling stupidly. 'I offered her chicken for her dinner... today, only today.'

Corrie gasped and said, 'No... no, you said every day if— '

'I don't know where she gets it from,' Cornelis interjected.

'Get out of my house.' Petronella said, deepening her tone.

'Did you hear from the boys?' he asked.

'Corrie, please go to the kitchen,' she pleaded. 'Kees is missing,' she said, lowering her voice and rubbing her head.

'He's fine, don't worry,' Cornelis said. 'Corrie, listen to your mother.'

'Why, in your opinion, is missing in action fine?'

'If he were dead, they'd tell you.'

She took the wrapped food from his hands and pushed him into the hallway. 'Go to your new... whatever, I don't care. Get away from my children and me now.'

Cornelis turned to the hallway and strolled to the coat stand, but Petronella opened the front door, and pushed him through the vestibule and out the door. She returned, pulled the coat from the hook, tearing the loop. She raised the wrapped chicken to throw it after him, but reconsidered.

She remembered how Cornelis had thrown his sister and her husband out months ago and how proud she'd been. How quickly things had changed. She threw the overcoat into his face and slammed the door shut. 'Come,' she said to Corrie, who stood sobbing by her side; she wrapped her arm around her shoulders and said, 'Come along, let's get you and Punica a clean plate,' she said, her voice shaking. 'I'm sure you two would love roast chicken and chips for supper.'

CHAPTER TWENTY-TWO

Kees

Kees writhed out of the hollow tree trunk. In the distance, orange light squeezed between the trees, sparkling on the snow. Sunset or sunrise? he removed his wristwatch to check; both were wrong. Putting the wristwatch into his pocket, he felt the soft handkerchief against his skin. He took it out with the tips of his fingers without letting the contents escape. His body trembled. He must stay out of Schachner's clutches and find a way home. If he disappeared, they would assume he was dead.

Kees sat on the snow and rolled his head back against the tree trunk – When I was a toddler, my birth mother hung a cardboard sign with my name around my neck. She put me on a red velvet seat and told me to stay put. Mama said the train would soon start moving, and when it stopped, I was to get off. She got up and disappeared.

I wanted to scream her name so she'd come back and take me home, and though my voice rumbled inside my throat when I opened my mouth as far as it would go, no voice came out. The train moved to the rhythm of my heart. When I was desperate, it screeched underneath me, and the whole wagon shook to contain me. I sat by the window and watched the snow erase my past. On the glass, reflections of the strangers around me loomed out of the whiteness. Their faces questioned me, but they did not ask. The train finally stopped, and I shoved to the edge of the seat, plopped onto the floor, and squeezed between the bodies wearing skinned fur overcoats, cold on my cheeks, black and brown.

A hand helped me avoid a gaping hole between the train and the platform as I climbed the steps backwards, but the hand was not attached to any arm. When I looked up, their faces turned away. I shuffled between strangers, desperately searching for my mother.

A man and a woman appeared before me.

The man smiled and called out my name. The woman sat on her haunches before me and read the sign hanging around my neck out loud. She said, 'Cornelis Mandemaker? Is that your name?' The man said he, too, bore that name and how glad he was that I had arrived safely. The woman said I looked younger than she had pictured me in her mind, and I must be exceptional to travel by myself and not have been lost from them. She kissed my forehead, and her breath smelled sweet, like apples. She held something behind her back. She kissed me again and produced a rabbit. My hands refused to take the stuffed toy. It slid from me onto the icy black ground. She picked it up, said, 'No matter,' and left it on a bench at the station for another child to find.

Ab touched Kees's arm, his shaking body.

'Where did you and my sister go?' Kees asked. 'At night, I saw you sneak away.'

Kees slid his hand into Ab's hand and held it for a while. Ab's hand dissolved. Kees looked aside. Ab had disappeared, and he was alone.

He pulled his backpack over to him. It was covered in bullet holes. He shivered from the cold and noticed his uniform was drenched in blood. He struggled, heaving his backpack onto his back. He reached for his rifle and ran back to the river. He remembered going to a slaughterhouse with his birth mother. She bought meat not fit for consumption. He remembered they were hungry, and she'd make soup from unfit meat. His mother was pregnant. Her belly made her waddle like a duck. He had escaped her hand and ran into white-tiled chambers filled with men busy at work. He'd tripped over a hose for spraying off blood and filth and fell into a puddle. The workers were all doing different jobs; some removed entrails and others sliced carcasses in half. The workers had not detected him. Kees had entered their work domain, which was not meant for a three-year-old's eyes to witness.

A cow hung above Kees by one hind leg, kicking and twitching; its eyes were filled with horror. Its throat pulsed blood onto him, soaking his clothes. Cows mooed in panic, and saws screamed and screeched on bones. Kees opened his mouth wide, his voice scraping his throat. But the clamour drowned him, and no one heard him. Men's voices shouted, and a man picked him up from behind, lifted him high into the air with stretched-out arms, and brought him to his mother. The man wore white clothes with a big red stain on the front and the sleeves speckled with blood. His boots left red footprints on the floor. He wore gloves made of metal mesh. Like gloves knights wore in the olden days. On his head, he wore a white cap.

Kees was inconsolable, walking home screaming at the top of his lungs. Pieces of bone gritted between his teeth and tasted of metal. His face and hair were red with blood, and lumps of yellow animal fat stuck to the soles of his shoes and made them slippery. His pants squished as he walked, and the inside of his shoes, too, overflowed with blood.

Kees struggled through the forest; every branch pointed him away from the river. He nearly stumbled over the body of the dead Russian soldier. Snowflakes caught in his thin Clark Gable moustache. His throat was a bloody mess, as if attacked by a wolf. Kees remembered how he had twisted the knife in the warm flesh.

Kees bent forward and vomited. He turned away and rushed to the river. At the world's edge, he pulled off his clothes as fast as possible and waded into the mushy ice water colder than the day before. He washed the blood from his body, kneeled on the muddy river floor, and washed his neck and head. The water coloured red around him. He swam out into the winter. A low mist rolled over from the hills towards him.

'Take me now,' he whispered. 'Take me,' he said calmly. 'I am ready to die.'

Willem had asked Kees to go to America. How his brother had loved American music. Kees should have said yes. He should have taken his brother and escaped to America. How he hated his father for not knowing better. Where would Willem be now? He imagined him wearing a Nazi uniform. That must be wrong. His brother was at school; he wouldn't enlist in the SS. He wouldn't if he wanted to go to America. But he saw his brother travelling the route he had taken – the train, the boat, the marching over Russian territory.

'Where are you?' Kees whispered.

Kees had offered his flesh to the hungry, one gesture he thought he owed his father. The water was cold enough to stop his heart, but it didn't. His heartbeat slowed but would not stop. How far did he have to swim for his body to become paralysed? He stopped swimming and turned onto his back. The sky was light blue, cobalt, with dark clouds like mountains, their hearts vanilla yellow. Pink streaks floated diagonally across the sky from the horizon.

He felt a presence watching him and lifted his head to look towards the shore. The doe stood beside his clothes. She observed him while her jaws chewed. He swam towards her, and she did not bolt away. The half-frozen water moved against him. He stared at her eyes, and the doe's face dissolved into a girl's. The Russian girl he had seen before regarded him as he swam towards her. He scratched the ground underneath with his fingernails. From here, he'd have to get up and walk to her. Was he naked? He couldn't remember. He got onto his haunches and stood up; his skin was cold.

'I heard you whisper,' he said.

She gasped and looked at his chest and body. She walked to him, staring at his stomach, and touched his skin. He watched her fingers circle a deep gash in his side. She walked around him, tracing her hand along his body, and touched his back in the same way as if encircling wounds.

'The bullets went into your back and came out of your stomach and chest,' she said. 'The cold of the water stopped the bleeding.'

'I... I felt nothing,' Kees said, contemplating her eyes. Sunflower petals surrounded her pupils. The irises were turquoise and emerald green, like the needles of fir trees.

'You must get dressed' – she reached for his clothes – 'or you will freeze to death.'

He waved his hand to stop her.

She picked up his shirt, frozen stiff, and gave it to him. He forced his arms into the armholes and pulled the shirt over his head. The material cracked, and red crystals dispersed into the air. He pulled up his trousers, pulled his coat over his shoulders, stuffed his feet into his boots, and lifted his rucksack onto his back. He picked up his rifle and looked at her.

'Follow me,' she whispered.

She took him into the woods. The trees glittered like silver, and he caught the scent of green tea and fresh fir needles. She took him to a cabin and told him to undress. She built a fire. As the flames danced, he lowered the backpack to the floor. He undressed. She opened a wooden chest at the foot of the bed and pulled out a pair of trousers and a rough blue shirt. 'They were my father's,' she whispered as she handed them to him.

Kees closed his eyes. He was losing reality; at least he knew what was real. He threw his uniform into the fire and turned, wanting to explain he should be dead, but the house was empty. She had disappeared.

A pain pierced his tongue, and it swelled inside his mouth. He rushed to the mirror above the dresser and opened his mouth wide. His tongue was purple and swollen like an egg; his lips folded dryly on his teeth. He wanted to curse but could not form any words. His heartbeat sped up, and beads of sweat formed on his face. Breathe through the nose, breathe. His heartbeat trashed his ears and pulsated in his head as he squeezed his tongue to stop the swelling. But he couldn't. His tongue didn't fit back into his mouth. Something moved underneath the skin – a creature or a bird, its feet with long sharp nails pushed and writhed.

Kees's eyes grew wide with fear.

The creature struggled to get through the skin. Kees gagged. But realising he might choke if he vomited, he concentrated on controlling his stomach. A tiny silver beak punctured a hole, and a silver head pushed out through the wound and ripped the skin. Kees slammed his hands down onto the dresser to steady himself. A bird wriggled out through the oozing blood, crawled up on wobbly legs, and staggered to the tip of Kees's tongue towards its reflection in the mirror. The bird spread its wings and flapped them, observing itself from different angles.

Kees checked his pocket for the bird his mother had given him on his first night at the house on Kerk Street. The bird was to keep him safe, a bird of silver and marble he always had with him. Before he reached into his pocket, he realised the coat was burning in the fire. The bird leapt into the air, flew towards the door, and crashed against it. It fell fluttering to the floor; it flew up and crashed into the door again. Kees turned back to the mirror. His tongue was normal, with no trace of a wound. Turning back to the door, he saw the bird lying on the wooden floor, gasping for air.

He walked over, picked it up, opened the door, and held out his hand. The bird stood on his index finger and sparkled in the light. The girl was at the door, her arms were filled with logs. The bird flew up and fluttered away. Her eyes did not follow it; she watched Kees intently.

He cried. He knew he was losing his mind.

She ushered him back inside. She rushed to the fire and pulled his clothes out with tongs, but the flames pulled them back. Kees shuffled to her and dropped to his knees beside her, staring into the fire.

CHAPTER TWENTY-THREE

Kees

Before dawn, Esther slid from under the cotton sheets, dressed, and went out into the cold. Kees needed the time alone and pretended he was asleep. When he heard the door softly close and heard the snow contract underneath her feet, padding further away into the forest, he got up.

He swept the old ashes from the grid, searching for the bones of Ab's finger. When he found them, they were black as charcoal but still in perfect condition. He brushed them clean, blowing the last particles of debris away, and wrapped them afresh in a tiny square of clean cloth. He dropped them into his pocket.

Using fresh logs from the basket, he started a new fire. Straightening and stretched out, he wrapped his arms around his chest; he hugged himself and cracked the bones of his vertebrae one by one, working from his lower back towards his shoulders. As he lifted the kettle from the dresser, Kees squeezed his jaws, imagining the pain he would soon inflict on himself, and tried to prepare for it. He scooped the kettle through a tub that Esther filled with fresh snow every morning and hung it above the fire. He needed boiling water to sterilise his carving knife.

He stripped his upper body, hanging his shirt and vest on a chair, and lifted his left arm. The Nazis had tattooed his blood group on his skin, A+ in gothic lettering like the devil's birthmark, about ten centimetres above the inside of his elbow. He took his carving knife from his pocket and laid it on the table. He missed something; he still needed a bandage afterwards to stop the bleeding. His eyes searched the dacha and settled on the bed; the sheet lay crumpled between the blankets. He tore a strip off, rolled it up, and laid it beside the knife. He needed something more and searched for scissors. Not in the cutlery drawer. Once more, his eyes scoured the dacha. On the windowsill, he saw Esther's sewing box. On top lay an old rusty pair of scissors. He took them and laid them by his knife. With everything ready, he squatted by the fire, throwing on more logs so the water would boil faster.

His face warmed.

Watching the logs turn to black porous flakes, he regretted burning Petronella's letter. But Kees could not erase the words from his memory. He stood up and stretched himself, his arms pulled out to the sides, his fingers spread wide. He rubbed his face hard. He regretted his naivety. Why couldn't he accept that Ab and Punica loved each other?

The water bubbled, and he got up and picked up a rag from the mantelpiece. He lifted the kettle from the hook using the rag, walked to the table, poured water into a bowl, and set the kettle down. A thick cloud of steam swirled towards the ceiling. He picked up his knife, checked the blade to see if it was sharp enough, and dropped it into the steaming water. Bubbles formed on the grey and black steel. He waited a few minutes, took the knife with tongs from the scalding water, and laid it on a clean towel.

He dabbed a corner of the cloth into the water and rubbed the skin around the Nazi tattoo. His heart pounded as he prepared himself for the pain. He inserted the tip of his knife into the skin below the tattoo. Clenching his jaws, grinding his teeth, he cut underneath the inky letters, slicing, sawing the tattoo free from the fat and muscle underneath it until a loose flap of skin hung on his arm. The wound burned, and he let out a subdued groan as the sweat burst from his pores. Blood poured from the wound; he lowered the knife into the bowl, the water turning red. Black blotches formed before his eyes, and the dacha spun around him. He clutched the table edges, tightening his muscles, gasping and whimpering as he tried to calm himself.

He had to get this over with, or he might lose his nerve, so he picked up the scissors and raised them to the loose hanging flap of skin. The blood streamed down his arm and coated his fingers as he tried to cut the flap free. But the scissors were blunt, and he needed to open and shut the blades twice, pulling the flap out. He groaned like a bear. The dacha spun faster now. He clenched the sides of the table but could not stand erect any longer. He sank to his knees, pulling the table with him. The kettle scattered across the floor, and the bowl smashed to smithereens.

When Esther returned, she rushed to him, dropping two rabbits she had killed.

'What have you done to yourself?' She removed her bow, sliding it over her head, and laid it and her quiver containing her arrows by her side. She touched his face so he'd focus on her.

'I couldn't stand the devil's mark on me any longer.'

She raised his arm and studied the wound. 'Let me,' she said, taking the makeshift bandage from his hand and wrapping it around his upper arm. She took the outer part of the strip between her teeth. Holding the corner, she tore it into two strips and tied the ends around his arm. The blood soaked through the white cotton. Her eyes widened when she saw the bloody scissors lying by his side, the strip of flesh caught between the blades.

'But they'll know when they see the wound. Everyone will know. They will come looking for you.'

Kees felt like sobbing and fidgeted with his knife, trying to restrain the tears from rolling from his eyes. He pushed himself off the floor but stumbled as he tried to find his balance. Esther took his arm and eased him back onto the bed. She helped him dress. 'Stay there a minute and gather your thoughts,' she said.

She hung the rabbits on a hook by the door, straightened the table, cleaned the floor, and returned outside to slaughter the rabbits.

She fried the meat, adding a few dried bay leaves and a clove of garlic. Kees lay on the bed, watching her. He loved the look of deep concentration sketched across her face when she was busy and her delicate hands fluttered about the work. The scent of her cooking filled

196

the cabin. His stomach rumbled for food even though the wound felt as if a molten rod still burned his skin.

While they ate, Esther said, 'I want to show you something. Are you up for a walk?'

'Of course,' Kees said, losing himself in the fantasy.

She cleared away the dishes.

'Where is your father?' Kees asked.

Esther dried her hands, walked to a chest behind the bed, and dug out an old wooden box. She pulled her chair closer to Kees, held the box in her left hand, and sat beside him.

'This is my Papa,' she said, taking out a photograph. She showed it to Kees. A man dressed in a Soviet army uniform stared into the light projected on his face. He stared to the left of the camera, avoiding the lens.

She held up another photograph: an idyllic picture of a young woman holding a toddler on her lap, and beside her, a girl of four. They wore lovely floral summer dresses, and the children wore white broderie Anglaise aprons.

'And this is my Mama. I'm on her lap, and my sister stands beside us.'

The woman and the children in the photograph sat by a lake. The trees were covered in leaves, throwing a camouflage of shadows onto their faces. It was a warm summer evening. 'I'm so glad I have these photographs of my family. Otherwise, it would be as if they never existed.'

Another picture, two girls sat side by side at a table. They were drawing. In their hair, they wore giant satin bows. Burgundy or maybe bright crimson, Kees thought, deciphering grey shades in the black-and-white photograph. She turned the picture over. On the back were Russian letters. 'It says, Varenka eight years, Esther four years,' she read. 'Rumours were going around... at the start of the blockade.' She paused a long while. Kees cupped her hands. They were freezing.

'My father knew of a way to get out of the city,' she continued. 'He thought the forest would supply enough food for me. He thought our greatest enemy was starvation. The situation in Leningrad was hopeless. The citizens would die if they stayed. But few could muster the courage to leave everything and find a way through the blockade to escape the city. The authorities didn't much care about us and ordered the police to shoot anyone for looting. In the Badaev warehouses, they stored enough food to feed the city. But as luck would have it, the first bombs the Germans dropped destroyed those warehouses. People were so hungry that they went there to find something edible under the sand and the soot and the rubble. The food had turned into rubbish, but at least after cleaning off the sand and soot, they'd have something to eat. The police shot anyone on sight who dared sneak into the ruins. They killed many of our people.'

'I didn't know,' Kees said.

'The newspapers didn't report it, but everybody knew anyway. The newspapers only reported what the authorities told them to report. We were only to read about the battles we had won. They had spies everywhere. If we talked about how bad it was getting, the police arrested us.'

'Did your father die in those warehouses?'

She turned her face to him, 'Do you keep bones of deceased people on you?'

'What do you mean?'

'I found a finger in your coat. When I returned last night, you burned your coat in the fire? I saw you.'

'He was my friend. I loved him like my brother,' Kees whispered.

'Did you do it out of love... or barbarism?'

Kees thought deeply. Barbarism? He did love Ab. 'How could it be barbarism if you love someone so much you keep a piece of them with you?'

Esther stared at him, her face solemn. She did not seem to understand. 'My father died trying to save me. He got me out of the city. I heard gunshots, and we ran for our lives.'

'I wanted to keep my friend's soul with me.'

'My father's soul is within me,' she whispered. 'I keep his memory deep within my heart.'

The fire cracked. Snow and ice fell from the branches and tumbled onto the roof. In the distance, a wolf howled.

'Come with me. I want to show you something.'

They dressed for the winter temperatures. They left the dacha and entered a winter wonderland. It had snowed profusely during the night, and Esther handed him two large oval rods woven with string and kept two for herself. She fastened hers to the soles of her feet, and he did the same after her example.

Esther led him to a turquoise pond with a dark circle in the middle.

'It looks like your eyes,' he said. 'The same colour as your irises. Only the yellow of sunflower petals is missing.'

She laughed and strolled off, his gaze following her. He saw something move in the dusk, hovering between the trees, a glistering of eyes catching the light. He discerned the doe that had visited him in his dreams. She stood there staring at him, with Esther hopping through the snow between them; her contours softened and were out of focus. His eyes returned to Esther. She took a bow and arrow from her backpack, pointed the arrow at the doe, and flexed the bow.

Kees could not move. His body froze stiff like Wolf's corpse was the day after he died, having lain in minus zero temperatures throughout the night. He watched her release the arrow and saw it pierce the air towards the doe. But a stag with antlers metres wide appeared from nowhere and walked towards Esther. The hair on Kees's neck rose as he saw the stag. Kees screamed, rousing the birds. The crows screeched with their low, hoarse voices scratching the sky.

The arrow bore into his forehead, and silence plummeted on him from the blackened sky. He watched the orange light – a flickering of flames – the sound of wood cracking from heat, the walls devoured by fire.

Esther's dacha exploded.

CHAPTER TWENTY-FOUR

Petronella

Petronella held a photograph of Punica in her hand, taken before the invasion when she was about eleven. She was dressed in a black leotard and wore black leather ballet shoes. She smiled into the camera; her wavy blonde hair hung loosely about her shoulders. Corrie and Ab's little sister, Eva, stood on either side. Both girls only reached Punica's shoulders. The photograph was taken in the garden. Sun-dappled leaves created flickering shadows on their smiling faces.

Petronella remembered the day Punica announced she wanted to be called Punica instead of Maria Cornelia and that she was leaving ballet classes. After turning thirteen, she fell in love with adventure books for boys and their handsome heroes. Petronella remembered how Punica had tried to convince her to let her leave ballet. She would never be as graceful as her mother, she had said. Shoulders back; head held high; chin up. 'I've practised a million times,' she pleaded. 'I need more excitement in my life. Always the same jokes. Madame's exaggerated dancing and Miss Goud's overenthusiastic piano playing. If you know the concept, it becomes too tedious for words.'

'I enjoy their jokes,' Petronella said.

'You're middle-aged, Moeke,' she said and strutted off.

'I'm not that old,' Petronella whispered as she threaded her embroidery needle with scarlet satin thread.

'Oh, and by the way,' Punica said, turning and leaning against the doorpost, 'I've changed my name to Punica. Maria Cornelia is so biblical and boring, and we already have a Corrie in the family.'

Petronella sighed, 'Punica,' she whispered, packing the photograph of her daughter with the others in an old shoebox to take with her. 'Punica, you were my little ray of sunshine. Why won't you tell me what happened during those weeks in Amersfoort?'

Petronella took out two more photographs, this time of Cornelis from when he was young, taken before she met him. She held each in each hand. He was maybe eighteen and in his early twenties in the other. His eyes and smile exuded more confidence than anyone his age. He wore a Dutch army uniform and sat on a leather chair; the copper studs glistered underneath his crossed legs. A Parsons terrier, with brown patches over its eyes, lay at his feet. She wondered what its name was. Cornelis had never talked of a dog or any other family pet they might have owned when he was younger. She pushed the photograph into the box between the others and took out another.

Cornelis's hair was blacker in this one, curly but tamed and parted in the middle. He stood, leaning his left elbow on a high stool at his side. He held a cigarette between his index and middle finger in his right hand. Around his wrist, he wore a broad black watch with a massive case. He was right-handed. Why wear a watch on the wrong wrist? The room looked grand, the walls behind him painted with flower arrangements. He stood on an Arabian rug. There was no dog at his feet in this one.

How fascinating he was when she met him. He had changed so much under German rule, having morphed into a selfish man. Why did some people transform into strangers while others remained faithful to their character and integrity?

She put the photograph in the box and put the box in her suitcase. She walked to her wardrobe, opened the doors, and peered at her clothes. What should she pack? She had no idea how long she'd be away. The Germans had ordered all non-essential workers to evacuate the city. They gave her one day to pack a lifetime of memories. She returned to the bed and sat down. She could only take what she could carry, but there was no knowing if the Allies would bomb the house. They had destroyed the medieval centre of Nijmegen, and many homes and lives had been lost.

She loved this house with its history before she loved the man who owned it, but she was content for sixteen years in the life she had built with Cornelis. She didn't regret the years before the war. Not even when he surprised her on her wedding day with a son he expected her to raise. One son turned into two sons; she would have also taken the girl if his first wife had asked her. Petronella had raised those boys and loved them like her own. But they had never been hers; Cornelis had taken them from her before she knew what was happening.

Where was Willem now? She had received a message from his school that he hadn't shown up for his apprenticeship in Poland. It said he disappeared on his way there and asked her to send word if he returned home. But she hadn't heard from him after the initial letter telling her what he called terrific news, and he'd be leaving soon. The school had forwarded her letters to the farm where he'd be, but they had returned them unopened with the words in loopy letters across the front of the envelope: Return to sender. Addressee unknown. Kees was also missing somewhere on the Eastern Front in Russia. But in her heart, she knew her boys were both still alive.

She got up from the bed and brushed imaginary dust from her skirt. Blackie jumped up, anticipating a run through the fields. Petronella ignored him and glanced around the room. She loved the master bedroom, the Chinese theme, the windows looking out onto the road, and the dressing room with the windows facing the garden. If she cocked her head in the corner of the side window, she could see the fields beyond the garden wall.

She walked out onto the landing, with Blackie following, and into Corrie's bedroom. Corrie was busy packing and smiled at her mother. Petronella returned to the landing and hesitated at Punica's open door. Punica sat on her bed, her hands in her lap, staring into space. Blackie thrust a paw onto Punica's lap, and she raised her hand to his head, stroking him, but kept her eyes focussed on something invisible on the wall by the windows.

Petronella turned to go to Kees's bedroom. She had kept it as he had left it. Little skeletons suspended from the ceiling on strings caught her hair. She smiled and reached up and pulled one down.

How masterfully he had carved it; how beautiful its wings were. She embraced it, hugging the tiny creature, and wandered into the adjoining bathroom, holding it to her heart. The boys' bathroom was now much tidier and cleaner than when they were at home. She smiled at the memory of the mess those two made. Via the bathroom, she walked into Willem's room. It was a lovely light space. She examined the musical instruments he displayed on stands along the wall: his guitars, saxophone, and drums. He had taken the box piano upstairs to practice on in private. She laughed. They had heard every false note but pretended not to when he reappeared with his hair a mess as if he had been conducting fifty musicians on a stage. If only she could take his priceless musical instruments with her to keep them safe for him until he returned.

She strolled onto the landing; her heart broke for the family they had once been and what they had become.

Petronella might as well leave now; leaving was inevitable anyway. She walked to her bedroom window and watched the streets fill up; a stream of evacuees was leaving the city. People were taking mattresses on bicycles and pushing carts loaded with non-essential items – memories they could not leave behind. She rushed into her dressing room and picked up her wooden box. How could she forget her magical box with the bird carvings? She put the tiny skeleton in the top drawer of the box and stuffed it beside the photographs in her suitcase.

She walked onto the landing and called out to her daughters. 'Come along, girls. Let's cook a meal together. Let's feast on the food we cannot take with us.'

Corrie ran out into her arms, followed by Blackie. Punica appeared at her door, looking solemn. Where had her lovely smile gone? Petronella walked to her and knitted her arm in Punica's. 'Let's make pancakes,' she said, sounding joyful. 'Your favourite.'

Blackie barked twice.

'Mine too,' Corrie said. 'In case you're wondering.'

Petronella laughed and tickled her side. 'How could I forget?'

They hopped down the stairs, the three of them, their arms hooked. Petronella noticed Punica took the last step, but she said nothing.

Blackie ran toward the backdoor, whining to get out. Mrs de Vries and Nienke sat at the kitchen table wearing their coats and shawls. The kitchen was immaculately clean around them. Petronella glanced at four brown suitcases standing underneath the shelves with the ceramic pots where they used to keep their sugar and rice, coffee and tea, and all the food that had been so normal and now was such an expensive luxury.

'You're both leaving us?' Petronella gasped. And before she let either answer, she added, 'You've stayed so much longer than I've been able to pay you, but you are part of my family.' Her eyes filled with tears. 'I... of course, you both must go.' She wiped her face. 'But where will you go? I hear the Germans won't let you go to the west or to Belgium, Mrs de Vries, where your family lives?'

Mrs de Vries stood up. 'Nienke offered to put me up. She's returning to her family in Friesland.' She forced a smile and looked at Punica and Corrie. 'You have enough to worry about with those two. You can't be showing up in Apeldoorn, dragging us along too.'

'But—' Corrie interjected.

'I'm sure' – Mrs de Vries laid her hands on either side of Corrie's face – 'a lovely family will take you in. I'm certain the nicest family is what you deserve.'

'Are you leaving us... now at this moment?' Petronella asked.

'Yes. We want to get to Dieren before dark, and Nienke's received a telegram from her family. They said they'd collect us at the town hall later this afternoon, so they'll get home before curfew.'

Petronella embraced Mrs de Vries for a long while. When she took Nienke in her arms, Nienke sobbed. Punica sank to the chair where Mrs de Vries had been sitting. Nienke and Mrs de Vries, in turn, hugged Punica from behind as she stared into oblivion.

Mrs de Vries and Nienke picked up their suitcases and left the kitchen; they walked through the hallway and the front door, leaving it wide open behind them. Their bikes waited for them by the garden gate. They heaved their suitcases on top and tied them with string, one onto the handlebar and one onto the back carrier, with a soft bag on top.

'Is the string strong enough?' Petronella asked.

'We will be back once the fighting has died,' Mrs de Vries said. 'I promise.'

'We'll help you get the house back in order. Don't worry,' Nienke said.

Mrs de Vries looked at the open front door. Petronella's eyes followed hers into the house, but Punica did not appear.

'I love this house,' Nienke said.

Mrs de Vries and Nienke soon disappeared into the crowd. Petronella wrapped her arm around Corrie's shoulders, trying to glimpse them, to wave.

A relentless sea of people walked along the road away from the river. Petronella took the wheelbarrow, and they joined them. Corrie held Blackie's leash and had taken Punica's hand. Petronella's eyes brimmed with tears as she watched her daughters follow the others before her; she didn't know where they were going or what awaited them.

Some refugees discussed finding a place at the Historical open-air museum in the woods outside Arnhem. Evacuees had moved into the exhibits of farmhouses from olden times. Others said it would be useless to try to find a roof there as it was packed. They walked along Sonsbeek Singel and up the Sweerts de Landas Street towards Schaarsbergen. The Apeldoornsche Weg would be too busy with evacuees and German soldiers setting up their heavy artillery.

Pushing the wheelbarrow up the hill was harder work than Petronella had expected, and not knowing where they were to sleep made it feel even heavier. What would have been twenty-five minutes by bike now took two hours. Exhausted, they arrived at Schaarsbergen, where a man in a white cap with a red cross on the forehead said they could spend the night in a school gymnasium.

The Red Cross supplied blankets. Petronella spread the blankets on the floor, claiming a square of two metres for herself and her daughters. Corrie played with Blackie outside. They weren't the only family taking a pet. Some had taken cats in small baskets. One family had taken a goat, but the father took the goat into the woods and slaughtered it. He roasted it at the back of the school playground, offering everyone a meal of fresh meat. The children ate first and afterwards played hide and seek, newly energised by the meat.

Throughout the night, there was a distant shooting. Polish and Canadian soldiers waited to attack the city. Punica stared into the darkness, her scared eyes glistening in the dim moonlight. Petronella wrapped her arm around Punica's shoulder, cuddling her. 'You're not alone now. I promise I won't let anyone hurt you or your sister or let anyone take you away from me,' she whispered.

They listened to Blackie bark. They didn't allow pets into the gym, so Petronella had tied his leash to the wheelbarrow and urged him to lie underneath. The fighting must terrify him.

'But what about Kees and Willem and Ab?' Punica whispered. 'You couldn't protect them?'

How could she tell her daughter it was all her father's doing? 'Try to sleep now,' she whispered. 'We have a long trip ahead of us tomorrow.' She tucked the blanket around Punica. It was freezing in the gymnasium. Petronella watched the moonlight cross the ceiling, the ropes and the rings, a memory of how life used to be.

Every time Petronella sank into sleep, a cough from somewhere in the hall would yank her awake, and she'd wonder about the shells exploding in the city. Had they damaged her house?

When the sun changed the light, she quietly packed their possessions, letting her daughters sleep a little longer. Punica awoke the first and sat up, followed by Corrie.

'Come on, darlings,' Petronella whispered, 'Get dressed.'

They walked along Konings Weg to the old Apeldoornsche Weg, a road through the forest. There, they joined the long rows of evacuees once again. Punica and Petronella took turns pushing the wheelbarrow.

'My legs are sore,' Corrie complained. 'Can I climb on?'
'They're strong enough to carry you a little further, darling,' Petronella said. She took Corrie's hand and coaxed her to walk with her.

Rain slashed across their cheeks, turning them pink. Petronella had hidden the blankets from the gymnasium under her suitcases. She wrapped a blanket across each of her daughters' shoulders. Corrie gasped at the idea of her mother stealing blankets. But Petronella hushed her. Of course, she should have taken them from home, but she had taken nothing they needed, she feared. The sky was grey and heavy, like a pillow stuffed with snow. She glanced at the other evacuees. A nun pushed a pram loaded with suitcases. A woman tried to carry a suitcase that was too heavy for her. A man wearing a white apron over his suit held a white flag. Old people followed him with handbags or satchels, obviously only containing what they could carry.

In the villages, people stood in their gardens, watching them walk past. A woman offered glasses of water; others provided sandwiches. One man dressed in a farmer's overall and cap, a cigarette hanging from the corner of his mouth, offered them a bowl of soup he spooned from a milk can. The soup warmed them, and they rested on the grassy verge, watching other people walk by. Corrie let Blackie finish her soup, much to the chagrin of a woman queuing. Petronella ignored her.

After walking for seven hours, they arrived in Apeldoorn, where the refugees gathered in the square, not knowing where to go or what would happen to them.

Word went around to report at the library where civil servants from Arnhem had created a makeshift office. There, they registered their names and organised beds. Petronella parked her wheelbarrow, lifted Corrie on top of the suitcases, and told Punica not to let Corrie out of her sight. Petronella entered the hall and asked a woman nearest her where she should go.

'We're all waiting to hear who'll take us,' she said.

Everyone looked worried.

A boy of about Willem's age walked in, looking around at the waiting crowd. He wore a brown jumper and a shirt and tie. Underneath his tweed suit, he wore traditional wooden clogs covered in mud. Behind his thick glasses, his enormous grey eyes took in the scene. He raised his hand to his mouth and bit the nail of his pinkie. Petronella nudged him with her elbow.

'We are to wait here until they find families willing to take us in,' she said.

'Are you looking for a place to stay?' the boy asked. 'My mother sent me. She wants me to choose a pleasant family. And you seem pleasant. Would you like to come to our farm?'

'Of course,' Petronella said. 'Is it far?'

'Putten. But I have a horse and cart,' he added when he saw Petronella's face sink. 'And I have blankets,' he said. 'They're dry.'

'It's not your turn yet,' the woman said to Petronella.

'Oh, that would be wonderful,' Petronella said. 'I have two daughters waiting for me outside. And we have a dog,' she said, raising her eyebrows, 'but he's no trouble.'

The boy nodded. 'My mother said to take a family of no more than three. You will share the attic, and we also have a dog, so I don't think it will be a problem.'

Petronella smiled. 'I better register. What is your address?' She turned to the woman and smiled. 'I'm sorry,' she said, heading to the makeshift counter.

After she had told the secretaries where she would be staying, she walked out with the boy. She introduced her daughters, and he took the wheelbarrow from her and pushed it to his cart while Corrie held Blackie on her lap. Corrie laughed as the boy pushed the barrow, speeding up and slowing down abruptly so she'd have to grab the sides. Blackie didn't like it much and jumped off, so Punica took his leash.

'And here is your chariot,' he said. He stopped by a wooden cart and a sturdy horse with short, muscular legs. Petronella lifted Corrie onto the back of the cart.

'My name is Bert,' he said to Punica. 'Bert van Buren.' He reached out his hand to shake hers.

Punica ignored his hand and squeezed her lips, looking away. Petronella shook his hand instead and whispered, 'Punica is a little shy.'

'And my name is Corrie, in case you're wondering,' Corrie said.

Petronella laughed, and Bert grinned. 'Pleased to meet you, Corrie. Punica, you can climb in via the wheel,' he said. She climbed in and shuffled, avoiding his eyes, over to Corrie. Bert gave her Blackie. The horse trampled the ground, rocking the cart as Petronella climbed in. She sat on the suitcases, grabbing the sides of the cart to avoid falling out. Bert sat on the drawbar, urging his horse to walk onto the road, forcing everyone standing there aside.

Petronella wanted to ask him about the village they were going to, but unsure what his answer would be, she stayed quiet. Punica had relaxed a little since they left Arnhem, and she didn't want to alarm her. They left the town centre through the stream of people arriving, and once they turned away from the main road, they entered the vast countryside and could see for kilometres and kilometres with not a hill in sight. The wind swept in from the north, and the temperature froze. Although it was September, it had become winter.

Petronella was glad she had taken the blankets. The girls' faces were so white with cold, and their lips blue from the open cart. They turned onto a clay path leading to a farmhouse with a smoking chimney. Orange light lit the windows. Red trees flanked the farmhouse, and moss covered the thatch roof; the windows had green shutters with red-painted diamond shapes. The girls lay curled up on the floor, wrapped in a mountain of blankets. They had fallen asleep. Petronella woke them and smiled at their sleepy faces. 'We're here,' she said, gesturing to the farmhouse behind them.

Bert directed the horse to the side door and said, 'Hu.' The horse stopped, and Bert jumped down. He strolled to the door, opened it a crack, and called out for his mother.

Soon after, a woman rushed out to greet them, pulling on a coat. She was a little older than Petronella. She wore a light blue blouse and a beige cotton skirt; her shawl had a crocheted flower pattern along the border. She wore make-up like the American movie star Bette Davis and didn't look like a farmer's wife. She smiled the friendliest smile Petronella had seen all day.

'Come in, come in,' she said, offering her hand. 'I am Johanna van

Buren,' she said, shaking hands with Petronella, 'Come in. I've prepared the attic for you. 'It is warm enough and comfortable enough, I hope. And I've food ready.' She turned to her son. 'Bert, call your brothers and your father. Dinner is ready. I've cooked erwtensoep with boiled, smoked sausage, and have some Hete Bliksem left over from yesterday. I hope it's enough?'

It smelled delicious. 'Oh, I'm so indebted to you. Let me pay for the food?' Petronella said.

'Nonsense,' Mrs van Buren said. 'The weather has turned so cold today; you'd think it was the middle of winter. We eat dinner at one in the afternoon, but I thought you'd want something warm when you arrive, so I've swapped supper and dinner around, just for today.'

'Come in, yes, yes, take the dog in with you,' she said, seeing the girls hesitate at the door.

Bert lifted the suitcases from the cart and put them on the floor inside the door. 'Do you want them upstairs, Mam?' he asked.

'Leave them for now. You can unharness Floortje first,' Mrs van Buren said.

Petronella smiled. She felt so grateful and stood at the door with her two daughters as they took in this strange new place smelling of burning wood, cattle manure, wet clay, hay, and a lovely meal cooking on the stove. Smoke from the grid puffed into the room as one of Bert's older brothers entered from the cold. In a chair nearest the warmth, an older woman sat, her lips wrinkled and curled around her gums as a soft pink pouch gathered by a string. Petronella smiled at the old lady, but her eyes did not register her.

'Is that Jan?' she called out in a screechy voice.

'No, mother, it's Jeroen. Will you go out and help your father finish up?' Mrs van Buren said to the boy.

She turned to Petronella. 'He has been reading his books all afternoon,' she said, smiling. 'He misses the lectures at university.'

'Who are they?' the woman asked, pointing at Petronella and the girls standing by the door. 'Do I know them?'

'This nice family will be our guests for a little while. I told you evacuees were coming to stay,' Mrs van Buren said. She tucked a blanket around the old woman's legs. 'They are...' she paused. 'I'm sorry, I haven't caught your names?'

'Oh, I forget my manners,' Petronella said. 'This is Corrie and Punica, and I am Petronella Mandemaker,' she said.

'And I am Jo,' the woman said, smiling, offering her hand again.

'Punica's actual name is Maria Cornelia, in case you're wondering,' Corrie said.

Mrs van Buren smiled. 'Will your husband join you?' she asked. 'We could make room for four.'

'I... I'm a widow,' Petronella said, squeezing Corrie's hand, trying to tell her not to contradict her for once.

Corrie looked at her mother's face, her eyes bulging. Petronella cleared her throat. 'Can I help you with anything, Mrs van Buren?'

'Oh, please no, and do call me Jo. I have everything under control. You are Punica?' she said, turning to her. 'What a lovely name.' She shook the girls' hands and said, 'You are all very welcome here. Very welcome indeed... Come sit down, warm yourselves while I finish cooking.'

A child's screech sounded from upstairs. Jo smiled. 'The little ones are awake. I'll be right back,' she said. Five minutes later, she reappeared with a baby on her arm and holding a little boy by the hand. The boy turned behind his mother when he saw Petronella and the girls in the kitchen. 'Don't be so shy, Careltje,' Jo told the boy. She let go of his hand and lowered the baby into a pram, standing by an armchair. The boy rushed to stand behind his mother. 'Come on,' she said. 'Sit with Oma.' She ushered him away. 'I need to feed her,' she said to Petronella, gesturing to the baby.

'Don't mind us,' Petronella said. 'Shall I set the table for you?'

'Yes, so kind of you.' She sat opposite the old lady and unbuttoned her blouse. Corrie blushed and turned towards her mother. 'The plates are...?' Petronella asked.

'In the cupboard above the counter. The cutlery is in the drawer next to the sink.'

Punica and Corrie rushed to help their mother. Petronella counted out her usual six plates. Jo watched Petronella and said, 'There're

211

eight of us plus three guests that makes eleven plates... Yes, five boys of which two should be at university but are home because of the war. And our little darling is a girl. We were so grateful after all the boys.'

Petronella lifted the soup plates to the counter and reached up for the dinner plates.

Mrs van Buren said, 'We eat soup and dinner from the same plate, or the washing up will take until morning.' She turned to the baby on her breast. 'Aren't you the hungry one,' she said.

'Hungry?' the old woman asked.

'Are you hungry, Mother?' Jo asked her.

'No,' the woman said. 'I'm never hungry. But I could eat a horse.'

Jo smiled and looked down at her baby again.

Petronella spread a tablecloth over the table and divided the soup plates across the tabletop. Punica followed her with knives and forks, and Corrie followed with spoons.

'Corrie, would you go out and see what's taking the men so long?' Jo asked.

'Yes, I'd love to,' she shouted, her eyes wide, plopping the spoons on the table and running to the door. 'Come on, Blackie.'

'Check the stables. They should be finishing up by now.'

'Wait,' Petronella said, 'Put on your coat first. It's freezing outside.'

Nearly a half-hour later, Corrie came back with the boys and Mr van Buren.

'They have calves,' she said, her face radiant, 'and a cat and a dog Blackie has made friends with already, and guess what? They have kittens too... And chickens and a rooster.'

Bert sat at the table, but the other boys shook Petronella's and the girl's hands and introduced themselves. Mr van Buren was as friendly as his wife. He told Petronella and the girls a little joke about each of his sons as they introduced themselves. Petronella waved her hands as if conducting an orchestra, 'I'm pleased to meet you all,' she said. She laid her hands on her daughters' shoulders. 'We all are.'

'Come, sit,' Jo said, lowering the sleeping baby into the pram. She walked to the stove and lifted the pot with soup onto the table. 'I'm famished, so let's eat. And maybe after dinner, René can play a tune for us. Don't you love music, Punica?' She spooned soup onto a plate and reached it to Bert, who placed it before Punica – 'It always amazes me when René blows a tune out of that saxophone of his?'

Punica nodded, lifting the spoonful of soup to her lips.

After dinner, and after René had played his saxophone and Punica had helped Jo wash the dishes, the boys finally hauled the suitcases to the attic. It delighted Petronella to find a straw-filled mattress ready for them, with clean, white sheets smelling of fresh lilies. She added the blankets she had taken. The attic had no electricity, but an oil lamp would do them fine. A rug with a biblical scene hung from the beams, and with the yellow light on it, it came to life. Corrie wanted to sleep beside it, and Punica slept in the middle.

Petronella awoke at dawn when the cock called out across the landscape. She dressed, awoke the girls, and told them not to dawdle. She rushed downstairs to see if Jo needed a hand preparing breakfast.

Five days later, the resistance attacked a German convoy killing a high-rank Nazi, and the Nazis ordered all men, women and children to report to the square in the town. The Germans split them into two groups. They drove the women and children into the church and the men and boys into the village school and the Egg Hall.

Petronella tried her best to comfort Jo, who feared for the lives of her sons and husband. Her elderly mother-in-law wept, sitting on the floor, unable to comprehend what was happening and why they took her from her beloved armchair by the fire.

At nine in the evening, the women were sent home. Petronella sat up with Jo while waiting for the boys and their father to return.

'How will we get Hannes, Geert, and René out, and my poor Jan... and Bert just turned sixteen? You should be thankful you don't have sons,' Jo said. 'Boys are a worry in times like these.'

Petronella lowered her hand into her pocket and folded her fingers around the cigarette case. She wanted to tell Jo the truth about her stepsons, but how could she explain when they both wore the Nazi uniform? She remained silent, staring into the fire.

At dawn, they heard Blackie bark in the farmyard. Jo rushed to the door and saw a boy from the village. 'Come in,' Joanna said, 'Come in... come in,' but her words trailed off as her eyes fixed on the red sky above the village and the black clouds of smoke. 'What's happening?' she asked with frozen lips out of breath, her face white from shock.

'They're burning houses—'

'Are they coming our way?' she cried.

'The Nazis have shot six men and a woman, and...' the boy hesitated.

'Oh, my God!' she wailed.

'They've paraded the men through town and loaded them onto the train. People are saying they're going to Neuengamme.'

'Where is Neuengamme?' Petronella asked.

'Oh, my God,' Jo wailed, sinking to her knees. 'What will become of us?'

'Let us go to the village together,' Petronella said. 'We might get them back.'

'They're gone,' the boy said.

'What will become of Careltje and Josje? And the farm?' Jo wailed.

Petronella knew she was right and shuffled back to her chair. She sat down, staring into the fire, her mind churning over thoughts of how to save at least Bert. He would have been safe if his birthday had been next week instead of last Tuesday. She remembered his face when he asked her to accompany him in Apeldoorn. But it was no use, no use, she thought. In the five days they had now lived here, she had come to love this family and felt responsible for this terrible turn of circumstances, as if her lie about being a widow somehow was to blame for everything that had happened.

The next day, Jo could not bear not knowing where her family was, so she saddled the horse and rode into town. Petronella offered to accompany her.

'Stay with my mother-in-law and my children,' she said.

Within the hour, she returned. The village was closed off by the Germans. The refugees told her the men were on the train to Germany. 'They burned over a hundred houses,' she said. 'But why Putten?' she sobbed. 'The assassination was nearer Nijkerk than Putten.'

A week later, Cornelis tracked his wife down and showed up at the doorstep wearing his NSB uniform. Jo answered the door, returning white and distant. She sank into her armchair by the fire without uttering a word. Petronella went to see who was at their door so late in the evening. When she saw Cornelis, she closed the door in his face without uttering a word to him.

Petronella closed the inner shutters of all the downstairs windows and returned to the seat opposite Jo. She was embroidering a shawl for her. She finished it, said goodnight, and retreated to the attic.

Petronella thought she might faint, clenching the railing as she waited for the staircase to stop spinning. She tried her hardest not to panic, but Jo's face, the boys' faces, and their father's haunted her. Petronella should have explained about Cornelis that she had left him after Punica returned from Amersfoort, but she couldn't find the right words.

Petronella took another deep breath and climbed the rest of the stairs. She would leave before dawn. The mere thought of having to face Jo filled her with so much shame. Petronella slipped off her shoes and slid underneath the covers next to Punica.

As soon as Petronella had settled, Punica turned over and lay on her back.

'Are you awake?' Petronella whispered.

'Yes, you woke me.'

'I'm sorry. Darling, we have to leave tomorrow.'

'What is it, Moeke?'

'Your father was at the door,' she said, trying to contain her tears.

Punica sat up. 'Did you turn him away?'

'Yes,' she said, 'but it changes nothing. We have to find another place to stay,' she said. 'The Nazis have sent all the men from the village to concentration camps, and your father shows up in his Nazi uniform—'

'The Germans killed a boy from my school,' Punica said. 'He was sixteen like Bert.'

'At the camp?' Petronella asked.

'Yes,' Punica murmured. 'They killed him for no other reason than they wanted to kill him. They kicked him in the chest as he struggled to breathe. He choked to death on his own blood. I can't get the sound out of my head,' Punica said, pressing her hands to her ears. 'They kept on beating him. I heard his skull crack. And the Dutch guards did nothing. They watched, wearing their...' Punica took a deep breath, 'wearing their stupid Nazi uniforms, just like Papa. They did nothing to help us.'

Petronella stroked a wisp of Punica's hair behind her ear and laid her palm on her cheek.

'I don't understand how someone can do this to another human being. I don't understand. What happens to someone's heart to become so... so empty of sympathy... or feelings? Are people born sadists? I look at Careltje's face and try to decipher what's inside his little head. Did those murderers have those smiley eyes, too, when they were babies? How can those joyful creatures turn into executioners? What happens in those heads to turn them into monsters? Father made monsters out of Kees and Willem.'

'They might have stayed true to their hearts,' Petronella said.

'Why didn't Mr van Buren, or Hannes, or René or Geert or even Bert, who was the youngest and the most impressionable, become Nazis? They stayed true to their hearts. Not Willem nor Kees,' Punica said.

Punica tucked the blanket around Corrie, raised her legs above the coverings, and climbed over her mother. She sat on the chair. Petronella threw her a blanket.

'Wrap it around your shoulders. You'll catch your death,' she said.

'Moeke, it happened right under your nose, and you did nothing.'

'Darling,' Petronella said. 'What are you talking about? What happened?'

Punica closed her eyes and rubbed her forehead. She drew a deep breath and pushed the air from her lungs. 'Do you remember when I went to Ab's house, and you came after me?'

'Yes, of course.'

216

'You discovered their bodies, didn't you?' Punica said, 'Ab told me. He told me everything.'

'He told you what happened?'

'They were all dead.' Punica's voice changed and became monotone.

Petronella felt stiffness crawling over her face. She wanted to light the oil lamp and warm the attic, but she was shivering too much to get up.

'Ab didn't tell me how. But I can guess. His father was a dentist. Ab said they died quietly.'

'Yes,' Petronella gasped, the memory of the family crammed into her mind. She slid to the side of the bed and lowered her feet to the wooden floor.

'How did they die?' Punica said. 'I want to know.'

'Eva slept. She was in her bed, tucked in and surrounded by her dolls. She seemed to be asleep. When I—' Petronella's memory flashed back to the master bedroom. 'Broken glass cracked underneath my feet. A vase with red flowers lay scattered like bloodstains across the carpet. I... I remember thinking I should fetch a towel from the bathroom. Dear Father, I thought. How worried I was about the water seeping through the floorboards and making yellow stains on their ceilings. Sarah lay in bed.'

'They were our friends, Mama. We should have taken them in like we took Ab in. They would have been safe at our house.'

Petronella rocked herself. The bed creaked underneath her, and moonlight caught her hair every second or so.

Silence.

'Go on,' Punica whispered.

'Sarah lay in bed with her back to the door – to me – facing Abraham sitting in the armchair by her dressing table. The smell of that room was... a syringe lay on the bedside table. Sarah's arm was bare, and her sleeve pulled up. Underneath her arm was a rubber cord; Ab's father must have tied it around her arm and loosened it to let the poison spread through her bloodstream. Abraham sat facing Sarah's beautiful jars and pots and powder puffs. I... I... the white and gold gilded mirror which reflected so many images of love and happiness in that bedroom,' Petronella hid her face with her hands, slid them to her temples and squeezed her head. 'The top of his head was shot off.'

'You thought Ab did it?'

'No, of course not. My heart went out to Eva, just a little girl Corrie's age.'

'You wrote Kees a letter? You gave it to him at the station, didn't you?'

'Darling?'

'Mother,' Punica said. 'You were so wrong about Ab. He discovered his family before you did. Don't you realise? He found the suicide note his father had written, begging him to flee. Try to go to America, it said. Mother, don't you see? Mr van de Berg knew the Germans were coming for them. He tried to protect his wife and daughter from the Nazis. No one ever returns from the concentration camps. Ab tried to run away, as his father had instructed. But where was he to go? If I had been older, I would have left with him. Together, we might have had a chance. But with half our family becoming Nazis, what other way was there for him to escape?'

'Darling, it doesn't matter what I wrote because I didn't give Kees the letter.'

'I saw you write the letter the morning Ab left with Kees. I saw you hold it in your hand as you stared into the distance before you put it into your handbag and put on your coat. What was in the letter, Moeke? What did you tell Kees?'

'I took the letter back home with me. I wasn't sure—'

'No, it had to be more. Shall I tell you what I think? I think you wanted to protect Kees. You told him about Ab and what happened to his family. I think you made it sound as if Ab murdered them. Even if you didn't want to, you still made Kees suspicious of Ab, didn't you?'

'I never sent the letter. It doesn't matter what I wrote because I never sent it.'

'Kees has always been your favourite, your special wedding present. You told him what you thought was the truth to protect him. Do you realise your letter caused both Kees's and Ab's deaths?'

'They're not dead. Listen to me. They are not dead. We have had no confirmation of their deaths. They could have deserted for all we know. Anyway, it doesn't matter what I thought or wrote. I did not send the letter.'

'Ab wrote me letters. Lots of letters. And if you weren't always so busy embroidering, you would know.'

Petronella gasped. 'You loved him?'

'I... I've always loved him. Kees teased me endlessly when I was a child. But not after Ab confronted him with his jealous behaviour. Ab wrote me so many letters. We were soulmates. I know he didn't die in battle. They hadn't even reached the front lines when his letters stopped coming.'

Punica rubbed the back of her head. 'Ab knew the Nazis censured his letters. We understood each other. I deciphered what they were doing and how Kees was coping. I knew Ab was in danger. He feared Kees. It must have been your letter that set his mind churning.'

Petronella stirred, opening her mouth to talk.

'Ab asked me about the letter Kees had received.' Punica said. 'Ab knew if the truth about him came out, he would be dead. Ab didn't trust Kees anymore, he told me. I think Kees told his commander. Enough Jews were hanging from telegraph poles for Kees to know Ab wasn't safe. Kees betrayed his bosom friend in the most horrific way possible. Kees should never have enlisted. He was a coward and he caused the death of his best friend. Your world revolved around Kees. It was always Kees, Kees first, and Kees last. But did you know him? I mean, truly know him?'

'We don't know what happened,' Petronella whispered, her heart beating in her throat. 'I promise you; I swear I never sent him the letter. There must be another reason for their disappearance.'

The sun rose above the trees and lit Punica with orange light.

'Then, there is only one other explanation. Someone else found the letter and sent it to Kees.'

Petronella's cheeks glowed. She rubbed her forehead. That letter, oh, how she wished she had burned the damn thing.

'I think the man who calls himself my father, found the letter in your handbag, read it, and sent it to his son in your name.'

Punica rocked herself. The floorboards creaked underneath her as the seconds ticked away; she stopped and lowered her feet onto the floor.

'Mother, I am not going with you tomorrow. I am staying here to help Jo with the farm. She has no one else to help her. You will understand.'

CHAPTER TWENTY-FIVE

Willem

Willem heard bombing far away. He squeezed his eyes to slits so he could peer through the dry snow into the distance. Plumes of smoke floated above the frothy hills. He slinked into the woods to his left and ran between the trees towards the fighting. He was so close now. Out of breath, he rested, his back leaning against a tree. Black blotches danced before his eyes from exertion. He heard Tommie's voice in his head.

'We aren't going to the farm for our internship, are we?'

Willem remembered Tommie's face, so naïve, so inquisitive.

'Do you mind?' he asked. Willem always asked him if he minded, but only after Willem had changed their plans without including Tommie in the decision, and there was no way back. Tommie never complained, even when he had been looking forward to something. He had often sat in the cinema expecting a particular movie to start, only realising when the title splashed across the screen that Willem had once again changed his mind about which film to watch. But this time, it was different – this time, it was big.

'I was looking forward to a roll in the hay with a Polish milkmaid. You had promised me?' Tommie said.

Willem burst out laughing. 'You're not built for milking a hundred cows daily in sub-zero temperatures,' Willem said. 'And besides, those Polish milkmaids have faces like dogs.'

'You're saying I'm built for walking thousands of kilometres through the Russian winter to find a brother who probably doesn't want to be found?'

'He does… and anyway, what is Huckleberry Finn without his Tom Sawyer?'

'Alone,' Tommie said.

'Exactly.' Willem kicked a clump. He thought hard about how he could make a joke out of it, but he couldn't think of any. Maybe Tommie was right, but leaving him at the school with those tough boys wanting to win at everything wouldn't have ended well for him. He felt he needed to keep Tommie close, to keep him safe. Willem reached for his cigarettes and offered Tommie one. Tommie lifted it to his lips while Willem struck a match and lit Tommie's and then his own. They sucked smoke into their lungs and blew it out as forcefully.

'I was planning on taking the boat from Danzig to Königsberg,' Willem said, taking out a map and trying to include Tommie in his plans. 'I've marked Kees's journey. He has written me a detailed account of his trip, describing every minor little thing he saw along the way. God, he's such a sucker for detail,' Willem said, trying to ease the mood between them. 'He described every hill along the way, every farmhouse and every tree even,' he laughed. 'It wouldn't be hard to follow his directions. Consider it a scouting trip with a treasure at the end.'

'Where do you think he is?'

'Somewhere here,' Willem said, pointing to a grey area on the map connecting two large stretches of land, with left and right of it a sea.

'We're going to St Petersburg… to fetch your brother home? Do you know how far that is? We would be away for weeks… months. Can a human being even walk that far?'

'An Übermensch can. An Übermensch can walk anywhere,' Willem said, dubbing Naumann and his German accent, shouting like a Nazi.

Tommie's face turned serious.

'So, what will my treasure be at the end of it? Or is your brother my prize as well?'

'Not exactly. Kees is in trouble. I need to help him.'

Willem felt the silver bird in his pocket. He couldn't tell him about the birds and the family myths. Willem wasn't like Kees. He had always thought of Moeke's stories as entertainment and her way of comforting her stepsons when they were so lonely away from their mother, but now he wasn't sure. The bird had appeared between his clothes in his suitcase, and he was sure Kees hadn't given it to him or that he had packed it. And it certainly wasn't amongst his things when he left the school at Schaarsbergen. How did it get there? If he discussed the bird with Tommie, he'd think he'd lost his mind, leave him, and return to that godawful school. But there was the fact Willem thought Tommie wouldn't be safe at the Nazi school. Willem believed the school would be the death of him, so letting him go back wasn't an option.

After a long pause, he said, 'Kees needs me to collect him; I can feel it in my bones.'

'So, we're deserting because you feel it in your bones?'

'We're not deserting. We're only students; we haven't signed up for anything yet. We can go wherever we please.'

'Well, tell Naumann that—'

'We are free to leave,' Willem insisted. 'There's nothing they can do to make us return if we don't want to. And after we pick up Kees, we're out of here – first stop will be America.'

'America?' Tommie said, raising his eyebrows.

'Yes, America.'

Tommie squeezed his lips into a stiff white line, contemplating what Willem said, nodding as the idea took hold of his mind. 'Sounds great,' he said. 'I wouldn't mind not seeing my old man again, and America sounds fine. Why didn't you tell me sooner?'

From Cologne, they took the train to Berlin, and in Berlin, they lost the rest of the school group when they had to walk from one end of the city to the station on the other end to get the connecting train to Danzig. The other students should have been on the platform for the train to Danzig, too, but they weren't. Willem gathered they must have missed it or were waiting for them at another location, as instructed by their teachers. This information must have been missed because he had been so preoccupied with running away to Russia. Either way, he was glad he didn't have to sneak away from them. At Danzig station, a sea of farmers with horses and carts awaited their interns. Willem and Tommie walked through them, not acknowledging their questioning gazes, even though they wore the Reichsschule uniform. They made their way to the docks and found a ship going to Russia. But it didn't take passengers, and especially not school children, the captain said.

They altered their plan and rushed back into town to change their clothes, stealing from bleaching greens and clotheslines. As luck would have it, when they returned to the docks, this time looking for a job, a ship to Königsberg lay waiting for the cook to show up. The captain said if they knew their way around a kitchen, they had found themselves a job, and soon, they were on their way to Russia.

They enjoyed themselves, cooking whatever came to mind. Tommie's speciality was mashed potatoes, and Willem was great at frying eggs. They cooked vegetables in milk, which was Willem's idea: he had seen Mrs de Vries boil white cabbage in milk and serve it with melted butter and a powdering of ground nutmeg. They fried pork chops, sausages, and whatever meat they found in the cooling cell. They weren't anywhere close to being professional chefs, but no one complained. The former cook had been an alcoholic. Willem and Tommie were so successful that the crew saluted them when they left the ship and were sad to see them go.

Tommie loved the adventure and was as enthusiastic as Willem about finding their way over the vast countryside. At night, they slept in haylofts, old sheds, and abandoned houses. On the odd night out, they covered themselves with branches and dry leaves to keep warm. They ate whatever they could find, stealing from farmers along the way. Sometimes, they found old rusty tins of food in larders of abandoned houses and stuffed as many as possible into their rucksacks.

The weather changed, and Willem and Tommie woke early from the cold. Unable to sink back into sleep, they got up before dawn and resumed their journey. They patted their hands crosswise on their upper arms to warm up. They heard a horse and cart in the distance, the sound rumbling towards them but still invisible along the twisty, muddy road behind them.

They scanned the area surrounding them. Sedges grew in clumps along the shore of a lake, with glistering spiderwebs clinging to the long stalks. A deer drank at the water's edge. It looked up at the boys as they listened to the sounds of the land. Overhead, a hawk screeched while riding air currents. A splash at their feet as a fish disturbed the water's surface. Tommie stepped onto the tall grass and peered into the water. 'Could we catch one of those?' he said. 'I'd love to eat one for breakfast.'

Willem checked his compass, 'You'll have to catch it with your bare hands,' he mumbled.

A horse and cart emerged from the trees, sniffing clouds into the air. An old man sat hunched on the wooden cart, holding the reins as his elbows rested on his knees. He pulled his cap low over his wrinkled eyes and tried to ignore them.

Willem waved to him. The man held his gaze on the road and stared into the distance. Willem walked out, moving in front of the horse to stop it in its tracks. It was an old, sturdy animal with long hair growing from its short legs. Willem stroked its face. The man cursed Willem in Polish or Russian or some other Baltic language they didn't understand, waving his hand for Willem to move away.

Willem placed his hand palms together by his chest and bowed his head to the man as if praying or begging him. He asked, pointing to himself and to Tommie, if the man would take them on his cart. The old man slanted his head and proceeded, smacking his gums, urging his horse to walk on. It walked around Willem, but Tommie blocked his way, bowing his head. The man sighed. He peered at them through narrowed eyes. He hesitated a minute, sliding his cap away from his forehead and scratching his balding skull.

He motioned for the boys to pull up their sleeves.

The boys looked at one another, not knowing what the old man wanted. He motioned for Tommie to come to him and pulled at

225

Tommie's sleeve. He pointed to the inside of his upper left arm and again reached for Tommie's sleeve, pulling it up.

'I think he wants us to show him our left arms,' Tommie said.

The man gestured the sleeve wouldn't go high enough and to take the coat and whatever they were wearing underneath off.

Tommie pulled at his sleeve cuff and pushed his arm from under his coat. His arm was bare, and the old man inspected it. He checked his armpit and the skin on the back of his arm. He seemed satisfied. He motioned for Willem to do the same. Willem showed him his bare arm. The old man inspected the skin as he did Tommie's; he spotted a mole the size of a black beetle. He scratched it with the yellowed nail on his index finger. Willem clenched his teeth. The old man motioned for both boys to dress and shoved over to the side of the cart. He waved his hand that they were welcome to climb aboard.

'What was that supposed to mean?' Tommie whispered to Willem, trying not to move his lips as if he were a ventriloquist.

'I don't have a clue,' Willem replied, sitting in the middle.

Willem and Tommie curled up into their coats, trying to warm themselves. The horse's hooves mumbled in the mud, and the ruffle of the cart echoed in the vacuum of emptiness and rocked them into a trance-like state.

Sometimes, a lonely suitcase, discarded doll, or cuddly toy lay on the verge. Willem peered into the distance and distinguished shadows on the road that plunged into the reeds and bushes along the water's edge as the cart came closer. Thinking they were stray dogs, Willem didn't pay them much attention. As the sun warmed the atmosphere, Willem saw that the shadows weren't dogs but children diving away to hide. He saw them huddled between the reeds, their eyes widening as they passed them. Young children lugged suitcases and bags and sometimes carried toddlers and babies.

The old man mumbled, 'Wolfskinder. Keine Eltern.' He motioned his finger across his throat as if cutting it.

'No parents,' Tommie said, translating the words into Dutch. 'Wolf Children... what are wolf children? Where are they going? Ask him where they're going?'

The old man raised his shoulders, gesturing 'Who knows?' He tried to smile. 'Too many,' he said.

Willem thought back to the two girls in the woods by Bensberg. Had they made it back?

The cart arrived at a fork in the road. The old man stopped the horse and motioned for them to follow the path into the forest.

Willem and Tommie got off and reached to shake the old man's hand, thanking him in German. They did the Boy Scout salute, not the Hitler salute, and the old man smiled. The horse turned away from the water's edge.

'Okay, let's get going,' Tommie said, marching towards the forest and the hills in the distance, 'and get this over with so we can leave for America.' He squeezed his lips to keep them from smiling.

'My father made me go to the Reichsschule,' Tommie said after about a half-hour of silent walking.

'Mine didn't make me go. He didn't try to persuade me not to go, either. I was different before the war started,' Willem said.

'Weren't we all?'

'I lived for my music.' Willem cleared his throat. 'Life used to be so much fun. My family enjoyed each other's company. We used to laugh so much. We lived in a fairy-tale house in the city centre. My stepmother tried to keep the war far away from us, and she would have been successful if it hadn't been for my father—'

'I was in Arnhem once. There was a wonderful house in the middle of the city, with gardens and fields. It had medieval parts, a walled garden at the front, and beautiful stained-glass windows. I was so jealous of the people living there. They even had a swimming pool. It was near the cathedral.' He said, 'If you walk from the church into town, you pass it on the right-hand side.'

'I know where it is. I live there,' Willem said.

'You live there? Your family must be wealthy.'

'Not at all. My father had one stroke of brilliance when he was younger. He always joked that it was his way of winning my mother's – stepmother's love. Anyway, I enrolled at the Reichsschule because I love music,' Willem said. 'Based on—'

'It's as good a reason as any,' Tommie said. 'We sang a lot of songs at school. Marching songs which come in handy, at times like these.'

Willem laughed. 'I thought I'd get to America if I enrolled. They said studying anywhere in the world was a possibility after graduation. I wanted to study music in America. But after getting a place in the Reichsschule, America declares war on Japan. And anywhere turned out to be within the borders of the Third Reich.'

'That's dumb.'

'Yep,' Willem said, saluting Tommie. 'That's me. Dumb. When you want something as badly as I wanted to go to America, you lose your common sense. Now I know there is no easy way. I've learned a lot since then. How quickly things can change. What was your reason?'

'My father was a member of the NSB. He said that my becoming one of the elitist forces would be the cherry on the cake. His cake.'

'You should have refused.'

'He whipped me daily... kept a special rod inside his sleeve. I was glad to go.'

'Inside his sleeve,' Willem said. Puckering his face. 'Do you have any brothers or sisters?'

'He didn't whip those, only me being the oldest. At least, I think that was why he beat me.'

'What about your mother?'

'Didn't whip her either. I was glad to get away.'

'I meant, didn't she stick up for you?'

'Nah, she told me I would never amount to anything from age four. My father was always going on about my brother, who is a year younger. I should be more like...' He waved his hands, dismissing the memory.

Willem wanted to change the subject. 'They're always on about Jews, aren't they? The Nazis.'

'Was your father an anti-Semite as well? Mine was.'

'The way I look at it, we are all flowering weeds in this brilliant garden called Earth.'

228

'My father used to be a farmer,' Tommie said. 'He wasn't much good at farming. Come to think of it, he failed at everything he did. Anyway, his milk cows got sick and died, one after the other. He couldn't even afford a vet to come to look at them. So we packed up and moved to Eindhoven.'

'A farmer moves to the city?'

'Yeah, my father had decided to become an electrician instead. He hoped to find a job at Philips, but you can't just decide to become an electrician; you need to learn something about electrics first.'

'And he called you a loser.'

'I found it hard to fit in at the new school. The other kids made fun of us and mimicked our country accents. I asked my father questions about his new profession. Too many questions, my father said. I asked if he had Jewish colleagues. The Jewish boys were my friends at school, you see. They stood up for me against the bullies. My father whipped me so hard. I was glad to get away from him and go to boarding school, even if I was to be his cherry.'

'At the Reichsschule, you had to be careful about asking questions, as well,' Willem said, shaking his head. The image of those caged people cramped into his mind. Nobody dared to ask questions. When they discovered those poor men, Mr Ros nearly cried but wouldn't dare enquire about them. He kept his mouth shut while the caged people starved. 'Our cook, Mrs de Vries, told us many Jewish families committed suicide to avoid the work camps. Perhaps they knew what would happen to them in Germany?'

'How can kids commit suicide?'

'I suppose their parents murder them in their sleep and then—' he shook his head.

'Jesus, that sounds scary. Do you know any Jews?'

'My brother's friend came to live with us because he was alone after his whole family was deported to work in Germany.'

'God almighty.'

'Yeah,' Willem said. 'I haven't thought about Ab's family much.' He sank into thought. How was it possible to have forgotten about them? He hadn't seen Eva since Sinterklaas, and her parents long before that. How could a family slip from his mind altogether? After he found Kees, he would write to Moeke and ask her if she knew where Ab's family was.

'What type of music do you prefer above other styles?' Tommie asked. 'Do you like Louis Davids, or wait, what were their names? They were Jewish, let out of Westerbork Concentration Camp to record a record in Amsterdam. The newspapers reported the story. Don't tell me, no, wait... it was Johnny and Jones? That same evening, they returned to their wives at the camp. You'd think they'd make a run for it.'

'I think there's something wrong with me,' Tommie sang.

'My mind keeps wandering,' Willem joined in. 'I've become another person,' he sang.

'I sing my Westerbork serenade,'

Tommie tried to follow but only remembered the last word. 'Serenade,' he sang, joining in.

'Along the railroad shines a silver moon,'

'On the heath, I sing my Westerbork serenade.'

Both boys stopped singing.

'Those poor caged people,' Tommie said, thinking the same as Willem. 'Do you think Mr Ros went back with food and water?'

'He said he would.'

'I don't know, the way he swore us to secrecy, he probably let them suffer.'

Willem rubbed his face hard. He didn't want to think about the caged people; he tried to think about getting Kees back and the three of them going to America. Maybe Ab would also want to go along. The four of them. Willem smiled.

It was dusk, the sky turning dark blue. Willem kept an eye out for a place to sleep.

'There's no way I'm sleeping rough in the open again,' Tommie said.

A roof bloomed from the white trees in the distance, as crimson as blood. Tommie pulled Willem's arm, pointing toward the house.

Willem smiled. The chimney wasn't smoking, so maybe no one lived there. They could build a fire and heat a tin of food to warm their freezing, tired bodies. As they approached, they saw the windows were broken. With their hearts beating faster – it would be empty, they hoped – they sped up. The walls were a metre thick, and the door was grainy old wood covered with turquoise scales of peeling paint.

Tommie strolled into the house.

'Be careful!' Willem whispered harshly. A gunshot pierced the silence. Birds scattered through the sky.

Tommie crumbled to the floor.

Time stood still. Willem froze. His legs could not flee or enter or do anything. He peered into the darkness and winced. An old woman sat in the corner on a mattress, holding a German army pistol with shaking hands. Her eyes were wide, the whites visible; her mouth a dark hole, no teeth, her face wrinkled like an old potato. A skeleton had found the strength to pull the trigger and was now pointing the gun at Willem's heart. Willem's mind slowed, and he glanced towards his friend lying on the floor, his face white, a dark stain blooming underneath his chest.

Willem raised his hands, surrendering, and shuffled towards Tommie, bending over him to check if he was all right. Tommie gasped for air; choking, frothy mucus simmered from his mouth. His right hand twitched at his coat button, the last twitches of a sixteen-year-old dying, and Willem knew... he knew he could not save his friend. All Willem wanted was to keep Tommie safe and take him to America. Oh, how he had failed.

Willem looked at the woman and felt so much hate; he tasted its bitterness on his tongue. He plunged towards her. She jerked back and pulled the trigger. Willem heard the click; the gun was empty. Only one bullet and his friend was dead. He grabbed the gun from her hands, twisting it away from her, and she groaned or yelped, or another indefinable sound came from her rotten throat as he rammed the handle across her head and knocked the hag from this earth so she would never kill another human being the way she had killed Tommie.

Willem sank onto his haunches, exhausted, and looked at his friend. His mouth contorted with grief, but he couldn't cry. What was he to do? He couldn't leave Tommie here. Not with the witch lying next to him. He hesitated a moment. The smell of mildew and the woman's faeces pounded his head. Aeroplanes roared over him, rumbling away into the distance. He lifted Tommie onto his back. But where could he go to bury his friend? The ground was frozen solid. Outside, wolves would get him and feast on him all night. He gently lowered Tommie back onto the floor and pulled Tommie's coat up to his face to cover him.

He took the woman instead. He lifted her into his arms like a bundle of firewood and walked out into the snow. He discarded her between spongy rotting branches and dead mushy toadstools. 'For the wolves,' he gasped.

Back in the house, he built a fire on the wooden floor. Lighting clumps of straw from the mattress with his matches and throwing them and scraps of clothing into a circle around Tommie, he kept feeding the fire, and the flames grew into a halo of light around his friend. Grabbing whatever he found, he threw on the fire, and, lastly, the filthy mattress, old blankets, a suitcase, and a wooden box filled with yellowed photographs of smiling people. Children with big bows on their heads and river-side picnics.

A thick layer of smoke filled the cabin, and Willem ran out coughing. He stood back and watched tongues of fire lick through the windows and between the roof and the walls. He waited, watching the flames trying to escape from the cabin, lifting it into a ball of light, spinning in the air on its one leg above the ground. Willem watched it burn, the fire slashing his face. He mumbled the song he had sung with his friend only a few hours ago and saluted Tommie as the flames devoured him.

Willem was as alert as ever, keeping his eyes peeled for any movement, whether close by or further away. He kept his eyes on the sky and watched what the birds were doing. The sound of the bombing grew louder, and he knew he was approaching Kees's battalion.

With his flashlight slashing the darkness, he finally reached a camp of dark tents. The place seemed like hell, with wooden planks forming makeshift paths over a mush of earth, blood, and excrement. A horrific, putrid smell wafted from the ground.

Lorries came and went, their headlights flashing as they transported a fresh supply of soldiers, food, and ammunition. And muddy motorcycles roared away with ammunition stuffed into their sidecars, puffing exhaust fumes into the air. Men with limbs missing and horrendous wounds returned and were taken into the light behind the canvas. Willem had never seen so much suffering.

He kept his eyes turned away from anything too gruesome to bear and asked around for Kees's commander, Oberscharführer Schachner. No one seemed interested in what this schoolboy was doing here. They pointed in the same direction, through the forest into the distance. 'Follow the noise,' they told him. They also said he would do better to turn back and go home, but he was determined to find his brother. He asked around if anyone knew Kees, but by the scale of the set-up, Willem estimated the chances of anyone knowing his introverted brother would be close to zero.

As dawn lighted the sky, Willem walked out from the field hospitable and slinked into the forest. A soldier, seeing him leave, called him back and offered him a coat he had taken from a dead Russian.

'Works better than the German coats,' he mumbled, looking the other way.

Willem took it and thanked him more than once. It didn't look like an army uniform coat, so he pulled it on over his jacket, even though it had bullet holes through the material at the back where white feathers escaped the lining.

Willem navigated through the forest and reached the German troops at midday, where he spotted a guard. He strolled towards him, singing one of the German marching songs he had learned at the Reichsschule. He wasn't sure the song would be enough to keep him alive, so he flapped a white handkerchief like a flag and called out Schachner's name. The guard confirmed he had come to the right place.

They sent word to Oberscharführer Schachner, and Schachner sent someone back to check Willem's identification. After verification, they brought the schoolboy who had ventured to Russia alone to their commander.

Schachner asked Willem whether he was hungry.

Willem nodded, so they arranged food for him. As he ate, Schachner said, 'They tell me you have walked all this way on your own?'

Willem nodded.

'So, you want to know what happened to your brother?'

Willem lowered his voice and said, 'I do.'

'Your brother has been in my company since training camp. He and his friend Mandemaker Two,' he said, pulling a cigarette from his breast pocket. 'It was a terrible business. They should check these softies thoroughly before sending them to me. Your brother cost me two fine men. Maybe even more. He always had this weird cold look in his eyes.'

'What do you mean?' Willem asked, shaking but trying to stay as calm as he could.

'It began with Mandemaker Two. Brink comes up to me and tells me that Mandemaker Two is a Jew. The boy was as blond as anyone and had blue eyes. He was nothing like a Jew. He said that if I didn't believe him, I should ask Mandemaker One. He'd tell me, he said. So I said, I thought you Dutch stick together? At that point, I had suspected Mandemaker One's nerves. He seemed twitchy. I don't know, never sleeping, never eating, dilated pupils. I suspected he took large dosages of Pervitin. He couldn't distinguish between real and fantasy; that was my opinion. Anyway, I wanted to hear the story from the boys themselves, not that I was interested in whether Mandemaker Two was a Jew or a Gentile. I shouldn't tell you this, but he was a good soldier. I don't care about ancestry; as long as I can trust a man to watch my back when we're out in the field, do you get what I'm saying?'

Willem nodded.

'So, the next thing I hear raised voices. I thought it was a dispute over food. We were all starving, and some men, unable to deal with a bit of hardship, had resorted to stealing food from their comrades. I was on my way anyway, so I thought I'd settle the dispute myself. And above and behold, I see your brother aiming his pistol at his brother's head. Mandemaker Two was sitting on his knees in the mud, begging for his life. What the hell was going on? Before I get an answer, your brother shoots the boy in the eye, and the boy dies on the spot. Mandemaker One tells me that someone called Moeke had told him everything. He rambled on about some letter he had received from her. Do you know who he meant?'

'Our step-mother,' Willem said.

'What could she have written to him to make him lose his mind and want to murder his brother?'

Willem shook his head, pulling the corners of his mouth downward. 'Did you ask to see the letter?'

'Of course, he told me he had burned it. Then he tells me Mandemaker Two wasn't his brother at all and that he, in fact, was a Jew.'

'A Jew?' Willem asked, pretending to be baffled.

'I decided to play along and asked him why he had fed me the whole cock-and-bull story about being brothers in the first place. And he said he hadn't, that everyone believed what they wanted to believe. So I asked him about having the same last names. A coincidence, he said. 'We have fifteen men called de Vries, so why not two Mandemakers?''

Willem couldn't believe what he was hearing and shifted on the log he was sitting on, pushing his hands into his pockets.

'I know.' Schachner rubbed his face hard. 'It's a lot to take in. It kept me awake at night, too, in the beginning. But I haven't finished yet. So anyway, I check his identification card,' Schachner continued. 'I didn't know what the truth was at that point. The next thing I know, Mandemaker One sinks to the ground beside Mandemaker Two and cuts off his finger. Have you ever heard of that before? There's lots of barbarism on the battlefield, but cutting off your brother's finger? And for what? That really got me, I can tell you.'

'Where is Kees now? Have you arrested him?'

'Wait, I haven't told you the worst. After a few days, Mandemaker

One seemed to be back to normal. He told me everything. He was open and communicative, and his eyes seemed normal and alert. I thought the terrible business must be true, so I assigned him a simple enough task with a new recruit. Nice guy. Ziegler, Wolf Ziegler. They seemed to connect, so I told Mandemaker to scout for us, to mark any irregularities on the map and take Ziegler with him. We expected them back the next day, but they did not show up; we waited forty-eight hours for them. What am I running here, a Kindergarten? I sent two men in after them. And what do they find? Ziegler dead, his throat torn apart.'

'Wolves?'

'No. Wolves go for the gut. He probably used the same weird little knife he used on the finger.'

'Did you find him? My brother?'

Schachner squeezed his lips, stood up, and, clenching Willem's shoulder, said, 'I'm sorry, boy, for having come all this way for nothing.'

'Kees might be alive, though?'

'Might be,' Schachner said. 'But not likely. Better go back to the Tross. Tell them I said to take you back with the wounded in the truck. They'll take care of you.'

'I'm free to go wherever I want,' Willem said, standing up. 'I'm not in the army.'

Schachner hunched his shoulders and gestured ahead into the forest. 'If you're suicidal, be my guest. But take my advice, go back. Even if he were still alive, he's not the brother you remember. He's not worth risking your life for.' He shook his head. 'It's up to you.'

Willem slept in the camp that night, snuggling into his jacket. At home, Willem would have thought it impossible to sleep under the sky in winter, but he knew he'd be okay unless the temperatures sank further. Willem wore two winter coats. Someone had laid an army coat over him, which helped him descend further into the unconscious sleep he had missed since the temperature plummeted below zero at night. He was glad he wasn't alone, that men surrounded him, even though they were Nazis.

The howling of the wolves and the scratching of the crows' voices at dawn awakened him.

As Willem got up, he noticed it wasn't an army coat that had covered him. Someone had given him a Russian sleeping bag stuffed with feathers. 'Schachner said to give it to you,' a soldier said as Willem examined it. Willem rolled it up to fit under the strap of his backpack.

Willem entered the forest by the path from which Schachner said Kees had disappeared. Schachner stood out from the others, watching him walk away. Schachner's eyes burned on Willem's back. Willem kept his gaze on the path before him; he convinced himself he needed no one, but his heart pounded from fear for the first time since Tommie's murder as he entered a kind of no-man's-land.

Willem zigzagged between shrubs and dwarf Siberian pines into the forest, still feeling Schachner's gaze on his back. Running between the large trees, he turned brusquely towards the company. No one watched him. What a schoolboy he felt. As if he was important to an Oberscharführer fighting a war! He was an ant, an insect, and nothing more.

As he slinked further into the forest, something changed. The trees were the same, spruces and Siberian pines powdered by snow, but the colours were different. Green trees changed to emerald; the moss on bare patches turned golden saffron, and the snow glittered on the twirling breeze.

He noticed the silence, too. No bombs, no shelling, no shooting, no machinery, no marching men. The scene was surreal, like in a fairy tale. Even if someone had asked him, he would be unable to describe what made it so: the colours or the slant of the incoming light? A mist hovered above the trees like a protective canopy.

He ducked below branches and climbed over dead trees. A river meandered away into the misty forest. He climbed down the slope and, on the shore; he noticed a rucksack with sheets of ice sticking to the sides and the bottom sucked into the frozen mass of mud and water. He pulled the back strap. The ice moaned and cracked but would not let it go. He sat down on his haunches, untied the string at

237

the top, and opened it to see if it belonged to Kees.

A notebook lay on top with a pencil tied to the cover with a string. Kees had written his naam and address on the inside cover. Flipping through the pages, he saw they were blank. Underneath lay a small green diary. On the left-hand corner of the cover, he read the year 1942 embossed in silver lettering. Kees had ticked off the dates as tasks completed until December, but there were no written entries. The handle of the carving knife stuck between his clothes and an empty pill tin beside it. He laid them on the snowy bank and picked up the long SS coat to check the pockets. He found a dirty roll of bandages covered in brown blood, containing something, a cigar shape but heavier. Unrolling it, he found a black – he didn't realise it at first, but when he turned it over and saw a fingernail, he realised it was a finger – the finger Schachner mentioned. Ab's finger. The skin was creased and hard. Willem gagged and threw it away from him onto the ground.

Willem knelt beside the rucksack, and saw a wooden box, the mahogany box where Kees kept his silver bird. He flicked the lid open. It was empty. He pulled the sack with all his might from the ice and turned it upside down, emptying the contents onto the ground. The marble and silver bird fell on his clothes and glittered in the sunlight. The lovely bird, Kees always believed, had a heartbeat. Willem remembered how Kees enjoyed sharing its secrets with Moeke. Willem dug out his bird from his inside pocket. He held both in outstretched hands, the tiny chick and the mother bird.

He saw movement from the corner of his eye. Startled, he jumped in fright. A doe bolted away. He gasped and lowered the silver birds onto the frozen river. He took off his rucksack, and the doe re-emerged from the undergrowth, watching him.

The ice on the water's surface was like glass. Not a speck of snow lay on it, and Willem stepped out. Fish in the depths swam underneath his feet. Something glittered at the bottom, and peering through the ice and the water, Willem discerned Kees's watch lying on black leaves. He pushed down with the toe of his right foot and ventured further, feeling his way as he slid toward the middle of the frozen river to where the ice grew thinner.

Sliding his foot toward the darkness, he saw a graceful hand beneath the ice. He crouched, staring into the depths; he made out the shape of a naked man curled up like a foetus suspended in the river's dark womb. The face looked so serene. Not frozen, whiter, a shade whiter, but healthy-looking pink on the nose and cheeks. Willem knelt on the ice and stroked his brother's face, so close but unreachable.

Everything changed. His hopes and dreams for the future, his plans. Everything froze in time.

Tears dropped from his eyes.

Something moved between the trees, and Willem glanced up in its direction. A doe trotted away towards a shadow lurking between the trees in the distance. He peered at it, and after a moment, he discerned a stag watching him.

ACKNOWLEDGEMENTS

When I first met my future mother-in-law, Corrie, I thought she looked like my French teacher in Ireland. Since I liked my French teacher, my mother-in-law and I initially hit it off. Yet, as my bond with my future husband deepened, I noticed she was constantly plagued by worry, incessantly checking up on her son and urging my husband to forgo any weekend outings so that she could have peace of mind. My father-in-law would mention that her worries were due to the war and give no additional clarification. For me, the Second World War was long before I was born and a thing of the past.

When my mother-in-law was widowed at 65, she started telling me about her personal experiences from her time during the war and how they had affected her life so horribly when she was a child. When the Nazis invaded the Netherlands, her loving family was divided into two camps. Her mother and her sister were against the Nazis, while her father and half-brother were pro-Nazi. She often talked of how her father had influenced her half-brother, Kees, a young lad, into joining the SS. Corrie was so ashamed of her father's Nazi ties that she never mentioned the war to people outside of her family. She frequently spoke of her mother's fearful reaction when her stepson told her the news of enlisting. It conveyed how little influence her mother had had on her stepson's life.

Not long after enlisting, Corrie's half-brother died on the Eastern Front, and his tiny diary with scarce entries became the only testament to his young life. She had always kept the diary hidden between her treasures in memory of him. Now I understood why she worried so much for her son's safety.

I wrote this novel as a tribute to my mother-in-law and all the women who had to witness their sons and brothers depart for war without fully understanding what they were getting themselves into. I also wrote it to honour Corrie's courageous mother because she got her children through a most dangerous period in time alive and well. The war, mentioned countless times by my family, has taken on a new meaning for me, and I shall never underestimate the effect it has had on so many lives of the people who have lived through such a dark period in history.

I want to thank my mother-in-law, Corrie, for all the beautiful stories she shared with me and my beta readers: Peter Curry, Marianne Verkamman, Patricia Burghout, Steve Miller, Johanne van Doremalen, and Mirjam van Rijn † for their time and helpful comments.

WRITTEN SOURCES

Beevor, Antony, *Arnhem: The battle for the Bridges, 1944*, (Viking, 2018)

Buckingham, William F., *Arnhem 1944*, (Tempus Publishing, 2002)

Gerritsen, Kees, *Leven in Arnhem In De Jaren 40*, (Uitgeverij Kontrast, 2019)

Groeneveld, Gerard, *Hitlers Jongste Hoop: Nazipropaganda voor de Jeugd*, (Uitgeverij Vantilt, 2019)

Have, Wichert ten, *Leven in Bezet Nederland, 1940 Verwarring En Aanpassing* (Spectrum NIOD, 2015)

Jacobs, Ingrid D., *40 45 Arnhem*, (WBooks en Gelders Archief, 2014)

Kamiénski, Lukasz, *Shooting Up: A Short History of Drugs and War*, (Oxford University Press, 2016)

Kistemaker, Henk, *Wiking:Een Nederlandse SS-er aan het Oostfront* (Just Publishers BV, 2008)

Liempt, Ad van, *Leven in Bezet Nederland, 1945 De Afrekening*, (Het Spectrum NIOD, 2020)

Lyklema, Hans, *Wakker Worden in de Oorlog*, (Uitgeverij Blauwdruk, 2013)

Marshall, Bonnie C., *The Snow Maiden and other Russian Tales*, (Libraries Unlimited, 2004)

Mukhina, Lena, *The Diary of Lena Mukhina: A Girl's Life in the Siege of Leningrad*, (Macmillan 2015)

Ohler, Norman, *Blitzed: Drugs in Nazi Germany*, (Penguin Books, 2015)

Oudheusden, Jan van, Schumacher, Erik, *Leven in Bezet Nederland, 1944 Verstoorde Verwachtingen*, (Het Spectrum NIOD, 2019)

Pierik, Perry, *From Leningrad to Berlin: Dutch Volunteers in the Service of the German Waffen-SS 1941-1945*, (Aspekt non-fiction, 2001)

Plicht, Elias van der, *Leven in Bezet Nederland, 1943 Onderdrukking En Verzet*, (Het Spectrum NIOD, 2018)

Schumacher, Erik, *Leven in Bezet Nederland, 1942 Oorlog Op Alle Fronten,* (Het Spectrum NIOD, 2017)

Slaa, Robin te, *Leven in Bezet Nederland, 1941 Het Masker Valt,* (Het Spectrum NIOD, 2016)

Steen, Paul van der, *Keurkinderen: Hitlers Elitescholen in Nederland, (*Uitgeverij Balans, 2009)

Reid, Anna, *Leningrad: Tragedy of a City Under Siege, 1941-44,* (Bloomsbury Publishing, 2011)

Vergunst, Nieske, Mathijssen, Lisanne, *Oorlogs Brieven: Een Familie in de Hongerwinter,* (Atlas Contact, 2016)

And numerous online sources, too many to mention

ABOUT THE AUTHOR

A.S. Mink was born in the Netherlands and raised in rural Ireland in the 1970s. Her short nonfiction pieces have been published in various literary magazines and newspapers, and her work has been recognised in several writing competitions. The Bone Sculptor has been longlisted for the Mslexia Novel Prize.

In her free time, she loves to walk through forests in rainstorms, and her favourite drink is tea – Earl Grey with a slice of lemon and a ginger biscuit.

The Bone Sculptor is her second novel.

Also by this author:
A History of Love and Now

SOCIALS

Follow A.S. Mink on socials

Facebook: asminkauthor
X: @asminkauthor
Instagram: @asminkauthor

If you enjoyed this book, please share your thoughts by leaving a review on **Amazon, Goodreads or with your book supplier**

Sign up for author alerts, exciting news and freebies at
asmink.nl

Printed in Dunstable, United Kingdom

75615303R00150